D0058006

ALSO BY LORA LEIGH

Rugged Texas Cowboy
Collision Point

LORA LEIGH

dagger's edge

St. Martin's Paperbacks

This is a work of fiction. All of the characters, organizations, and events portrayed in this novel are either products of the author's imagination or are used fictitiously.

DAGGER'S EDGE

Copyright © 2018 by Lora Leigh.

All rights reserved.

For information address St. Martin's Press, 175 Fifth Avenue, New York, NY 10010.

ISBN: 978-1-250-11034-3

Our books may be purchased in bulk for promotional, educational, or business use. Please contact your local bookseller or the Macmillan Corporate and Premium Sales Department at 1-800-221-7945, ext. 5442, or by e-mail at MacmillanSpecialMarkets@macmillan.com.

Printed in the United States of America

St. Martin's Paperbacks edition / September 2018

St. Martin's Paperbacks are published by St. Martin's Press, 175 Fifth Avenue, New York, NY 10010.

10 9 8 7 6 5 4 3 2 1

For first loves,

For last loves,

For the dream of love.

Special thanks for AB, advanced readers
and good friends.

prologue

Journey came awake gagging, the horrible taste in her mouth so vile she could barely stand it.

As she fought to bring her stomach under control, she remembered the moment she'd realized the danger she was in, along with her friend Teylor. They'd been in the garden talking. She'd needed help, needed someone to help her escape the engagement she was being forced into when everything had gone dark.

Gregor. She remembered the voice of Gregor Ascarti, one of the men who worked for her father, telling her she'd been warned to keep her bitch mouth shut. And she had been warned. Beau had told her when she'd overheard his conversation with Gregor not to speak of it.

Fear strangled her now. She struggled to make sense of where she was, to understand how she'd come to find herself in a dimly lit metal room.

Sitting up on the thin mattress, she forced her head up, forced her eyes to adjust to the dimly lit room. As she did, she could see her friend Teylor, struggling to sit up on the makeshift bed across from her.

"Teylor?" she whispered, her voice shaky. "Oh God, what happened?"

She blamed herself for this. In her desperation to be free she'd endangered her friend. Her only friend.

A broken sob escaped her as she fought back her tears. Tears. They wouldn't help. They never had in the past.

"We've been kidnapped," Teylor answered her, sounding far more lucid than Journey felt.

The battery-powered lights were dim, but Journey could see enough to be assured her friend was okay.

Teylor pushed her dark red hair back from her face and stared around the metal-enclosed room they were in.

"Where are we?" she asked, terror racing through her.

Teylor met her gaze, her expression almost resigned.

"It's a shipping crate," she stated. "The type they use for overseas shipping."

A shipping crate? Journey fisted her hands in the long skirt of her ball gown and fought to hold back her screams.

"Teylor, what's happening?" she whispered, trying to make sense of the danger she sensed they were in, and her uncertainty in the face of it.

Before Teylor could answer, the sound of metal

scraping against metal drew her gaze to the end of the crate where the door was slowly swinging open to reveal Ascarti and several other men Journey had seen meeting with her father, her grandfather, and Beau.

Other than Ascarti, she wasn't certain who they were, and she had a feeling she didn't want to know.

"Let's go," Gregor Ascarti ordered, his voice as rough and ugly as his face, as the other two pointed their weapons toward her and Teylor.

"You were supposed to be dead," she heard Teylor tell Ascarti softly as they passed him.

He grunted at the statement. "If you'd had your way, I would be. Fortunately for me, I think I might have actually survived. Unfortunately for you, perhaps. Now let's go." He waved a handgun indicating both of them should step into the darkness outside the shipping crate.

"How did you get into the gardens?" Teylor asked him.

"A little inside help," he answered her, amused. "Now be a good girl and let's finish our business. Then I can go about recouping my money from that little hit your friends made against my stash."

"What hit?" Teylor asked as Journey fought to figure out what the hell they were even talking about.

Ascarti laughed. "Let's go, Ms. Fitzhugh. Someone is very interested in talking to you."

Journey stiffened as Teylor pulled her closer to her, the name tugging at her memory and filling her with a sudden dread.

She'd heard the name Fitzhugh several times in the

past, and if she remembered correctly, it was one tied to a very violent and depraved person. As well as a much beloved family member and missing cousin.

They were led across a wide-open space to a brightly lit office, the doors thrown wide, and as Journey stepped inside, all she could see was the three men she'd always believed would protect her. Her grandfather Stephen, her father, Craig, and her fiancé, Beauregard Grant.

She heard her own cry, the denial that slipped from her lips, and felt her world being destroyed one second at a time.

"Father." She would have raced to him, would have fought the truth, if she were given the chance. Instead, rough hands gripped her shoulders, pulling her back and throwing her onto a tattered leather couch along with Teylor.

Her grandfather and father and Beau stood watching them silently. Grandpa Stephen was propped against the edge of an old desk, his arms crossed over his chest, his expression hard and cold. Her father grimaced in disgust as she whispered his name again, a plea that this not be true filling her voice. Only Beau remained aloof, unaffected as he stared at her.

Her grandpa was watching Teylor rather than her though, an amused, faintly condescending smile on his face.

"I remember that look," he told Teylor. "The same look your dear mother had when we caught up with her in Nicaragua. I believe she may have actually cried, though." The pleasure in his voice was terrifying to

Journey. "And I would have thought by now you would have explained who you are. The daughter of our dear, departed Francine. Tehya Fitzhugh."

"That's not true," Journey cried out, shocked, certain her grandfather had to be mistaken.

Teylor wouldn't have hidden that from her. It was the same as a lie and she knew how Journey felt about lies.

"It's true," Teylor, or rather Tehya, stated softly. "And they're the reason Mother died."

It couldn't be true. They had to be playing one of their elaborate games like they played with their children. They couldn't kill. They wouldn't have. But they had. She saw in their faces, in the cruel, vicious smirks on their faces.

She turned to her grandfather, her father, enraged. "What are you doing? Father? Grandfather? Have you lost your minds?"

The look her grandfather flashed her was one so hard she could only stare back at him, terror flashing through her.

"If she opens her stupid mouth again, gag her," her father ordered the men standing behind her.

Gag her? She stared at the two men she had always loved. She hadn't been close to them—they were very standoffish, even on a good day—but they'd always looked out for her, hadn't they? She'd believed they'd loved her, despite their often harsh demands. At that thought, vague memories of when she was younger, of conversations that had made little sense to her, began to swirl within her mind.

Conversations that had frightened her, made her distrust them before the fear had forced her to forget the words.

As she stared at them furiously, she was aware of Beau unfolding his crossed arms and allowing them to hang carefully at his sides.

"You killed my mother," Tehya said then, the words sinking into Journey's soul with slashing horror.

Her grandfather chuckled then. "She thought we were there to help her. That her father had sent us after she contacted him." He smiled with satisfaction. "She was rather upset to learn that wasn't the case." He turned to her father then. "We did enjoy our last hours with her though, didn't we?"

Journey stared at them, uncomprehending. Her aunt had been found in the jungle, tortured and raped to death. She lifted her gaze to Beau, praying she'd somehow heard wrong. The gleams of regret and compassion in his gaze, the pity, sliced at her soul. And in that moment, she hated him. She hated him because he knew, he knew what they were, and he still stood with them.

Journey was afraid she was going to be sick now. This was her family. They weren't exactly loving. But this . . . this was beyond cruel. They were monsters.

"Now, my dear, it's like this." Her grandfather's expression became harder, something evil glowing in his gaze. "If you want to ensure your dear cousin Journey has a reasonably content life from here on out, you'll answer my question and do so without a fuss. Refuse me, dare to attempt to lie to me, and she'll die with you."

They wanted to use her now? Use her against her cousin? Just as they'd sold her to Beau and used her against him over the years?

"I'd rather die," Journey cried out, enraged now as she surged to her feet in an attempt to run, to escape what was happening.

Hard hands caught her, the two men behind her attempting to hold her still as they struggled to restrain her. She fought with everything she had, desperation, fear, and a rage unlike anything she'd known racing through her. They struggled to hold her still until Beau stepped to them, grabbed her arms, and jerked them behind her, enabling one of the men to tape her lips securely.

She glared up at the man they'd forced her to accept as her fiancé. The man they thought they could force her into marrying and she hated him. He'd been a friend once, long ago. When she'd been a child. He'd never been someone she'd dreamed of being with or marrying. That fantasy was reserved for someone far darker than this man. Someone far more dangerous.

Hatred and fury spilled from her as tears of rage ran down her cheeks. She kicked out, her foot connecting with Beau's leg, though there was no reaction, not even a wince to give her a measure of satisfaction.

"Now that we've taken care of that," her grandfather sighed before turning back to Tehya. "Did you understand the rules for her continued safety? Or do you have questions? Or do you want to be as stupid as your mother?"

Tehya's mother. This couldn't be real. It had to be a

nightmare. As they continued to threaten Tehya, demanded a code that accessed her inheritance, Journey could only sob. Impotent rage raced through her, pulling a haze of red before her eyes, making the conversation seem distant, almost slurred.

It was all about money, she realized. Her aunt Francine's inheritance as well as Tehya's. Money that should have never belonged to her grandfather and father to begin with. They had been behind her aunt's kidnapping, her death, all to steal control of the Taite fortune, and now they wanted what had been put back for Tehya and her mother as well.

Journey couldn't stop crying. She heard every word, but processing it was another matter. How was she supposed to process this? Make sense of it?

She stared at Tehya, daring the woman she knew was her cousin to give them anything. She'd rather die. She'd rather face hell than let them have what they wanted because she knew they were going to die anyway.

For a moment, she wished she'd gone to Ivan Resnova for help, rather than Tehya. Tall, dark, powerful, he'd been at the party as well, and she'd seen him watching her. She should have asked him for help. Ascarti would have never attempted to kidnap them had he faced Resnova rather than Tehya.

As she watched, her grandfather's fist clenched when Tehya wouldn't give him what he wanted and he stared at Journey. She saw the intent in his eyes and hated him for it.

Just before he would have struck her, Beau stepped in front of Tehya.

"Journey's mine," he stated. "I won't have what I want from her affected by your treatment of this one."

At that demand a hard knock sounded on the door, and moments later more of her father's men entered the room, tossing two who appeared unconscious to the floor. And within moments, hell began erupting around her.

Lights went out, throwing the room into darkness. Gunfire swept through the room as she felt Beau throw her to the floor, and when it was over, finally over, black-clad masked men had her father and grandfather, along with Beau, in handcuffs.

Journey felt numb, defeated. Her hands were released, the tape removed from her lips gently, and she was pulled quickly from the warehouse to a van outside. As she entered the vehicle and turned back, she saw him.

Ivan.

He strode through the night, black hair surrounding his face, his dark blue eyes finding her, holding her gaze as he paused. The world narrowed down to that one moment, that connection as his gaze held hers. Like an invisible line pulling at them, reaching out from her, needing him to take her away. Just for a little while.

A frown pulled at his brow as he watched her, his lips forced her name, like a whisper that only her soul heard. His fists clenched, his expression hardened, and then he took a step toward her.

The door to the van quickly closed.

"Everything's going to be okay, ma'am," a gentle

female voice assured her from behind the dark mask. "You're safe now."

But she wasn't safe, Journey thought. She'd never be safe again and she knew it. Nothing in her world would ever seem safe again.

Ivan watched the van door slide closed and paused in the instinctive move to rush to the young woman inside the vehicle. She was like a siren calling to him. She had been for years. And this time, the impulse to go to her was nearly impossible to refuse.

He wanted to rescue her.

Shoving his hands in the pockets of his slacks, he lowered his head, drew in a deep breath, and forced himself to turn away from her. She belonged to another man. Not that the bastard deserved her, but she wore his ring, had promised herself to him. He had no business interfering in that.

Besides, she was the daughter of the men revealed as the enemy he'd searched for for over twenty years. The two men responsible for the vicious murder of his mother, his aunt's rapists, the men who had struck at his daughter and attempted to destroy her. She was their daughter. Granddaughter.

And he wanted to fuck her so bad it was like a hunger, he admitted to himself. A hunger he wasn't entirely comfortable with.

"Looks like you have a little obsession going on there, boss." Ilya, more friend than assistant, stepped from the shadows, the dragon tattooed over the side of his face flexing dangerously.

"Those eyes of hers." He grimaced. Green, gem bright. Those eyes pulled at him.

"Hungry eyes," Ilya murmured, moving into step with him as he headed for the warehouse.

Hungry eyes.

Desperate eyes.

Eyes he saw in his fucking dreams . . .

chapter one

Four years later
Outside Boulder, Colorado

This was dangerous.

Journey Taite, now known as Crimsyn Delaney, stared around the guest room as she rubbed her hands over her arms, wishing she could chase away the chill spreading through her.

The Resnova estate was smaller than many she'd stayed on, but she had to admit it had an understated elegance rarely seen. She liked that. The rooms were warm, a gas fireplace gracing this one, and a small sitting area across from the bed.

Rugs were scattered over the hardwood floors; the beds were sinfully comfortable, the blankets that covered them downy soft and inviting rest.

It wasn't what she expected from a crime lord, especially a Russian crime lord. She expected flash, very little class, and found something she admired instead.

Unfortunately, it was probably the most dangerous place she could be.

If there was a single place on the face of this earth that drew together all the forces she considered a threat to her life, then this was the place. And here the concentration of individuals most likely to realize exactly who she was, was the highest.

Noah Blake and Riordan Malone and Ivan Resnova. Though, thankfully, the first two had left the day before, along with Ivan's daughter, Amara. She was stuck here for the moment because Amara had made her swear to wait until her father made arrangements for her to return to New York before leaving the estate.

This was what she got for trying to help a friend, she told herself, pacing the room. Sticking her nose in where it didn't belong. She should have learned better years ago. But had she?

Evidently, she hadn't.

The only good thing to have happened was Amara's safety. With the death of the Resnova servant who seemed to have masterminded the problems Ivan's daughter, Amara, had faced, that part of the problem was taken care of.

Now to find her way out of the estate without anyone learning her true identity.

It had been four years, she told herself. She was no longer a fresh-faced twenty-two-year-old though she still looked younger than her twenty-six years. At twenty-two she'd looked like a teenager. A naïve, rather stupid teenager. Not that she was displaying more common sense now than she had then.

Noah Blake and Riordan Malone hadn't realized who she was though; that was a plus. At least they hadn't seemed to. And from what she knew of those two, if they even suspected her name was something other than Crimsyn, then they'd have called her on it before they left the estate that morning. Ivan was suspicious of everyone from what her friend Amara had told her over the past year that they'd worked together, but she was confident the identity she'd paid so much for would hold up.

She'd have to disappear after she left here though. Perhaps use some of the carefully hoarded funds she'd hidden away when she ran four years ago to buy another name, another past. Honestly, she'd begun to like this identity though.

She liked the way Ivan Resnova called her Syn. The dark quality of his voice, the way his gaze seemed to flicker with hunger.

Stupid, Journey. Stupid, she told herself as she paced back to the balcony doors and stared out onto the snow-packed grounds.

She should have never come to Boulder. No matter the danger to Amara or the danger to herself because of their friendship, she should have remembered how little Lady Luck cared for her.

That mercurial bitch hated her.

She was so screwed if she didn't get out of here. If there was one man in the world who had a reason to hate her the most, it was Amara's father. Because of her family and her father's and grandfather's involvement with Ivan's father decades ago, Ivan had nearly lost his own daughter, as well as his life.

Because of her father, Craig Taite, Amara had nearly been taken from him as a child and given to a white slaver known as Sorrel. Simply because she'd been born a girl rather than a boy.

Because of her father, Ivan had been forced to kill his own father and countless men he'd been raised with as well as those he had counted as friends before the betrayal.

Because of the Taite family, he had nearly lost everything he'd held dear, and he'd spent countless years working to destroy a family that always seemed one step ahead of him.

Until four years ago.

Her stomach roiled at the memory of that night as she fought to push it back. She didn't want to remember the night she'd learned the evil that ran in her bloodline. Not that she could forget it for long. News stories still ran about the remaining family. Her brother, her sister, and her cousins.

The Taite wealth was all but nonexistent now from what she read, the Queen's support stripped, their titles taken.

Not that she cared about the wealth or the titles. She'd cared about the sense of family, and learning it was no more than an illusion had nearly broken her.

Watching the thick, heavy fall of snow that had begun once again, she drew in a deep breath and tried to reassure herself she would make it out of there before she was discovered. That was all she had to do: make it out of there, get a bus ticket, and then disappear.

Maybe she'd go someplace warm. Florida or California. She liked the idea of California; it was warmer there. Maybe it would be easier to find a job and to hide.

A quiet knock at the door had her turning quickly, barely controlling her response to the sight of Ivan standing in the doorway.

He shouldn't look so good. He should look like a father, dammit. Maybe some gray hair, at least an ounce or two of fat on his leanly muscled frame. But oh no, the jeans he wore, cinched at those lean hips with a leather belt and paired with a black silk shirt, sleeves rolled partway up his forearms, emphasized the power of his six-two frame. Thick black hair brushed rakishly back from his face, deep midnight blue eyes, and a face that wasn't classically handsome but rugged and wickedly sensual.

She wanted to clench her thighs against the response she had to him. She'd never, at any time, responded to a man as she did to this one. Her body sensitized, her breasts felt achy and tight, and between her thighs she could feel herself growing damp. Never, at any time, had she so wanted a man to touch her.

"Yes?" She cleared her throat as he stepped into the bedroom and closed the door behind him with deliberate care.

Her heart was racing now, nerves gathering in her

stomach as she fought back an instinctive fear of what was to come.

"Tell me, Ms. Delaney, what are your plans now that this is over?" he asked; the low pitch of his voice only made her nerves worse.

This. The deaths of the men attempting to kill his daughter. Yeah, fate hated her. They hadn't even been tied to the Taite family. She'd simply been at the wrong place at the wrong time with his daughter.

She shrugged at the question. "Return to my job," she lied. "My life. Why?"

Stepping farther into the room, he stalked to the fireplace, where he leaned against the surrounding brick, arms folding over his chest as he watched her closely.

How many times had she dreamed of him? Dreamed of him holding her, his strength supporting her. So many years, she knew, and now, rather than reaching out her only choice was to run again. Because she couldn't bear to have him know who she was. "You've lost six months of your life," he pointed out. "The apartment you had is no longer available, your belongings disposed of by the apartment manager, and your position at the DA's office has been filled."

She frowned, her fingers tightening as she linked them in front of her.

"There are other apartments, other jobs, and things can be replaced," she told him, keeping her voice calm.

Hell, she knew better. Nothing was ever easy but it sure as hell beat a forced marriage to a man she had no desire for.

"Where will you live?" he asked then as though simply curious.

Ivan Resnova was never simply curious. According to his daughter, he was at his most dangerous when he pretended to be.

"I have friends . . ."

"Family?" The question was asked so smoothly she nearly stuttered over her response.

"A few cousins." She finally shrugged, remembering the identity she'd paid so much money for and fighting to contain her growing frustration. "I'll be fine."

It was as though he were rubbing her nose in the fact that the obstacles she faced were rather difficult.

"Hmm." The murmured response had her lips tightening as she fought to hold on to the temper he seemed to ignite without trying.

"Is there a point to this interrogation?" she snapped before she could stop the words.

Dammit. She didn't need to piss him off further. Amara wasn't here right now; he could kill her, have her body disposed of, and simply tell his daughter she'd left the estate.

His brow arched, mocking amusement touching his lips.

And still, he was so handsome. The deep, dark blue eyes, thick black hair. His features were that of a fallen angel's, dark skinned, savage lines, and determined angles.

"Doesn't every interrogation have a point?" he mused lazily.

He was dangerous, she reminded herself, far too dangerous to allow herself to be comfortable with him. She had to remember this man could destroy her.

"Then get to it so we can be done with it," she demanded, steeling herself to pretend unconcern. "I'm sure I have better things to do than stand here and be questioned by you."

"Like what?" That amusement filled his voice now. "We're in the middle of another snowstorm at the moment, and other than minimal security and staff, we're pretty much alone. Humor me."

Yeah, she'd get right on that.

"Humor me and get to the point." She sniffed irritably.

Taking an attitude with a crime lord wasn't the smartest thing to do, but he just pissed her off. She wasn't a twenty-two-year-old child anymore. The four years she'd been running from her past had taught her a few things at least.

He pissed her off now though, and made her wet. A hell of a combination, wasn't it?

"What do you want to compensate you for the past six months and to ensure I don't have to kill you to keep you from running your mouth about it?" His demeanor went from amusement to icy control.

She stared back at him for long moments, knowing he'd said exactly what she thought he said, but unable to explain why it hurt so bad to hear the words.

"Wow. Just call me a money-grubbing whore and have it done with," she told him with far more calm than she felt. "Honestly, I thought I'd consider myself lucky if I just got out of here while I was still breathing."

Bastard.

She could feel her temper burning now, and though she was certain it would be far better to push it back, she found it impossible to do so.

"As if there was any other option," he snorted as though disgusted by that fact. "Amara would no doubt check on you from time to time, just because she's nice like that. I'd never let my daughter suspect I'd killed a friend."

Of course not. He loved his daughter, didn't he? How could she have forgotten that? That didn't mean she was safe by any means.

"If I'd wanted anything in compensation, I would have asked your daughter," she pointed out with a haughty little sneer she'd learned from her mother. "Keep your money, Resnova. I don't need it, nor your insults. And I damned sure don't want my life and my safety further inconvenienced by my running my mouth, as you so crudely put it."

Her fingers curled into fists; the need to plant one of them in his face again was nearly overpowering.

"I find that rather hard to believe," he murmured, suspicions shadowing his expression.

"I don't give a damn how you find it!" she snapped furiously. "Amara is my friend. Helping her was helping myself. I'm alive. I can return to my life. And you can take your offer and go to hell."

She should have expected this, she told herself. Ivan

and men of his ilk only knew the power of their money. There was no such thing as friendship or loyalty that didn't involve some type of payment.

She should have run the opposite direction of the Resnovas. When the men working with Amara's abductors six months ago had come after her as well, she should have just headed to California then. There was nothing in New York to hold her. It was just a place to stop, to rest, nothing more. The last place her family or their investigators would think to look for her.

Ivan was watching her doubtfully now, obviously unable to believe she wanted nothing.

"How much?" he asked her again.

Her teeth clenched.

"Fine. Whatever." She flipped her hand toward him angrily. "Just write yourself a check, whatever you think it's worth, and give me a ride to town in the morning and you'll never have to remember I existed. How's that?"

She didn't have to cash a check; she could just burn the damned thing.

She hated him.

She wanted him . . .

She hated herself because she wanted him to touch her, to kiss her with those sensual lips, touch her with those long-fingered, broad hands, surround her with the warmth of his body.

She wished she could find some way to shed the pain, the aching loss, for just a single moment out of time instead of having this man make it worse, intensify it. For the first time in her adult life she wanted a man to touch her, and he just wanted to pay her off and get rid of her.

She glared at him, letting the anger build instead of the hurt. Hadn't she hurt enough yet? Hadn't she lost enough?

He watched her silently now, his expression giving nothing away as he stared back at her. But she could feel the suspicion, the growing sense that he was playing some game, had some agenda she wanted no part of.

"This storm is expected to last through the night and now into the morning as well," he suddenly announced. "Getting you into town will be impossible until the day after tomorrow at the earliest. Think about it and we'll discuss it again before you leave."

He straightened, his arms dropping from his chest as he moved closer to her.

Journey watched warily as he paused beside her, his gaze on the snow outside the balcony doors, his profile implacable.

"Was there something else you wanted?" She couldn't help the confrontational tone.

Her father had warned her countless times that her temper was going to get her in more trouble than she could get herself out of one day. For a moment, the memory of a vicious blow to her face, her father's cruel gaze, the icy mercilessness in his expression, and her own horror flashed through her mind.

She flinched and moved a few steps from Ivan, desperate to lock the past away again, to run from it just as hard as she was running from those searching for her.

His head turned, those dark blue eyes watching her intently.

"Who are you running from, Syn?" The question shocked her, terrified her. He asked it so gently, as though he understood her fear, as though he wanted to help her.

If she didn't get out of this house, out of his life, then he'd end up destroying her.

Ivan watched as Syn's face paled and her green eyes darkened in fear. She wasn't as good as she thought she was at hiding the fact that she was running.

Oh yes, he knew who she was now, and he was rather shocked by the fact that he hadn't recognized her. Though, in his defense, four years had wrought just enough changes in her delicate features that he could be excused for that. That added maturity, as well as the shorter hair and the thinness of her once curvier body, had allowed her to slip beneath the radar and away from those searching for her.

He was one of those searching. He'd had a team tracking her since the night she'd disappeared, though the trail had grown cold a year after they'd begun their search.

Craig Taite's younger daughter was still a beauty though, perhaps even more so than she had been at twenty-two. And so very young. Twenty-six. It was a crime that she had to carry the weight on her shoulders that she carried, that she had the knowledge of the monster her father had become.

It was a shame that she would now face her father's

crimes in ways she'd avoided since she'd begun running. He couldn't allow her to run farther though. As long as she was out there, undefended, knowing the things she possibly knew, then she was a liability to some dangerous people.

He turned to her, watching as she swallowed tightly, her deep green eyes meeting his before shifting, touching her lips, then dropping before she quickly turned away and pushed her fingers restlessly through her hair. But not before he saw the flush that washed through her cheeks.

His lips quirked in amused knowledge at what he knew she'd seen.

Oh yes, she could make him hard. Instantly. There was something about her fiery nature, about that shy, innocent gaze, that filled him with raw lust. Just as it had for years before she disappeared. She was his secret fantasy, his flame-haired dream lover.

He would have ignored it. He would have pushed her right out the door along with Riordan and Amara to avoid it if it hadn't been that overriding hunger.

She wasn't leaving the estate, but the question of how to hold her there was one he had yet to answer to his satisfaction. He had no desire to lock her in the basement but he knew from years of searching for her just how resourceful she could be.

"I've been running from your daughter's enemies, it seems!" she snapped, shoving her hands in those cheap-assed jeans she wore. "And as you seem to be stuck with me a while longer, I'll be sure to stay out of your way."

She'd once had access to the finest clothes, the softest fabrics, and she was now wearing clothes he knew for a fact that she'd picked up in Boulder during her stay at the homeless shelter there.

A fucking homeless shelter.

The Taite fortunes weren't what they once were, but her brother and her mother's and brother-in-law's family were slowly repairing some of the losses with her former fiancé's help. There was even talk that the title might not be stripped from the family after all, rather than merely allowing the public to believe it had been.

"Did I ask you to stay out of my way?" he queried, keeping his voice soft as he tried to contain a fury that had twenty years to brew inside him.

And he had to balance that black fury and his daughter's demand that he protect this woman she called her friend. Protect her. This woman whose father and grandfather would have seen his daughter sold as no more than a sex slave when she was but a child. The same two men who had murdered his mother while Ivan's father laughed at her screams for mercy.

"Let's say I consider it prudent to stay out of your way," she informed him with an indignant little glare.

He found himself restraining a grin.

"I told you I wouldn't harm you. At least not without cause." He faced her, arching a brow as she frowned up at him. "Do you intend to give me a reason?"

She wanted to roll her eyes. He could see it in her expression.

"Trust me, Mr. Resnova, I have absolutely no intention of that." There was a flash of disappointment in her expression that bothered him, he found.

Damn her. Her father would have destroyed Amara had he had his way. Yet Ivan's conscience, his own child, would never allow the same to be done to Taite's child.

This was the price of raising the sweet, loving child who stared at him with such trust. Amara believed in him and it was a belief he had worked hard to ensure.

At least that was the reason he was giving himself. He couldn't allow lust to excuse the fact that he'd never hated this young woman. From the time she was sixteen she'd drawn his interest. At eighteen, she'd begun drawing his lust.

That didn't mean there weren't other ways to make certain the elder Taites suffered. They were imprisoned, but Ivan knew that imprisonment was far more comfortable than it should be. And they were far more arrogant and superior than any prisoner should be.

How superior would they be when the prisoners known to have been part of the supposed Resnova criminal organization reported that the missing Taite daughter was sleeping with their boss? When news of it was flashed through the news services and society pages?

The idea had him tensing, had the lust he fought to keep banked burning brighter, hotter.

Stephen and Craig had tried to destroy him for the better part of his life. Their hatred for him, their inability to steal his organization or bring him to heel, enraged them. He was no more than a dirty Russian thug, Craig had once sneered at him over a phone line. One far beneath his notice.

"Is there something else you wanted?" Journey asked when he said nothing more.

No, not Journey, his Syn.

His lashes lowered as he wondered what it would take to turn that innocent little blue blood into a woman whose sexual knowledge glowed in every graceful movement of her body? A woman who knew her sexual power and her ability to use it.

It took far more than just having sex. Far more than just a lover, Ivan knew that. It would take releasing that inner core of hunger he'd noticed rising each time he saw her before her disappearance. It would take ensuring she saw herself as more than just a one-night stand or a mistress.

"And if there is?" He tipped his head to the side, watching her carefully. "Would I be risking that pretty little fist again?"

She packed a punch, he thought in amusement. The night he had brought her to the estate that fist had punched into his face, busting his lips and, he swore, perhaps loosening a few teeth.

Surprise flared in her green eyes as a flush worked from her neck to her hairline and sensual awareness filled her eyes. Innocent, curious awareness.

The blood beat hard and fast in her neck, her breasts rose and fell in agitation, and she gave her head a little shake, as though suddenly uncertain.

"I d-d-don't understand . . ." she said with a little

stammer, her breathing jerkier, her expression less confident and confrontational than moments before.

He'd bet several of the sizable fortunes he possessed that she was a virgin. If not a virgin, then not far from one. He watched the blood beat at the vein in her neck, the way her gaze locked with his, uncertainty and innocent sensuality filling her expression. Her breathing was heavier, her breasts rising and falling as sexual excitement began pulsing through her.

In his life, he'd never seen a woman experience that first moment of pure, overriding lust. But he saw it then. He watched the flush that colored her face, the darkening of her eyes, that moment of distress when the hunger overrode caution.

"Don't you?" he asked, moving closer, staring down at her, allowing her to see the hunger in his expression.

And her nipples were hard. They were stiff and tight beneath her too-thin T-shirt. He knew a woman's body, knew their responses, and his little Syn was primed for a lot of sinning.

And he was just the sinner to show her the way.

chapter two

Brain cells were crashing, hormones were raging, and Journey was certain she could feel her common sense melting beneath the dark, wicked look on Ivan's face.

No, not dark and wicked, his expression was carnal.

She couldn't breathe. She felt frozen in place.

She swallowed tightly and nearly choked on her own spit.

"Stop." It was all she could do to force the word past her lips and make herself step away from him. How she managed it, she had no idea. She felt like a frightened rabbit faced with the ravenous wolf. The meal he'd make of her would destroy her.

Unfortunately, away from him put her closer to the bed, something those wicked blue eyes didn't miss.

The corners of his lips quirked with a knowing, mocking smile. The sensual knowledge in his gaze, in his expression, threatened to steal her breath.

A woman needed a little sexual experience to deal with Ivan Resnova and the pure, carnal wickedness he was capable of projecting.

"Join me downstairs." He wasn't asking. "We'll have dinner and a drink and watch the snowfall in the solarium. Alexi has a fire in the fireplace and the snow's beautiful as it falls outside the glass walls. We can have a drink and have Alexi put us together a light meal."

Dangerous. He was so dangerous.

"I would make a really bad one-night stand, Ivan," she burst out, unable to hold the words back.

His lashes lowered, the male hunger gleaming in the dark blue depths intensifying.

"You should let me be the judge of that," he murmured. "But I can be a rather greedy man, Syn. I doubt one night would be enough."

She was going to suffocate if he kept saying things like that, because the words, the look on his face, had her heart racing, her breath coming hard and fast. She couldn't get enough air to combat the effect of him.

Confident arrogance. He wore male strength with subconscious grace. It was a part of him, all the way to his bones. It wasn't a learned art but a natural part of who he was, and it was dangerous.

"You're playing with me," she accused him as confusion, arousal, and anger mixed in a chaotic mess.

He knew what he was doing, and he knew the effect it was having on her, no doubt. But he couldn't know how badly she needed to be touched, to be held, to be warm. He couldn't know that she had wondered what it would be like to feel his lips on hers, to feel him touching her, since she'd first seen him just after her father's and grandfather's arrests. He couldn't know how many times she'd fantasized about him.

"Playing suggests it's a game." His voice was a dark, sensual rasp. "What I have in mind is no game. Simply pleasure." His hand reached out, the tips of his fingers caressing over one side of her face. "Or are you still dreaming of happily-ever-afters?"

Happily-ever-after? Now wasn't that one a joke?

"I'm not a child." She flashed him what she hoped was a suitably insulted look. "Nor do I engage in delusions concerning my life. I'd appreciate it if you'd remember that."

There was no such thing as a happily-ever-after for her, and she knew it. What man could possibly love a woman whose family was as stained by blood and depravity as hers? What man would want to risk a life and children with a woman who carried her genetics?

"That's a good thing," he murmured. "I'm no white knight, love. But a white knight could never give you the pleasure I could give you either." He stepped back, though the lust in his expression remained. "I'll be in the solarium if you decide to join me downstairs."

"And if all I want to do is watch the snow?" Dammit, she sounded breathless. Uncertain. She hated that.

A slow, wicked smile curled at his lips. "There's no pleasure in rape or in coercion, love. Unless you come to me willingly, without games and without lies, then neither of us will find true satisfaction. Come, watch the snow if that's all you want. The choice is yours."

Then his head lowered and before she could even think of avoiding him, those wicked, sensual lips brushed against hers.

Journey froze, shocked by the heat and sheer pleasure she felt at the caress.

It wasn't the first time a man's lips had touched hers. It wasn't the deepest kiss she'd ever had. It was the most shocking. Staring into his eyes, watching them darken, feeling just the brush of his lips . . .

She was dazed, more uncertain than she'd ever felt in her life.

"More?" he whispered against her lips as she felt his palms against her back, his hands, broad and so warm through the thin material of her T-shirt.

He was so warm and soon, so very soon, she'd be out in the cold again. What would a kiss hurt?

"More . . ." It was barely more than a breath of a sound, and in it she could hear her own need.

How pathetic. To hunger so much for the touch of a man she feared was no better than the one she was running from. The difference though: this man made her hungry in ways she'd never been before.

She should have considered her answer though. Should have considered the nature of the beast holding her. Before she could do more than gasp his lips covered hers, his tongue stroked past them, touched her own, and the waves of sensation that tore through her stole reason.

Lips parting, a moan whispered past the kiss as Ivan's lips slanted over hers, he deepened the caress, deepened the pleasure she found herself helpless against.

She couldn't believe this was actually happening. He was kissing her, pulling her closer, surrounding her with his arms, and lifting her closer to him.

He was tall. So tall she felt defenseless, felt intensely feminine. She felt overwhelmed, sheltered.

Bad idea. Very bad idea.

If she was discovered, the repercussions wouldn't be pleasant. If this man ever learned who she was, he'd probably kill her himself.

But she was helpless, ensnared.

She hadn't realized how desperately she needed to be touched, how cold and hungry she was inside.

She stilled in his arms for just a second as she felt a tidal wave of need suddenly erupt inside her. Instinct took over and her lips parted, her fingers fisted in his silk shirt, and she found herself on her tiptoes as she fought to get closer, to taste more of him.

She'd never been kissed like this. With such experienced male lust and determined sensual intent. He didn't make allowances for the experience he had no idea she didn't possess. One hand gripped the hair at the back of her head, the other pressed into the small of her back, lifting her closer to him, and the engorged length of his erection pressed into her lower stomach between the layers of clothing separating them.

He was warm, hard, strong.

His lips moved over hers, demanding a deeper kiss,

leading her along a path of wicked delights, and her body was more than willing to follow the dark sensuality pulling her in. He wasn't gentle. His lips slanted across hers, his tongue spearing between them, licking, tasting her as he let her taste as well.

Pleasure overwhelmed her, mesmerized her. He led her past her fear of the unknown and her own inexperience with sensual temptation and sensations she could have never imagined existed.

Those diabolical lips slid to her neck, stroked, tasted, his teeth rasping, her senses held hostage to the most incredible pleasure. And she was weak, so weak.

She knew he was undressing her. Her t-shirt was jerked over her head before his lips returned to hers, the clasp of her bra released before she realized it, and one broad, callused palm cupped her sensitive breast, his thumb rasping her nipple.

Oh God . . .

What was she supposed to do? She needed to do something, anything to return the incredible pleasure she was feeling.

"That's it, baby," he groaned as she felt her back meet the mattress of her bed. "That's it; just let me have you."

Hard hands tugged at hers, pushing them above her head as she forced her eyes open in time to watch him shrug the silk shirt from his shoulders.

"How beautiful you look," he crooned. "My perfect Syn."

Bronzed flesh, a light mat of hair covering his wide chest, hard, heated flesh. Her fingers curled into fists, the need to touch him battled with her inexperience, her uncertainty, and the weakness that swept through her.

Rising to stand next to the bed, he quickly loosened his belt, then the slacks he wore, and a second later shed them before her stunned gaze. Not that he gave her time to do more than glimpse the erection he released. And he sure as hell didn't give her a chance to consider what she'd seen.

She was on the verge of voicing an objection, or at least considering one, when he bent to her, his lips returning to hers for several deep, hungry kisses as he released the band of her jeans.

Those kisses . . .

She moaned, arching to him, the tight, sensitive points of her nipples raking against his hair-roughened chest and sending pleasure lancing at her senses.

She had to touch him. Feel the heat of his flesh, the flex of powerful muscle beneath. As her hands clenched on his biceps she felt her jeans being pulled from her. They cleared her hips, her thighs, leaving her naked, undefended before him.

For a moment, fear of the unknown threatened to swamp her, to dilute the mesmerizing sensations wrapping around her.

His lips slid from hers, kisses moving along her neck, holding her spellbound, wrapped in a heated warmth she couldn't fight. His tongue stroked against her flesh, his fingers cupped the mound of one breast, then those diabolical lips covered the painfully tight peak.

"Ivan . . ." She was barely aware of breathing out his name, but she was intently, intensely aware of his lips closing on the peak, drawing the hard bud into his mouth and sucking her with hungry demand.

Oh God. No one had ever touched her there, not like this. She'd been groped, pinched, a time or two, but this?

She arched to him, holding on to him for dear life as her neck tipped back and she fought to just breathe.

Just breathe.

Because it was so good. Because the sensations were like being trapped in the most exquisite chaos, spreading a heated warmth clear to the depths of her bones. This went beyond pleasure.

Her hands slid from his shoulders to his hair, spearing into the thick black strands to hold his suckling mouth closer, to feel the sensations deeper. His tongue rasped the peak, licked it, caressed it. His hand shaped the mound, plumped it, held her nipple in position for his mouth to devour her.

A moan broke past her lips as he moved, only to turn into a shattered cry when he turned his attention to her other nipple. Fingers of electric ecstasy raced from her nipple to her sex. Her clit was swollen, as tight as her nipples; she could feel the wet heat spilling from her, preparing her.

"Sweet Syn," he whispered, his voice decadent with the sound of male lust. Rough, dark, the hunger that filled his voice had a moan escaping her.

She was shaking, she realized. Forcing her lashes up, she stared up at him as he levered himself away from her, staring down at her, the deep blue of his eyes appearing black in the dim light of the room.

"Come up here, baby," he whispered, easing her up along the bed as he pushed her thighs apart and eased between them.

Then his lips were on hers again, kissing a path down her body until they met the mound of her sex.

"Ivan . . . wait . . ." she whispered at the same second his tongue licked over her clit.

Sensation tore through her. Pleasure, so much pleasure. Her fingers locked in his hair, the distant realization that she was pushing his head closer, that she wanted nothing more than to feel that caress again, shattering her.

Lifting her legs until her knees were bent, her feet flat against the bed, he proceeded to still any thought of protest. He destroyed the ability to think. His hands slid beneath her rear, lifted her, and showed her just how wicked, how carnal, he could be.

He kissed, licked, moaned against the bare folds between her thighs and within seconds had her screaming his name as her body began to vibrate with a surge of pure rapture. She was trying to cry out his name, so breathless, so lost in the sensations tearing through her mind, that she wasn't even aware of him rising between her thighs.

The pressure at her sex at first was lost within the storm tearing through her. His lips came over hers again, his tongue plunging past them as the pressure became heavier, thicker, pressing inside her.

He was taking her, so slowly. The strange, heady

blending of ecstasy and fire made distinguishing between pleasure and pain impossible. His erection stretched her flesh apart, spreading it, burrowing deeper.

"So damned tight . . ." he groaned, tearing his lips from hers, burying them against her neck as she arched closer.

Pleasure and pain.

The sensations building inside her were so intense, unfamiliar, so blinding, she didn't have a chance to understand exactly what they were. She had a moment to regret her inexperience, to wish she could make him feel the power, the fiery, lashing sensations as she felt them. To please him as well.

In the next second he pulled back and returned with a thrust that tore through the thin veil of her virginity. She heard herself cry out. Not for the pain, though there was the surge of flaming heat mixing with the ecstasy.

She could barely breathe, she wasn't even certain she remembered how to breathe, when he stilled over her.

She thought she heard him curse, the sound torn, filled with conflict. His large body was tense above her, so hard and thick inside her.

"Don't stop . . ." she gasped, needing, desperate, to ride the brutal waves of sensation she could feel threatening to break over her.

One hand slid to her knee, lifted it until it rested over his hip as he thrust inside her again, going deeper as her inner muscles tightened with involuntary spasms around the intrusions.

It shouldn't be like this. It shouldn't ride that border of pleasure and pain with such a fine edge. She shouldn't be begging for more. But she was, a whispered cry, desperate whimpers, as she writhed beneath him.

"God. Baby. Easy," he groaned at her neck as he took her deeper, filled her more. "Sweet . . . So sweet . . ."

The thrusts quickened, deepened, until he pushed in with one hard lunge, filling her to her limits, the feel of his flesh throbbing inside her so hot . . . He was heating her from the inside out and she craved more. Her body was begging for more. Her inner muscles were clenching and unclenching, rippling around the invading force as a rough, desperate growl sounded at her ear.

Then he was moving. Moving and intensifying those sensations, building them, making them race inside her, to build and build like a storm growing out of control, tearing through her mind. Tighter and tighter with each hard thrust, each caress of her inner flesh.

The impalements were hard as he moved between her thighs, thrusting through the brutally clenched flesh, stretching her, taking her. She arched, shuddering as the sensations inside her became more forceful, like a tornado of sensation racing out of control. Brutal. So hot—

Then it erupted in a conflagration she was certain tore the life from her body. She couldn't breathe. She was only barely aware of Ivan tightening above her.

All she knew was the brutal heat exploding through her, rapture imploding outward, and stealing her mind, perhaps her soul.

Conscious thought was lost, unwanted. Hard shudders wracked her body with each inner explosion, jerking her hips against his, dragging a cry from her lips with each one, a shattered male groan from his.

How long it lasted she didn't know, didn't care. She'd remain there forever if she could, always warm, always safe.

But nothing lasted forever. She knew that. She'd known that for years. And reality intruded, though it did so with a hazy veil of exhaustion.

She moaned in protest as she felt Ivan move, felt her body fight to hold on to him as he retreated. She drifted on a cloud of such satisfaction as he gently wiped her thighs that she couldn't force herself from it. She was simply there until his warmth enfolded her, sheltered her, and allowed her to drift into sleep.

Just for a little while, she told herself. As long as he held her, she'd be safe. No one defeated Ivan Resnova. No one dared. She could sleep safe, warm, just for a little while. She'd run again when she woke, before he could realize the deception she was practicing. Before he could ever learn who she was and she had to see the revulsion in his eyes.

Just for a little while . . .

She was gone.

Ivan stared at the empty bed and he knew she hadn't just left the room. Her pack wasn't lying on the stool at the end of the bed, nor were her boots sitting on the floor behind it.

Damn her.

He'd told her he'd be back in a few hours. He hadn't told her where he was going. The trip into Boulder had been necessary though. The two men who had nearly taken the red-haired temptress the night he and Ilya had jerked her off a dark street in Boulder had been found. Unfortunately, they were in no shape to talk. A bullet in the brain would do that though.

Stepping to the bed next to the table and the note propped against the lamp, he picked up the stationery, read it, then let his fingers crumple it slowly.

"Ivan, security reported Miss Delaney left . . ." Ilya stepped into the room, only to come to a stop at the look Ivan shot him.

Rage was burning inside him and he had no idea why, other than the fact that he wasn't quite finished with her yet. Not quite yet.

"How long has she been gone?" He had to force the calm into his voice, force back the fury pounding at his brain.

"She left thirty minutes after our departure. She was picked up by a young woman one of the guards recognized from the coffee shop," Ilya reported. "She would have had to have made the call before we left."

Yes, she would have. She knew she was leaving even as she lay in that bed when he walked in after his shower and promised to return to her.

He should have known, he admitted to himself. Something almost fearful had flashed in her gaze, but he'd marked it down to the sexual excesses of the night and early morning. She'd been a virgin, but never had a woman been more eager to learn the pleasure to be found in his arms.

"Find her!" There was a snap in his voice, despite his efforts to hold it back. "She'll leave Boulder as soon as possible. Find her and bring her back."

Surprise reflected in the other man's gray eyes as the dragon tattoo at the side of his face flexed as though in warning as his jaw tightened. It was a look Ivan had seen when the other man had caught him leaving Crimsyn's suite that morning and realized Ivan had spent the night there.

For some reason, Ilya had developed a protectiveness toward the girl while she was at the estate. A protectiveness that could end up causing problems if the other man wasn't careful.

Rather than protesting, Ilya gave a short nod, turned, and left the room.

When he was gone, Ivan glared down at the note, each word clearly branded into his brain.

Thank you, but it's time for me to go . . .

No goodbye or signature. Nothing. Just that one simple sentence.

Time for her to go? He didn't think so. And he'd quickly show her how ill-advised it was to run from him. He enjoyed the chase, the hunt, and once he caught her he'd damned sure enjoy that even more.

chapter three

Ivan watched Journey as she waited tables at the crowded diner. She was pale; dark circles shadowed her eyes despite the makeup she wore. Her face was a bit thinner, or at least appeared so from the way her red-gold hair was pulled back from her face into a tight ponytail.

She looked more delicate than she had a month before, more haunted. More frightened. She had far more reason to be frightened than he'd imagined when she'd been at his Colorado estate.

No doubt she was also preparing to run again. She only stayed in one place long enough to make enough money for another bus ticket before she disappeared. She used a different name each time she ran, kept her head down, and worked for next to nothing for under-the-table wages.

She was terrified.

Her eyes kept checking the windows of the diner, searching the night outside, her body tense and ready to run. She had good reason to be scared. She had good reason to run.

"She already has a bus ticket," Ilya stated from where he sat in the front seat of the dark SUV far enough from the diner that she wouldn't see them sitting in the vehicle. "Max questioned the staff at the bus station. Flashed her picture. She bought it just before she arrived for work under yet another name, heading for Los Angeles."

Elbow propped on the armrest between the back seats, Ivan rubbed his forefinger over his upper lip, his gaze narrowing on Journey now.

He had two men sitting in a booth next to the door, two more positioned at the back and front entrances in case trouble arrived before he made his move.

She had no idea what she was doing or where she was going, he'd realized in the last four weeks, but she was obviously more frightened than she had been before coming to Boulder a month ago. Before that, she'd usually stayed in one area longer, actually held a proper job, and had the money to purchase a fake ID.

What had happened to change that?

Hell, the better question was why had she begun running to begin with? True, her father's betrayal of her and the knowledge she'd more or less been sold to the fiancé she had four years ago would have been a shock. The family wasn't destitute despite her father's and grandfather's arrests and imprisonment. The humiliation of it would have run deep, but the rest of her family were handling it fine.

The fiancé, Beauregard Grant, wasn't really a bad sort, a bastard and an ass but instrumental in revealing the crimes committed by the two men who headed the Taite family. That fiancé now ran the Taite companies and the family was still taken care of, so why had the younger daughter run as she had?

And why had she found herself in New York working with Ivan's daughter, Amara?

There were far too many questions and not enough answers. Just as he couldn't identify who she was running from now, he could find no proof that her former fiancé was behind her fear. There were no signs that her father and grandfather were behind it either.

"What are you going to do, Ivan?" Ilya questioned, his tone quiet, curious.

To be honest, he hadn't yet made up his mind. That damned woman was like a hurricane when she was pissed off, dangerous as hell. He hadn't forgotten her little fist slamming into his face the first time he'd literally kidnapped her off the street.

Nor had he forgotten the night he'd taken her virginity.

His erection flexed at that thought. The lust that had come into being that night had been like wildfire. Impossible to fight, destructive as it burned inside him and refused to relent. He woke in the middle of the night, his fingers clenched around the hard flesh, memories of her tormenting him, testing his patience.

And no other woman would do. He'd learned that

quickly enough. No other woman smelled like his "Syn," tasted like her, sounded like her. And no other woman had ever been brave enough to play the game she'd played with him where her identity was concerned.

"Ivan." Ilya drew him from his thoughts and pulled his attention to the closed-panel van that moved slowly through the parking lot.

It was the second time it had made a pass along the far edge of the parking area. If it did as before, it would circle the diner.

"Carter, tail it," he spoke into the communication link he wore at his ear.

He watched as Carter and his partner pulled out in a compact sedan and followed the van.

"She'll be off in five minutes," Ilya told him. "That van will back."

And they had no idea how many men would come for her.

"Tobias and Sawyer, join Mac and Cameron," he ordered the two men he knew Journey would recognize. "We'll pull around back to the kitchen entrance. Carter, stay on that van."

Ilya started the SUV when Tobias and Sawyer stepped from the pickup they waited in closer to the diner. He eased the SUV from the parking spot and pulled around to the back of the diner as the other two men neared the doorway.

After he pulled the SUV just beyond the back entrance, he and Ilya stepped from the vehicle, leaving the doors open, and waited just a few feet from the exit.

They didn't have to wait long.

The back door flew open and Journey tore from the diner, right into his arms. Catching those lethal little wrists and dragging her close, he glared down at her pale features, giving her just enough time to realize who he was.

"Me, or the men in the van that will be pulling around here in about two minutes flat. Make the choice now," he snarled as her eyes widened and the fear in her features increased. "Now."

"You." She wasn't in the least relieved to see him there though. It was more a choice of the threat she knew versus whatever she was running from.

After Ivan pushed her ahead of him and into the back seat of the SUV, Ilya was pulling around the diner when the link at Ivan's ear activated.

"Van's pulling in again," Carter reported. "Heading around back."

They intended to do just as he and Ilya had. Catch her exiting the diner through the shadowed rear door.

"Stay on them," Ivan ordered. "I want to know who the hell they are and who's pulling their strings. Tobias and Sawyer, you're with me. Jake and Mac, join Carter and watch your asses. Get burned and you'll deal with me."

Something none of them wanted to do.

Deactivating the link, Ivan pulled it from his ear and tucked it into the pocket of his leather jacket before turning to the little imposter huddled defensively against the door next to her. She looked prepared to jump from the vehicle if he so much as startled her.

He had to grin at the thought. Child locks on the back doors were amazing inventions. He'd learned to appreciate them in past years.

As he turned to her, the privacy window between the back and front seats lifted, ensuring his privacy. The executive-level SUV had been built to his specifications, with his comfort and needs in mind.

The windows darkened further as he flipped on the dim light and simply stared at her. The incredible green eyes watched him warily, her pale features somber, those lush lips thin with the control she was exerting over herself.

Small fists were clenched in her lap and the tension that radiated from her was nearly thick enough to cut.

"You've not been sleeping," he stated calmly as he leaned back against the corner of the seat and stared at her. "Or eating well, it appears."

Surprise gleamed in her gaze for a second before the wariness returned.

"Why are you here?" Her voice was as tight as her body.

He arched a brow and let a grin edge the corners of his lips.

"We'll discuss that later." *Much later.* "Take your hair down before I do it myself. It's a wonder you don't have a headache."

Surprise again, and this time it lingered longer in her gaze as she frowned back at him.

"What does my hair have to do with anything?" The argumentative tone assured him she had no intentions of doing as he asked.

He didn't ask again.

Reaching out, he did it himself, holding her head still the second it took to pull the hair band from it and leave the loose, fiery curls tumbling around her face and shoulders. Before she could strike out at him he was back in his own seat and surveying his handiwork in approval.

"Damn you, Ivan!" That temper of hers shot into her expression and brightened those pretty green eyes. "That was uncalled for."

"I told you to do it before I took care of it myself; you were the one who wanted to argue over it." He shrugged at the accusation. "I rarely ask twice, Syn. You should know that."

Syn. No, that wasn't really her name, but damn him if it didn't suit her.

The look she gave him was filled with anger now. He preferred the anger over the wariness and fear.

"No, you just force others to do it!" she snapped. "Why the hell are you here?"

"It appears I'm saving your ass, again," he grunted. "What the hell are you running from, baby? And don't bother to tell me 'nothing,' because I'd be very irate to hear that lie fall from those pretty lips."

"Irate" didn't even come close.

Her lips trembled, once, before she controlled them. For a second, the memory of those pretty pouting curves surrounding his cock nearly had a growl tearing from his chest.

"Fine, it's none of your business then." Anger filled

her voice. "And for the life of me I can't figure out why you assume it is."

Because she was the daughter, the granddaughter, of his greatest enemies.

Not that Ivan had known who they were until four years ago. It had taken years to learn the identity of the men who haunted his and his daughter's lives and murdered his mother.

"You're my daughter's friend," he finally answered as though the reason were completely logical. "It wasn't hard to figure out you were running from more than my enemies or what you saw in New York when you lit out of Boulder as you did."

Disbelief completely filled her face now. She blinked twice, pushed her fingers through her hair, then shook her head as though the situation were simply a lost cause.

"That's your reason?" she finally asked, resigned doubt filling her voice.

"Well." He laid one arm along the back of the seat and smiled at her, anticipation surging through him. "It definitely factored in."

It hadn't rated as high as the hunger bounding through him to feel those pretty lips against his flesh again or see the shock in her eyes when she found something she was certain was depraved was instead too good to deny.

A flush mounted her cheeks as his gaze slid to her breasts, then back to her face.

Her nipples were hard. That thin shirt did nothing

to hide the tight little points beneath her bra. Her breathing was harder now, but he'd be damned if the innocence that had always lurked in her eyes, in her expression, had disappeared. It hadn't. It was like a beacon to the carnal lust that rose inside him and demanded he experience it again.

Breathy little moans, shocked, pleasure-filled gasps, the uncertainty even as she let him have his way. They'd burned down the night in that bed and she'd done something to him he couldn't explain. Something he hadn't realized she was doing until he'd stared down at her as he'd pushed his cock past those pretty lips and realized she had no idea what to do, but she ached to do it.

"Stop," she demanded. "This has nothing to do with sex and we both know it."

That was why his dick was iron hard, he thought mockingly, because it had nothing to do with sex.

"Do we now?" he murmured a second before he moved once again. Reaching across the distance, he gripped one wrist and pulled it from her lap, tugging her closer and forcing her fingers over his cock, letting her feel the erection tormenting the hell out of him. "Sure of that, are you?"

He wasn't sure of that at all.

Her fingers curled against the width of his erection as though the action were involuntary, her gaze going to where he held her grip.

"Ivan . . ." The breathy little sigh was rife with feminine need and uncertainty, wariness, and hunger.

The look on her face was one he swore he'd never

seen before. Dazed, filled with such hunger and need. There was nothing calculating, or knowing, just a woman's desire. Slightly confused, helpless, wanting . . .

He lifted his hand from her wrist to cup her cheek, the feel of her fingers trembling, caressing his flesh through his slacks, testing his control. But he had to taste her again, feel those pretty lips beneath his own.

"Stroke me, baby," he whispered against her lips, staring into her dazed expression, desperate to release the straining length of his cock.

He took the kiss he was aching for before she could protest, if she was going to protest, and let himself sink into the need raging through him. Damn, he hadn't had enough time to teach her how to take what she wanted, to stroke him, to explore him as he wanted to explore her.

This was why he'd never allowed himself to take a virgin. His desires were too dark, his needs too carnal. And he'd been helpless once he'd figured out just how innocent she was.

As his lips slanted across hers, he pulled her closer, holding her against him, one hand tangling in the curls at the back of her head, tugging at the strands just enough to give her a taste of heat. And she loved it.

A moan whispered past her lips, and the sound made him crazy, made him so eager to take her it was all he could do to keep from ripping her clothes from her.

He pulled back from her while he still had the control to do so, while he could keep from pushing her to her back and taking her like a damned animal. Her fingers were still caressing his cock, little tremors raced through her body, and her expression was dazed with the pleasure beginning to overtake her.

"Now, what were you saying?" he growled, hearing the whisper of his accent in his voice.

Breathing heavy, he watched her struggle, felt it in her reluctance as her fingers moved back from his erection and in the regret that flickered across her expression.

"You were lying to me about why you came for me." She moved back from him, her gaze never leaving his. "You wouldn't chase after a woman simply because she made you hard, Ivan," she all but sneered. "I know better than that."

"I'm about two seconds from pushing you back in that seat, ripping that skirt off you, and fucking you like a goddamned animal," he snarled, the challenge in her gaze pushing a button he hadn't known existed within him. "Don't push me right now, you little wildcat, or I'll do just that."

There was something in his voice, a darkness, a throb of complete sincerity, that had Journey easing back from him as she watched him carefully, uncertain now in the face of that pure, carnal lust reflected in his expression.

"It's not the only reason." She shook her head, certain of that but of little else. "I don't believe it's the main reason. So why don't you admit it."

She was terrified of the exact reason why though. Had he learned her true identity? Did he know she was

Craig Taite's daughter? Surely he hadn't, or he would have killed her by now. Ivan wasn't known for playing with his enemies. He was known for striking hard, fast, and with utter mercilessness.

"When you tell me who was in that van coming for you." The mocking dare wasn't lost on her. "Tell me, my little Syn, who else is chasing you?"

Who else was chasing her? She'd need a notebook for that one, she thought wearily.

She didn't need this now. Not when she felt so weak, when everything was so hopeless. She just wanted to find a place to hide, to sleep without dreams, either of the sexual or the terrifying, and find some peace.

"I don't know," she whispered.

At least it wasn't a lie. She had a feeling he could see through any lie she tried to tell. That was a distinctly uncomfortable feeling.

Lowering her head, she stared at her fingers, her thumb rubbing over the small circular scar that marred the inside of her left index finger. It was always there, a memory she couldn't escape, couldn't forget.

She didn't know who was in the van, she didn't know who sent them, but she knew her father was the reason they were after her. And if they caught her, they'd destroy her.

"What are you running from, Syn?" His voice wasn't filled with lust and it wasn't teasing. It was chilly, as cold as she felt inside.

"What I'm running from doesn't affect you or Amara," she told him, shaking her head because she knew the truth wasn't something she could tell him.

God, he was the last man in the world she could ever tell. He'd throw her to the wolves so fast it would make her head spin. There was no lust deep enough, strong enough, to still the hatred Ivan Resnova would feel for the youngest granddaughter of the man who had nearly destroyed his life more than once. Her grandfather hadn't been alone either. When her father had come of age, he'd been right there helping Stephen Taite in the depraved, horrendous acts committed.

"Let me be the judge of that," he advised her, his tone warning. "If what I saw tonight is an indication, you're not going to be able to hide for long. This makes twice I've managed to slip you from beneath the noses of whoever's chasing you. Run from me again and you may run out of luck."

The thought of that terrified her. The thought of Ivan ever learning her identity and staring at her with hatred though . . . It wasn't just the fear of what he would do to her; it was the fear of seeing the pure distaste that would fill his expression. For some reason, the thought of that hurt far more than the knowledge that he would likely kill her.

"Eventually, that's exactly what will happen." She was smart enough to know that. "You should have never come after me."

But if he hadn't . . . She had to fight the hitch of her breathing that would assure him of her pure terror. Whoever they were, they were determined; she gave them credit for that. They had somehow found her in Boulder and managed to stay on her ass ever since.

She couldn't figure out who they were or who had

sent them. She was too damned busy trying to stay one step ahead of them.

"Hmm," he murmured, and that sound sent a chill racing up her spine.

"Look, just take me to the bus station so I can leave." That sound he made, the tone of it, the hint of knowledge in it, had panic raging inside her. "If I had wanted your help I would have asked for it, don't you think?"

She would have never asked for his help; she didn't dare.

A dark, amused chuckle had her lifting her head, watching him cautiously, that fear rising inside her, tearing at her. There was no way to run, no way to escape him. At least not yet. And the danger that suddenly filled the interior of the SUV had the hairs prickling against her arm in warning.

"Ivan . . ." she whispered, wanting to beg now. "Just let me go."

She tried to force back the anger, the fear. They rose inside her pretty much neck and neck. Her mother had warned her for years that her temper was going to get her in trouble, and Journey had realized years ago she was right.

"No," he stated implacably. "We have a rather long drive ahead of us; would you like Ilya to stop for something to eat?"

He asked the question as though the earlier conversation had never existed. As though there weren't a chance that he knew who she was, that there weren't someone determined to kidnap her and do only God knew what.

"No, I'm not hungry, dammit . . ." the anger slipped.

"You're rather testy; perhaps you are." He smiled coolly. "If I'm not mistaken you're even thinner than you were in Colorado."

She clenched her fists, certain she wanted to hit him. Again.

"Don't play games with me, Ivan," she demanded, knowing she'd never survive if he kept this particular game up for long. "Give me the courtesy of that much at least."

Something shifted in his expression until his gaze was somber, intent. She wished she knew what he was thinking, what he saw when he looked at her. Something besides the ragged, exhausted woman she'd become.

"Then you do the same, baby," he demanded. "Tell me what I need to know to protect you."

That shocked her. He couldn't know who she was, no matter the certainty she'd felt for a moment that he did. If he did, he'd never offer to protect her, never want to protect her.

She shook her head wearily. "I don't know who it is. I swear it."

"Tell me what you're hiding, and we'll figure out the rest." His expression was devoid of emotion. It was cool, almost polite.

Journey stared back at him, taking in every nuance of his expression, recalling everything Amara had ever told her about her very dangerous father. And one thing she remembered was that the other woman said he was at his most dangerous when he appeared cool, polite. When he watched a person without a hint of emotion. Not hatred, not compassion, no hint of warmth.

He couldn't know, she told herself. If he did, he would have already killed her or he would have left her to her fate and allowed the men looking for her to catch her.

Panic sped through her, racing through her veins and kicking her heart into overdrive. The need to run, to fight, was like a fever inside her. And there was no place to run, no way to run.

"This isn't your problem," she told him, the chill that had filled her before he took her in his arms returning now that he was no longer touching her. "I'm not your problem. The best thing you could do for both of us is drop me at the bus station."

Smoothing her hands down her thighs, she turned away from him and fought the weariness trying to sweep over her. She was so tired. The constant running and fear were finally taking their toll.

"Well, for the time being, I think I'll make you my problem," he replied mockingly.

The sheer arrogance of the statement should have had her raging; instead, she could only shake her head at the sheer stubbornness.

Maybe she should just tell him the truth, she contemplated silently. What worse could he do than the men chasing her? At least Ivan would kill her quickly. He might be merciless, but she couldn't believe he'd torture her.

"You think it's so simple," she sighed. "With your

money and your power, you believe you can simply buy whatever you want and shoot your way through any danger. For the rest of us, life isn't always so simple."

Her life wasn't so simple anyway. Betrayal filled it. There was no amount of money or power that could protect one from the cruelty of others, especially family. Her father was a monster, her mother a product of the world she lived within. And the one true friend she'd believed she possessed had been lying to her in the worst way.

And in her naïveté, she'd honestly believed she could handle the danger she found herself in after she'd run.

"Well now, baby, let's see if I can't help you simplify your life a little bit?" His voice was as dark, as dangerous, as his expression. "We'll just see if we can't figure out who's chasing that cute little ass of yours and why they want it so bad." He leaned closer, the steely determination on his face sending a chill down her spine. "I'll just settle this little problem for you."

She shifted, closing the difference between them further as that damnable temper of hers sparked and exploded.

"Fuck you!" she enunciated clearly, teeth baring as she locked her gaze with his. "I don't need your help."

His eyes narrowed. "Well now, my little Syn, I don't mind if I do."

chapter four

His control was for shit.

He'd known the night he met her what that fire exploding from her gaze did to him. It made him hard, made him crazy.

Before he could stop himself his hand jerked forward, buried in the hair at the back of her head as he pulled her forward, his lips covering hers again. And this time, there was no hesitancy, no reluctance or fight.

Her lips parted, her fingers fisting in his hair as well, holding him to her as he jerked her closer.

Wait to have her? It was going to happen.

His lips devoured hers; tongue thrusting, burying against hers, he took her mouth as he turned, balancing her on the edge of the seat as he knelt in front of her. The snug skirt she wore was pushed to her hips, her panties ripped.

Her hands were at his belt, pulling at it, struggling to loosen it and the clasp of his slacks. Pushing her shaking fingers out of the way, Ivan finished the job himself until he was gripping his cock, the shaft throbbing in demand as he pushed between her thighs.

She was wet. Little cries parted her lips as she stared back at him, her expression filled with hunger, pleasure, and just enough bemusement that he knew she was as surprised by her own lack of control as he was by his.

When the sensitive head of his cock pressed between the bare, slick folds of her sex, he paused. Breathing hard, teeth clenched, he tried to leash the lust just enough . . .

"Oh God, Ivan. I need you . . ." The desperation in her cry was like a match to fuel.

He thrust forward, the thick crest burying inside her, sending flash points of pure, fiery bolts of sensation slamming into his balls.

"Fuck. Baby . . ." He groaned.

He turned her, pushed her back to the seat, and came between her thighs, rising over her and lifting her hips to forge deeper.

"That's my Syn," he groaned as the heated, snug inner tissue gripped him tighter. "Let that sweet pussy suck me in."

She was as tight as the first time, as hot and intoxicating.

Before he realized what he was doing he parted the front of her blouse by the simple means of tearing the buttons from their moorings.

It was a simple matter to release the front clasp of her bra, to lower his head and suck one hard little nipple into his mouth as he thrust inside her again.

God, it was good. Her wet heat clasped his erection, rippling over it, sucking him inside.

He could feel the sweat gathering on his brow, in the small of his back. The interior of the SUV became steamy with the warmth spilling between them as he felt it blazing through his body. She made him so fucking hot he couldn't bank the heat, couldn't dim it.

He'd hungered for her until he'd been certain the need would make him crazy. He could remember little else but the need that had tormented him for the past month.

Beneath him, his Syn arched to him, her fingers tight in his hair, holding him to her nipple, her legs wrapped around his back, her hips arching, taking him deeper.

Burying inside her should never be done quickly, he thought with hazy lust. It was done by destructive degrees, each push fraying his sanity as he fought to hold on to just enough to ensure her pleasure.

Groaning, his lips lifted from her nipple, his head falling to the seat next to her shoulder as finally he pushed fully inside her. Buried in to the hilt, balls drawn tight, his cock throbbing, his release hovering at the edge of his senses.

"So fucking tight . . ." he growled, his lips against her shoulder, the taste of feminine flesh touching his tongue as her hips shifted, her sheath rippling along his cock. "Ah hell, be still, baby . . ."

"I dreamed of you," she panted, the breathy, needy sound of her voice causing him to clench his eyes closed, to fight to hold on, just a minute. "I dreamed of you touching me, Ivan."

The husky, desperate tone of her voice, the need rising in it had his balls tightening with the need to come.

God, a minute.

One hand clenching her hip, he thrust against her. Pulling back until the crest remained inside her, he thrust against her, and he was lost. The pleasure was jagged strikes of pure sensation. Working inside her, thrusting, his breath clenching with the pleasure, he felt her tighten, heard her cry out his name, and lost his mind.

He'd never lost his mind in a woman's arms in his sexual life. He knew the dangers. He would have never allowed it to happen if he'd believed it possible. But as he felt her coming around him, the slick heat spilling along his cock, his senses exploded.

The world was a blaze of pure fiery ecstasy. It was a pleasure he couldn't resist, and he knew he'd willingly jump into this flame again and again. He'd be unable to stop himself, unable to resist.

Thrusting, groaning her name, he spilled himself inside her, pumping his release into her with a force that stole his breath after it stole his mind.

What had happened?

Journey fought to make sense of her own actions, her weakness where this man was concerned. As though when he'd taken her the month before he'd opened a part of her senses that she had no idea existed.

She was quiet as he eased from her, his still firm flesh retreating and sending a shudder of reaction through her at the movement.

Lifting her lashes, she watched as he quickly secured his slacks by the means of simply zipping them. His shirt might be missing a few buttons though, she noticed.

Before she could regain her breath or her mind, he reached down to the bag she'd seen on the floor earlier. A second later he eased her thighs farther apart and efficiently cleaned their combined releases from her.

He'd forgotten to wear a condom again, she thought distantly, making a mental note to discuss that with him. The birth control she was on wasn't the strongest, and she was certain he wouldn't want to actually conceive a child with his enemy's daughter.

"I have a shirt you can wear," he said quietly, reaching down again, and when he straightened he helped her up into the seat.

Tugging down the waitressing skirt, she let him help her remove the tattered remains of her blouse before helping her into the shirt. He buttoned it for her, saying nothing, his expression quiet, almost somber in the shadowed darkness of the enclosed space.

"I'm sorry," he finally said, moving to sit across from her, his knees enclosing hers as he leaned forward to brush her hair gently from her face. "I can't even excuse that loss of control, baby."

Baby. He kept calling her baby, as though she meant something. She'd remembered that during the long, lost nights she'd spent after running from him. The way he whispered the endearment, his blue eyes dark and reflecting a hunger that didn't always show in his expression.

"It was mutual." She finally lifted her shoulders when he said nothing more.

Should she be ashamed? She hoped not, because she couldn't find it in herself to regret it. She'd never known such pleasure, or such power, in simply touching a man. And being taken by him was something she couldn't have imagined. There hadn't been a touch or a moment in her life that could have prepared her for the effect Ivan had on her.

"You don't have to say that . . ." The regret in his tone made her feel an edge of fear, as though he regretted not just his loss of control but having taken her as well.

"I don't just say anything," she informed him, her voice still far too weak to reflect any sort of irritation. "I missed . . ." She started to say him, his touch. "Never mind. But it was mutual."

He just stared at her for long moments, no mockery or frustration, just a steady watchfulness she found nerve wracking.

"I'm a hard man, Syn," he finally said quietly. "I'm not a nice man, nor am I the white knight any virgin would dream of. Parts of my soul are so dark, even I refuse to peer into them. But if you trust me to help you, I wouldn't betray you."

He always kept his promises. That was the one thing his daughter, Amara, loved the most about him. Her poppa, as Amara called him, always kept his promises. He gave them carefully, with much thought, but when he gave them they were absolute.

She shook her head at this promise though. "I won't hold you to that," she promised him instead. "You can't help me, Ivan. No one can help me. The best thing you can do is release me. Let me go and forget you ever saw me."

Because it was going to kill her when he learned who she was, and the longer she stayed the greater the risk. The thought of seeing that hatred in his eyes destroyed her.

He eased back in the seat with a heavy sigh, pushing his fingers through his hair before shooting her a brooding look.

"What the hell am I going to do about you, Syn?" he asked her then.

And she didn't have an answer for him. He wouldn't do what was best, and that was let her leave. He'd destroy her when he learned who she was though.

He might even kill her . . .

Ivan watched as Journey rubbed her thumb over the small scar on the opposite hand. Just between her thumb and forefinger, the circular scar looked like a cigarette burn. When she was upset, he'd always know, because she'd rub her other thumb against it.

Reaching out, he gripped her hand and drew it to him until he could see the faint blemish marring her creamy flesh.

"That's a cigarette burn," he told her, pushing back the rage. "How did it happen?"

The tension that filled her body had her drawn so tight he was amazed she wasn't trembling.

"I didn't move fast enough." She shrugged as she met his gaze, then dropped hers.

It wasn't a lie, but it wasn't the truth.

"You didn't move fast enough to keep some sorry bastard from trapping your hand?" he growled. "It's an old scar. I'm going to guess a parent."

That bastard father of hers no doubt.

"I wasn't a very obedient child," she said softly, turning to look out the window as she tugged her hand from his grip.

"Neither was Amara." He could feel the fury burning closer to the limits of his control. "And by God, she doesn't carry any scars from the experience."

She pulled her hand back to her lap and stared down at the scar in the dim light.

"I was sixteen," she told him then. "I spoke to the wrong person at a party. When I was told not to do so again, I argued."

Him.

By God, that son of a bitch had burned her because she'd spoken to him at some fucking party. And Ivan knew it was him. She'd looked so uncomfortable, out of place and frightened that he'd asked her if she wanted to dance. He'd known she was just a kid, but there had always been something about her eyes that got to him.

"A boy?" he asked, almost strangling on the need to know.

"A man." A mysterious smile tilted her lips. The smile of a woman child learning her way. "It was worth the scar."

The pain that struck at his chest shocked him. *That scar had been worth it,* she said. That smile, the soft tone of her voice. What the fuck was he going to do about her?

"Should I be jealous?" he asked as though it were a possibility.

That smile again. Mysterious, totally female, even as she shook her head.

"No need to be jealous." She shot him a quick glance and in her expression, he saw rueful amusement. Not a lot, but enough to wipe the fear from her face. "It was a long time ago anyway."

Her expression sobered again, and she turned back to the window, watching the night pass as the SUV drove swiftly through the darkness.

"You can trust me, Syn," he finally said gently, knowing she wouldn't.

"I know I can." She nodded but he heard the fear in her voice. "I know I can, Ivan."

"But you won't?" And that just pissed him off.

"I do trust you." She turned to him again, her gaze meeting his, that trust, so innocent, and so wary, gleaming in the depths of her eyes. "But I won't involve you. Now please, just let me go."

His jaw clenched.

Damn her. Son of a bitch. He was going to paddle her ass for sure.

"No," he snapped. "Not quite yet."

He was starting to wonder if he'd be able to ever let her go?

chapter five

The next evening Journey still couldn't believe the sheer arrogance Ivan displayed in forcing her to stay with him as she stood at the glass wall overlooking a sheer cliff where it plunged down to the lashing waves of the Pacific Ocean.

Only pure, unadulterated arrogance and supreme confidence would give a man the boldness to live in a cliffside home in a state where earthquakes were the norm rather than a rare occurrence. As though he were daring Mother Nature to strike.

The house was beautiful though. The living area behind her was spacious and led to a monstrously large kitchen and dining area that would be perfect for entertaining. The house spread out to include three luxurious bedrooms with attached baths that were simply decadent. On the other side you stepped out to an impressive pool and patio area.

Glass surrounded the better part of the house, which made little sense considering he was suspected to be the head of a Russian criminal organization. What crime czar surrounded himself with windows? The fact that the property was enclosed by a high stone wall didn't excuse the deliberate challenge to danger.

As she watched the sun dip below the horizon, the splash of the sun's rays against the ocean as it seemed to sink into the water itself was spectacular. She understood the desire for glass when the view was so gorgeous, but it didn't excuse the lack of protective walls.

"There you are. I wondered when you'd make it out of your room." The sound of his voice was smooth, dark, stroking against her senses like black velvet and reminding her how much darker it could get as he touched her.

"There are a lot of windows here." She turned to him as she wrapped her arms across herself. "Aren't you afraid of someone taking a shot at you?"

He paused in the middle of the room, his brow arching in condescending humor. As though he believed no one would dare. He was crazy. It was that simple.

"The windows face the ocean and we're isolated enough that I feel fairly secure." The shrug was nonchalant. "Besides, no one's taken a shot at me in years."

"Surprising." She gave a droll little roll of her eyes. "Give me a gun and I'll take care of that. I'd hate for you to forget what it felt like."

His chuckle was accompanied by a gleam of mirth mixing with the sensual wickedness of his expression.

Dressed in his customary slacks and white shirt, sleeves rolled back on his arms, he looked as predatory as any other dangerous creature.

"I tried to leave." She glared at him as he moved closer. "Your henchmen refused to allow me past the front door."

His lips quirked as he moved closer. "They know how to follow orders," he murmured, stopping within a few inches of her and forcing her to stare up at him.

"I want to leave, Ivan." She kept her voice firm, her arms crossed over her breasts and her expression determined. "I'm not your responsibility and I refuse to pretend I am."

It took effort to keep her accent from her tone. She'd gotten better at it over the years, but during times of stress it tended to slip free. And the past month had been nothing if not stressful. Her first language was English, but the French influence couldn't be completely erased no matter how hard she tried.

"Allow me to pretend for you, then." The suggestion had her freezing in shock and staring up at him.

It was the last thing she would have believed he'd think, let alone actually suggest. She couldn't, wouldn't, be his responsibility; she didn't dare.

"Have you lost your mind?" Damn, the French nearly slipped out again.

Shaking her head, she moved away from him quickly, keeping her eyes on him as she put several feet between them.

"Strange, Amara never mentioned you were

unbalanced." She watched him suspiciously. "I would have thought she'd have told me that at some point."

There was something about the half grin that pulled at his lips that had the hairs at her nape lifting in warning.

What was he up to? Ivan did nothing without a damned good reason and she could find no reason for this. It didn't benefit him in the least.

"Amara does like to keep her secrets," he finally stated, stepping toward her again. "But then, she's not the only one, is she? You like your secrets as well, it would appear."

Did she like her secrets?

She hated them. She hated the fact that she had to run, to hide from her own family, just as she hated the fact that it seemed her family was a little too determined to reacquire her.

Who else could it be? They were desperate she honor the engagement to Beauregard Grant, the distant cousin her father had sold her to. Her mother was so determined that she go through with it that she had threatened to have her committed to a facility until she learned how to be a dutiful daughter. The fortune the Grants possessed now was imposing, especially considering the loss of the companies, titles, and respect the Taite name had suffered.

"All the more reason to allow me to leave." She frowned at him as he stopped again, far too close to her, his fingers cupping her shoulders, holding her in place.

"But I'm intrigued. *You* intrigue me, my little Syn."

His head lowered, his lips brushing her ear and sending a shiver racing through her flesh.

The heat of him . . .

She wanted to close her eyes and soak it up, wrap him around her, and allow herself to sink into his skin. He was so warm, and even after escaping Colorado's spring chill, she was still cold inside. So cold and alone, and tired.

The weariness had become ever deeper in the past weeks. Always running, staying in one place only long enough to make enough money and run again. And there was never enough money to run and to eat properly. If it weren't for the waitressing jobs she took and the free meals that invariably came with working under the table, she'd likely starve. Or already have been caught.

She was smart enough to know she'd been incredibly lucky the night before though. She'd been faster than she'd expected, and she wouldn't have had a hope of escaping had it not been for Ivan.

"Ivan . . ." She wanted to protest as she felt his lips caress her ear; she truly did. She wanted to pull away, deny him, deny his touch.

But she'd ached for him after she left his Colorado estate. And when she slept, she dreamed of his touch, of the pleasure, the mind-stealing sensations she had no idea how to fight or to keep from needing.

She was twenty-six. She'd been a virgin until he'd touched her. She hadn't been raised to accept touch as an everyday part of her life and she hadn't understood how weak it could make her, or how she could crave it.

Her skin actually grew more sensitive at just the thought of Ivan touching her, kissing her again.

"You were gone when I returned to the estate," he breathed against her ear. "I was hard, imagining you in my bed waiting for me. Only to find you'd run." His lips moved to her neck, brushing against flesh so sensitive her breath caught. "I'd spent hours imagining what I was going to do to that very lovely body."

She'd never been told she had a lovely body. Too curvy, unfashionably heavy, and downright fat, but never lovely.

"I had to leave," she whispered only to lose her breath as his teeth raked against the side of her neck, rasping the flesh with such erotic promise that her womb clenched with need.

She had no idea when she'd gripped his forearms, but she could feel the tough skin under her fingers as his hands flexed at her hips. And just as the night before, she could feel her sense of self-preservation evaporating beneath the pleasure she felt whenever he was near her.

"And now I've found you." His cheek, raspy with the shadow of a beard, brushed against her shoulder. "And I'll make up for the weeks of lost time." A lingering kiss to her shoulder had her lifting to her tiptoes to get closer as she fought to breathe now. "And I'm going to fuck you until you're too tired to run from me, Journey. How does that sound?"

Oh God . . .

Journey.

He called her Journey.

He knew who she was . . .

He was almost unprepared.

She was soft and sweet; melting against him one second, in the next she was tearing herself from his arms. Ivan barely managed to keep her from falling over the glass table at her side and still she fought him.

"Let me go." The cry was fraught with both fury and fear as panic gleamed in her pale expression and exquisite green eyes.

She wasn't pale now. Her face was flushed, her expression filling with desperation when he refused to release her but, rather, wrestled her to the couch, where he pushed her to her back and came over her, holding her by the most effective means of using his own body.

"You bastard," she screamed, half sob, half fury. "Let me go."

Holding her wrists in one hand above her head, he held her hips still by lying between her thighs, ignoring her kicking legs as he gripped one hip.

A man could tell a lot by the expression when a possible enemy believed themselves helpless, unable to fight, to escape. When all the secrets were laid bare and there was nothing left to hide behind, that was when the true depth of their strength and their weaknesses were revealed.

It took only seconds to realize Journey was no fighter. She didn't possess the instinct, training, or ability to get herself out of a wet paper bag, let alone kill a highly trained agent in a garden knee-deep with snow.

Watching her curiously as she fought while doing nothing to keep her from feeling the erection straining his slacks, Ivan simply held her to the couch and waited for her to run out of steam. It didn't take long.

Perspiration coated her face and neck, her muscles strained until they quivered weakly, and her screams turned to desperate rasps until her head finally collapsed against the couch. And as she stilled, he watched a single tear roll from her closed eyes.

That drop of moisture did something to him, something he wasn't certain how to describe, even to himself. The slow-motion track it made down the side of her face, leaving a trail of dampness, like a faint scar against her flesh, softened something inside him.

Those pretty green eyes flashed open then and the fury that burned in them had his dick flexing in demand that he take the challenge, the silent dare in the depths of her gaze.

"Do it," she snarled, her voice rough with the anger and the tears she refused to shed. "What are you waiting for? For me to beg? My begging days are long over, you son of a bitch."

She'd begged her father, he knew; it was in the reports he'd read. For years she'd begged him. She'd even begged when she realized the monster she faced in a dark warehouse when she'd learned he'd sold her to a fiancé she didn't want.

"If I remember correctly, you've already begged me," he reminded her as he fought the instincts raging at him to soothe her, to take the anger and coax it to lust instead. "You begged me in my bed, didn't you? 'Please, Ivan, lick me there.'" He kissed her jaw gently. "'Please, Ivan, harder. Take me harder . . .'" he reminded her. "Those are the only pleas I want to hear from those pretty lips." Lifting his head, he stared down at her again, refusing to relent when he saw the misery filling the depths of her eyes. "Are you ready to talk now? Or shall we lay here a while longer?" He lifted his brow mockingly. "I'll warn you though, my dick's only getting harder. I lay here pressed against that hot little pussy much longer and I'm going to fuck it."

"You want to talk?" The sheer disbelief in her tone was rather amusing.

"Killing you just seems rather bad form, all things considered," he murmured, and watched the wariness as it filled her expression. "Amara would of course become suspicious at some point. She'd be very angry with me." He allowed his lips to brush against hers as he stared into her wide eyes. "Besides, who does it hurt? Your *father*?" He sneered the title. "Your grandfather? As I understand it, you were only useful to them as long as you were a virgin. Something I've already taken care of. Correct?"

She remained silent, simply staring up at him, waiting. She was an intuitive little thing, wasn't she?

"You are far more valuable alive, in my bed, on my arm in public, and playing the besotted lover, wouldn't you think?" he asked, and watched her face leach of all color.

"No . . ." she whispered, the fear in her voice infuriating him. "You can't do that. Ivan, you can't . . ."

Couldn't he? Oh, he could, and he would.

"Why is that, sweetheart?" His lips brushed against hers again before he jerked back, barely avoiding her teeth as he chuckled at the attempt before staring down at her, his expression, his voice, hardening. "They're still conspiring against me even from their prison cells, and I suspect they're behind the others chasing you. Push them, piss them off, and they'll make a mistake. Once they do, the rest of their power structure will fall."

Journey stared at him, silent for long moments as she tried to process what he was saying, tried to push back the need burning in her body to make sense of the words.

"They'll kill you, then me," she whispered, the knowledge that he was willing to sacrifice her so easily slicing her with a sense of betrayal. "No wonder you have no plans to kill me yourself." Morbid amusement filled the sharp laugh that passed her lips. "You're going to let him do it for you."

Was her heart breaking?

The sudden pain that sliced at her chest echoed through the rest of her body as she stared up at him. She couldn't strike out at him, restrained as she was by his hard body and shackling grip. Could she have fought if she wasn't restrained? The shock that filled her went so deep, she wasn't certain she could.

A frown jerked at his brow, anger making the blue in his eyes brighter.

"Is that really what you think? And what do you think those bastards chasing you intend to do?" He jerked off her then, releasing her. And as she suspected, the fight that she would have normally felt couldn't escape the pain radiating through her.

She'd thought she couldn't feel more betrayed than she had felt by her family. The mother she believed loved her, the sister she'd thought she was close to, the brother she'd thought would always try to protect her, if he knew she needed it. And the friend she'd learned was the cousin they believed dead, a cousin who hadn't wanted her kinship known.

But strangely enough, she felt more betrayed now.

Sitting up slowly, she stared up at him, shaking her head slowly. "They're Beau's men," she whispered. "He's determined that I'll honor the engagement . . ."

He laughed at that. The sound wasn't one of amusement.

"No doubt Beau would love to secure the Queen Mother's regard by marrying the only Taite child she was fond of, but trust me, baby, that wasn't just a snatch and grab you've been running from. The men that came by that diner last night were a strike force, Journey. They were there to kill you or anyone willing to help you. They weren't taking chances."

That wasn't possible.

"Beau wouldn't have me killed," she denied. "As you said, he's desperate to reacquire the Taite title by marrying me. It will never happen; the Queen would never return it . . ."

"The title has yet to be taken, sweetheart." The brooding quality of his voice, the anger in his expression, assured her he wasn't lying. Besides, Amara had told her many times that her father rarely bothered to lie to enemies. "It's merely being held out of reach, subject to your arrival home. Alive. Those weren't Beau's men. You can trust me on that."

They weren't Beau's men?

"That can't be true—"

"I spoke to him myself." He didn't give her time to finish the objection. "Beau's men were in Colorado. I left, the morning you ran from me, to meet him in Boulder to identify them. They were found in a back alley, each with a bullet in his brain. He has another team following a trail I had an agent lay back to New York. The team that's stayed on your ass since you left here aren't my men or Beau's."

She rose from the couch slowly, panic beginning to bloom inside her. Turning from him, she moved to the wall of windows once again and stared at the tumultuous waves crashing toward land beyond the cliff's walls.

The men chasing her weren't Ivan's men or Beau's as she had believed? They were sent to possibly kill her or anyone who might help her?

She could feel her stomach roiling at the knowledge and had to swallow tightly to hold back the sickness threatening to rise inside her.

Someone had possibly sent assassins after her?

"Who?" She had to force the question from her lips. "Who sent them?"

He was strangely silent, and that very silence was an answer she had to fight to accept.

"Stephen or Craig?" she asked, turning back to him, her gaze meeting his. His eyes were still a lighter blue, but his expression was somber rather than angry. Compassionate.

"Does either of them make such a decision alone?" He spoke quietly, his voice gentler.

Pity.

She hated that look, hated seeing it. She'd seen it all her life. From her mother, her sister, even Beau. They'd pitied her all her life but never enough to warn her what was coming from the men who should have protected her rather than selling her.

"No, they don't," she whispered, rubbing at her arms as a chill raced over her. "They would agree when the decision was made."

They'd warned her, she reminded herself. The night they'd had her and her cousin kidnapped, they'd warned her they'd kill her before they'd allow her to escape. That warning had been followed up before she'd run from Maryland that night four years ago.

She was the daughter who had gained the Queen Mother's favor. The only child who could have enough influence to have their imprisonment moved to England or France rather than America, where they were confined.

Once out of America, they could use their influence there to have their sentence lowered or even allow home imprisonment despite the severity of their crimes.

"It doesn't make sense." She shook her head, unable to understand why. "If they kill me, I couldn't do what they want me to do. If I die, the Queen Mother wouldn't even consider aiding them."

"Beau's been given directorship of the Taite holdings due to his engagement to you and his experience in running his own family holdings. He seems to be actually charming the Queen Mother. They might feel they don't need you," he pointed out. "Or you could know something they're afraid you'll tell."

No, she wasn't trusted with secrets, Journey acknowledged fatalistically. It wasn't a secret she had but, rather, like her cousin, an inheritance that only reverted to the Taite family if she was dead.

How insane was that. Both her cousin's grandfather, as well as her own maternal grandfather, had been incredibly close friends. When Benjamin Taite had locked up an inheritance for his daughter or her heirs when his daughter had been kidnapped, her grandfather had followed suit. Both his granddaughters' inheritances were locked until marriage, or their deaths. Journey's went a step further. If she didn't marry before thirty, then the inheritance was released to her in full.

For thirty years the original amount had gained in interest and grown through careful stock choices. At thirty, if she wasn't married, then she'd have it without needing to rely on a husband's agreement should she want to use it.

"It wouldn't matter," she said, confused. "If they're after my money my grandfather placed in trust as my cousin's grandfather did, it wouldn't do them any good. If I died, the inheritance reverts to my mother, not my father or grandfather."

"And your mother refuses to believe your father committed the crimes he's imprisoned for," Ivan stated. "Perhaps he believes she'll use it to curry favor in having him moved to France."

A long shot, Journey thought, pushing her fingers through her hair as she frowned, still watching the water below. She'd seen her mother's face when she'd been told what her father had done, the way she'd stared at Journey, shock and realization filling her eyes.

"She wouldn't do it. He'd know better. Mother hated him." And she had. She'd stayed drunk for years to escape her father's petty cruelties.

"Then who would it benefit?" His voice harder, firmer, now. "Who would want to kill you for it?"

"No one." Journey turned back to him and lifted her chin, pulling her pride around him as she met the pity in his eyes. "My death would only benefit the family or business as a whole. And no one in the family would buy Stephen or Craig out of death if it was imminent. You have to be wrong."

He stepped closer, the pity easing from his expression though his eyes were no longer a navy blue but closer to a true blue.

"Tell that to the owner of that diner you were working at," he told her softly. "The men in that van came back searching for you. Before my men could catch up with them, they nearly beat him to death questioning him. Good old Marvin Worth is fighting for his life in ICU right now. Those men aren't playing, Journey, and neither am I. Whatever you have, Stephen and Craig Taite are willing to kill you to either ensure they possess it, or ensure your silence. And until we learn what they want and why, your life isn't worth shit away from me. Beau can't protect you; your family can't protect you. To kill a monster, you need a monster."

She trembled at the dark, wrathful tone of his voice.

"And you're a monster?" she whispered. She hadn't wanted to believe that. Hadn't wanted to know that the man she couldn't resist physically could possibly possess such cruelty.

"When I have to be," he assured her. "When I want to be, Journey, I can make Stephen and Craig Taite very, very afraid. If I didn't have the power to do that, they would have already killed Amara before killing me. And I'm the one person guaranteed to make them insane with rage at the thought of you in my bed. Trust me, my little Syn, I'm your only chance at living now."

Journey could only shake her head. God, how had her life become such a chaotic mess?

"How long have you known who I was?" She had to focus on something other than her imminent death or she'd go crazy.

The look he shot her was knowing.

"I've known since about two hours after I brought you into the estate," he scoffed. "Really, baby? Did you think that once you were there I didn't do a thorough background check? The identity you were using was good. It was damned good. Until you got to the part where Crimsyn Delaney disappeared at age twenty. An orphan with no family but a few cousins she'd never met? Then she pops back up a year after you disappeared? Of course, the DNA sample I managed to acquire and run against your cousins only helped. You should have been more careful when you nicked those pretty legs shaving, I guess."

Shit.

Dammit.

She ran through a litany of curses as she remembered the blood on the towel. She'd meant to rinse it out, but Amara had shown up at her door and distracted her. The towel had slipped her mind. Something that should have never happened.

"Does anyone else know?" Did her cousin, her family know? Beau?

"Now, why would I tell them?" he grunted. "They'd be here so fast you'd hear the sound barrier break. No one knows but myself and Ilya."

"Well, there's that at least," she sighed, pushing her fingers through her hair as she fought to figure out exactly what she was going to do. "For now."

God, she had no idea what to do. She had no idea how to handle this. She was drowning in the sudden shift of her reality and had no idea how to even hold her head above water.

"Journey, you will never be safe if you turn and fight. Running will only weaken you now. You know that," he warned her as she turned away from him and walked from the room.

It wasn't running that weakened her, she told herself. It was need. A need she couldn't run from and, it seemed, she couldn't escape either.

chapter six

She could play Beau's whore or she could be Ivan's.
Well, wasn't that a hell of a choice, Journey thought
as she wandered around the gardens next to the pool
area several hours later. Night had fallen, but the walk-
way was well lit, the lush grass well maintained.

Ornamental trees, flowering bushes, and beds of
blooms scented the air, providing a peaceful setting for
the grounds. She found very little peace amid it though.

She was too old for this. God, she should be hap-
pily married with several kids or knee-deep in the
landscaping design career she'd dreamed of. She
shouldn't be running, still stuck in some ways at
twenty-six and fighting for freedom.

She should have fallen in love by now, had her heart
broken at least once, matured in her dreams, and have
a plan for the rest of her life. Instead, she was trying
to decide which was better, sleeping with a man who

only wanted to use her for revenge, saving her life, it seemed, in the process, or marrying a man who had already informed her that he couldn't be faithful. That she wasn't woman enough to fill his sexual needs.

She was Beau's path to a title. She was Ivan's path to vengeance against her father and grandfather. And she had no idea who she was to herself.

The fact that she ached for Ivan wasn't lost on her. Lately, her need for him had only grown, her flesh becoming more sensitive by the day as dreams of that night haunted her. Her breasts were swollen, her nipples sensitive. And her sex ached, becoming moist and ready for him at any given thought of him.

The things he'd done to her, had encouraged her to do to him, were carnal, explicit. And he was a very vocal lover. His dark voice would deepen, his accent slipping further, and sometimes he spoke in Russian. He'd made her wild, made her forget her normal shyness, her uncertainty. As the night closed around them and he extinguished the lights, she'd felt a part of herself she hadn't known existed come alive.

She was paying for it now. As she wandered through the gardens she wondered how much more she'd pay for it. Because she knew the choice she'd make between him and her former fiancé. There was really no choice to make. The thought of having Ivan touch her again, take her, filling her senses with such pleasure that she couldn't resist it, made the choice for her.

It was dangerous, she knew. She'd no doubt end up dead. He didn't love her, she wouldn't be his first priority, and that was okay. She didn't want him to die for her. He had a child who loved him, family who depended upon him, and even if he was perhaps a criminal, she knew he loved his family.

And who did she have? The one time she'd called her family they'd only wanted her to come home, to return to Beau. Get married. She'd deserted them. They needed her to honor her promises. Even her brother needed her to honor her promise despite her objections to being nothing more than a road to the title he so wanted.

According to Ivan, going back was no assurance of safety though. If it were, the men sent after her wouldn't be coming to kill her but to kidnap her and return her.

Pausing, she moved into a small vine-covered area and curled into the heavily padded swing there. The gas firepit next to it lit automatically, the low flame casting flickering shadows around her.

Evidently, crime really did pay. Despite Amara's belief that her father wasn't really a crime lord of some sort, Journey imagined such a reputation came honestly. If "honesty" could be applied. And he was right; he was perhaps the only man her grandfather and her father had ever feared.

Her cousin Tehya had spent several days explaining Stephen and Craig Taite's past to her after their arrests. The years spent as the masterminds of a terrorist and white slavery business. The buying and selling of titled and blue blood girls and young women to men with enough money to purchase the bloodlines they wanted.

Who would want to kill her? Who would go to such

obvious expense as to hire a team of assassins to do the deed? They couldn't be a very good team, because she'd managed to stay one step ahead of them for four years. Because she knew damned good and well, both fate and Lady Luck weren't exactly on her side.

Four years of running, of fighting to find a life for herself, to find a place where she could put down roots, an identity that couldn't be tracked, and instead, she found herself here. In the arms of a man who considered her the enemy.

Yeah, she'd really done a good job there.

Hell, she'd thought she was just running from Beau's thugs, not assassins. And she'd believed she could have one night of pleasure before just disappearing again. She'd had the pleasure, and now it seemed she couldn't escape it, she thought mockingly.

But what pleasure it had been. Pleasure bordering on pain, carnal and intense and so very wicked. He'd taken her several times through the night, moving tirelessly inside her, driving her from one plateau of ecstasy to another.

She'd cried his name. She'd screamed it. She'd begged him to make her orgasm. And through the past weeks, she'd awaken from restless dreams of him, those pleas whispering into the night as she reached for him.

As she sat there, immersed in the flickering flames and her own thoughts, she was aware of one of the bodyguards, Elizaveta, pausing at the entrance, watching her silently.

This woman had just as much reason to hate her as

Ivan did. She'd been targeted along with Amara all those years ago, to be taken and sold for profit rather than raised as the beloved children they were. Though in Elizaveta's case, her parents had died in their fight to save her from that fate.

Lifting her gaze, she stared at the other woman. She was a weapon, she'd heard Amara say. Highly trained from childhood, and taught to fight, to kill. She and her twin brother always worked together, watched each other's backs, and ensured their survival.

"Ivan asked that you come inside now," the body-guard stated, her accent heavier than Ivan's. "It is growing rather late."

And he was no doubt ready to be serviced by his whore.

Anger spread through her like a living stain she couldn't escape despite her need for him. She ached for him as she'd never ached for anything, but at that moment she almost hated him for the choice he'd given her.

"So he sent you?" She managed to keep her voice polite despite the anger. "I should have come in before he asked that of you. I'll go in now."

Elizaveta had suffered enough; she didn't need the daughter and granddaughter of the men who had destroyed her life disrespecting her.

The other woman tapped her ear softly. "Grisha and I are on duty in the gardens tonight. He merely asked that we request you come back in when you were seen."

Elizaveta's voice was low, polite, but there was an edge of a sneer on her pretty lips. And she was a very pretty woman, Journey thought. She might be a weapon, but she was a beautiful one.

"Thank you for letting me know," Journey said, knowing there was nothing that could ease Elizaveta's hatred for her. "I'll go in."

She rose from the seat and moved to step for the opening.

"You should have told him who you were in Colorado," the accented voice said softly. "It would have saved him much trouble."

No doubt it would have.

"I didn't mean for him to follow me." She shrugged, uncomfortable. "Or to cause him any trouble. I wanted to help Amara . . ."

"Or yourself?" Elizaveta questioned her coolly. "Is that not more the truth? That is why you targeted Amara, to ask her father for help."

Journey held her gaze despite the weariness that mixed with the anger.

"At first," she admitted. "Because I was scared. I was tired. But after Amara and I became friends, I changed my mind. I decided I didn't want to die if his hatred extended to me."

She hadn't wanted to die at the hands of a man she'd already begun dreaming about. One who fascinated her as Ivan Resnova did.

Elizaveta frowned at that. "How could our hatred not extend to you, Ms. Taite? You are the daughter, the granddaughter, of the men who have killed his mother, raped his aunt, and nearly killed her. Because of your family he has lost many who he loves. Who we all loved."

"But not because of me!" Journey snapped back, the weariness evaporating in the face of such caustic regard. "And don't imagine either of Craig Taite's daughters felt any softness for him or from him, because I assure you, we didn't."

Elizaveta's lips curled in a mocking sneer. "You were a virgin when Ivan took you to his bed, were you not? I saw the stains on the sheets when he and Ilya raced to Boulder to find you. Sophia will not be able to say the same. Ivan's uncle, Gregor, still suffers the scars that cover his body because of your father and grandfather. Amara still suffers her nightmares. All you suffered was the lack of a father's love? Poor little girl. I weep for you."

"And I've wept for you," Journey whispered, realizing how it must seem to this other woman. "I've wept for you, Amara, Ivan, his aunt, and his uncle, and everyone else I've learned they nearly destroyed. I've wept for all of you. And if I personally could change it, take that hell from your lives, then I would. But I won't be punished by you for it either."

A frown struck between Elizaveta's eyes, the sneer fading to more somber lines.

"May I go in now, or would you like to grind what little pride I have left into the dirt while we stand here?" she asked when the bodyguard said nothing more.

She didn't speak, but Elizaveta moved back from

the entrance just enough for Journey to pass her. Keeping her head high, she moved along the path back to the patio entrance of the house and refused to look back.

She wasn't frightened of the other woman. She was wary of her; she had no doubt Elizaveta considered her the enemy. But from what Amara had told her and what Journey had seen for herself, Elizaveta's loyalty to Ivan was absolute.

Brushing her hair back from her face, she slipped into the glass-enclosed patio room and back into the living room beyond it, aware of the bodyguard following her.

Thankfully, Ivan wasn't waiting for her, and rather than asking where he was, she continued through the house to the guest room he'd shown her to earlier. The room wasn't as nice as the Colorado estate; it was more impersonal but comfortable. Not that comfort was going to help her much now. And she sincerely doubted it would help her much later.

And once he joined her, she wouldn't give a damn; of that she was certain.

Ivan heard the conversation between Elizaveta and Journey, never revealing to his cousin that she hadn't fully disengaged the comm link when she tapped it. She'd only disengaged the audio on her end.

At Journey's statement that she'd wanted to ask for his help, he poured himself a drink. When she told Elizaveta she had wept for them, her voice resonating with grief, he'd tossed the drink back and poured another.

He'd have to discuss this with his cousin. Even he acknowledged long ago that his war with the Taites had no bearing on the youngest child. Had he found her before she arrived in Colorado, he had no doubt he would have tried to help her. She wasn't to blame, no more than Amara was to blame for his crimes or his actions.

Once he'd seen her, had been foolish enough to touch her as he had in Colorado, he'd known he'd have to find a reason to keep her for a while though. That fact that someone was trying to kill her only enraged him. Just as he knew there were very few plans that would reveal what Stephen and Craig Taite would gain from her death.

There was no doubt they'd gain something. Once he'd begun asking questions last night and tapping a few sources he had outside the Elite Operations unit he worked with, he'd learned the Taite men had been up to some very interesting games.

There were already dozens of guards at the prison on their payroll, as well as the stronger of the prisoners. Until the unit had managed to put a stop to it, prostitutes were being brought in regularly; a few hadn't made it out alive.

It was their secret visitors who intrigued him though. The men, many foreign nationals and unidentified, were being slipped in for long meetings with the two men. Ivan had learned several of the prisoners he had on his own payroll had turned against him, as well, and were now providing the two Taites with information they gained from within his organization.

For the moment, he was allowing them to live. He needed them. They'd provide the perfect vehicle to bring the information to Stephen and Craig that Journey was sleeping in his bed. That the daughter Craig had so hoped to use as a bargaining chip with Beauregard Grant was no longer his to use.

From what he'd learned though, the assassins looking for Journey weren't theirs. There had been no order to kill her, and according to the few trusted sources he still possessed, Stephen and Craig were still hoping for a marriage between Beau and Journey.

That left far too many unanswered questions. He'd assume he could be wrong about the Taites and they were behind the order, because he couldn't come up with any other source who would benefit from her death. He'd put out an order for information from other sources though, those within the Elite Ops and several outside it.

Which was why he was sitting in his office watching through the security monitor as Journey entered her bedroom alone. Because the sources he'd gone to within the Ops had done as he knew they would: contacted the one man who could throw a wrench in all his plans.

Jordan Malone, husband to the cousin desperate to find Journey and provide her a safe haven.

He couldn't allow that. If she was taken from him, there would be no way to learn who was trying to kill her, and no way to push the Taites into revealing their ties within his organization or their part in the last attempt to murder Amara.

There was no doubt they were involved. The interrogation of the assistant district attorney had provided that information. Andru, the trusted servant they knew as Danny, had been on the Taites' payroll for years before his own brother, Alexi, had killed him when he'd managed to attack Amara in her own home.

As he refilled the glass from the bottle he'd placed on the table, his attention was drawn to the low ping of the computer. The notice of an incoming video call had a grimace pulling at his lips. *Bastards couldn't use a goddamned phone anymore.* Everything was video, revealing a man's expression unless he controlled every nuance of it.

There were times when a phone was far preferred.

Hitting a button on the keyboard, he watched as the video screen opened, revealing Jordan Malone and his wife, Tehya.

"Hello, Red," he drawled teasingly, focusing on Tehya's features. "Tell me you're tired of putting up with that bastard beside you and I'll rescue you immediately."

Her green eyes, so like Journey's, flickered with amusement as her husband scowled back at him.

"As I hear it, you have your own redhead in residence, Ivan," Jordan growled, causing his wife's gaze to chill and the amusement to disappear. "That true?"

Ivan frowned as though confused. "I'm partial to redheads," he admitted as though uncertain of the direction of the conversation. "Why?"

"Is it Journey?" Tehya wasn't one for beating around

the bush, it seemed. "If it is, get her ready to leave, Ivan, because I'm coming for her."

That amused him. He really didn't think he was going to allow that to happen.

He leaned forward on the desk, placing his folded arms atop it as he glared at both of them. "If I had Taite's brat she'd already be on her way to you," he snarled, not really lying. Journey was no brat, just a temperamental little hellion when she wanted to be.

Jordan's sapphire blue eyes met his wife's before he turned back to the screen. "The men we have searching for her tracked her to Boulder, then to California under the identity of Ellen Roberts. They glimpsed two of your men in the same vicinity just before Ms. Roberts disappeared."

What an enterprising little thing his Syn was. Even he was unaware of that identity.

"I can assure you, Jordan, I haven't heard that name before and I have no one named Ellen Roberts here. I'm in town for business and had received a report from the team your men glimpsed that they may have found Ms. Taite in Nevada City, but I haven't heard back from them yet. I called in a few sources within the Ops unit to track down any rumors that the Taites had found her. I assume that's why you've called."

Tehya's expression dropped as Jordan grimaced in regret.

"I was hoping you'd found her," the other man said regretfully. "Our men reported sighting another group, heavily armed, that seemed to be searching for her too.

It sounds as though her father is tired of waiting on her to marry Grant and may have decided to just kill her."

That was his assumption as well, Ivan thought, but he knew he couldn't depend upon it, just in case there was another enemy in play.

"Not according to several secure sources I have within the federal prison they're being held in," he revealed, watching the interest that darkened the other man's eyes. "The team I have tracking the girl reported the same group as well, but the information I received tonight says the Taites are still talking a possible marriage to Beauregard Grant. There's not been so much as a whisper of anything more threatening."

Jordan's expression turned thoughtful. "I'll check a few of my contacts outside the Ops and let you know what I hear. Maybe between the two of us we can come up with an answer. I have a feeling she's in a hell of a lot more trouble than she knows or we're guessing."

Ivan nodded, then asked about their small family. Several minutes were spent discussing more mundane issues before he excused himself from the conversation saying that he had a few more matters to deal with before turning in. There was a certain flow to their normal conversations that Ivan made certain to keep intact. Jordan was a highly suspicious man, as was his wife, and rousing those suspicions at the moment wasn't something he wanted to do.

Once the video call was disengaged he finished his drink, rose from his seat, and made his way from his office to the guest room where he'd taken Journey the night before. Opening the door, he stared into the dimly lit room, aware that she'd left the bathroom light on, the door partially opened.

She didn't sleep well in the dark. He'd begun to suspect that in Colorado as he passed her door each night and caught the faint light from beneath it at all hours. She preferred to be able to see past the shadows, while Ivan lived within the shadows.

She was stretched out on the bed, dressed in the white silk pajamas Elizaveta had bought for her that morning, her head pillowed on her arms as she slept. She looked like a fucking teenager and made him feel like a depraved pervert. The things he wanted to do to her would erase that innocence for all time, he knew. And the thought of doing them had his cock pounding in lust.

He'd been hard since the second he and Ilya had grabbed her on that dark street in Boulder. That hunger hadn't abated either. But it was doomed to remain unsatisfied tonight because he couldn't bring himself to wake her.

She'd been pale all day; the fact that she was exhausted wasn't lost on him. She'd fought to stay one step ahead of three different teams searching for her for a month, and it was sheer luck that he'd found her first.

The information that someone wanted her dead would haunt her now, and he knew it would take time to digest. Unfortunately, he had a feeling they might not have enough time for her to fully comprehend it.

Stepping into the room, he collected a throw blanket from the chair next to the bed and placed it over her, careful not to wake her. He'd let her sleep tonight; tomorrow was soon enough to begin the game he was carefully putting together. A game that would increase the danger for a while perhaps but would ultimately see her safe and her father and grandfather eliminated. Their deaths would be her only assurance of safety. They may not have put out the order to have her killed, but they were no doubt the reason for it.

"Ivan?" She came awake as the blanket settled around her, sitting up and staring at him in surprise. "Is something wrong?"

She pulled the pale peach cashmere throw over her breasts, but he'd glimpsed her hardening nipples beneath the material of the silk tank. He restrained his smile, staring down at her, wondering why in the hell this woman seemed to sink so deep inside him.

"I was merely checking on you before turning in." He sat on the edge of the bed as she propped herself against the headboard. "I didn't mean to wake you."

She shrugged at the comment. "It's not your fault. I don't sleep well anyway."

Unable to stop himself, he lifted a hand, moving slowly, and reached out until he could run his knuckles down her cheek. Soft, warm silk.

"You need to rest," he told her, lowering his hand to brace it against the bed. "And eat. You're letting yourself get run-down, Syn."

She almost rolled her eyes. He knew that look. It was one Amara tried on him often.

"You're obsessed with my health for some reason."

The light amusement in her tone pulled a small grin to his lips. "I'm a redhead. We're naturally pale."

No, she'd been naturally pale in Colorado last month. This was different and it concerned him.

"Perhaps," he murmured rather than arguing with her.

She was more relaxed than normal right now. She leaned back on the pillows propped against the headboard and watched him with those slumberous, witchy eyes. A little sleepy, a lot sensual, like a kitten contemplating whether or not to awaken enough to cause havoc.

"You should have had six kids and a wife who made your knees shake when she frowned at you." She grinned. "You worry too much about others."

He hid his surprise. That was something few saw, and even fewer recognized.

"I was barely thirteen when the woman my father brought to me conceived Amara," he told her, the memory no longer as bitter as it had once been. "He couldn't control me with his fists, so he thought to control me by other means. He succeeded. For a while."

The amusement eased from her expression, and he regretted that.

"I'm sorry . . ." she began.

"Amara was not the perfect child you seem to think she was," he chuckled, hoping to bring that smile back to her face. "From the moment she could crawl, she was like that battery bunny on television. There were six of us watching out for her, and together, we could barely keep up with her."

Journey watched him doubtfully now, but the amusement was returning.

"Amara?" she questioned him suspiciously.

"I swear it." He placed his hand on his heart as he grinned back at her. "She made a game out of driving us crazy, especially after we came to the states."

Before, while in Russia, fear had kept her contained. She'd known fear from a very young age, and the memory of that threatened the pleasant atmosphere he was attempting to project.

"I so admired her as a child," Journey said then. "For a few months, we attended the same boarding school in England. We didn't really meet while there, but I remember seeing her around. She was always smiling, and so proud of her poppa."

He grimaced at that. "I try often to forget you're closer to her age than you are mine. Only two years separate you and Amara."

She shrugged again, and the expression that crossed her face had his dick throbbing. Sensual, a little teasing, feminine and mysterious.

"That ball, where you asked me to dance?" she said softly. "I was quite smitten with you afterwards. I watched for you at each ball after that."

"And I noticed you watching me," he admitted, leaning closer, one hand bracing on the mattress at her hip, the other stroking up her bare arm. Skin as soft as silk, warm, and so incredibly soft. "What you didn't see was the way I watched you, love. The year you turned eighteen, I found myself unable to not watch you. To want you."

Journey stared back at Ivan, uncertain if she'd heard what she knew she'd heard.

"You don't have to lie to me," she whispered. "I don't need fairy tales, I told you."

His hand cupped her neck, his fingers callused, warm against her flesh as he leaned closer, his lips touching hers as he whispered, "We all need a little illusion in our lives sometimes, my sweet Syn. The fact that my dick stays hard for you is no illusion though."

Her breath caught, her lips parting as he pulled her to him, his tongue slipping past to stroke against hers, to stoke the need for his touch, his possession, higher. Reaching for him, her hands met the fine cotton of his shirt, the heat of his body diffused by the material. She needed that heat. The warmth of his body. His touch.

She felt as though she'd been cold forever, and when he held her, heat flushed through her, flames raced over her. And she loved it. She needed it.

She ached for it.

Her hands pushed beneath the parted edge of his shirt, her fingertips meeting hot, male flesh as his lips slid from hers to caress her neck.

The sensations . . . Oh God. It was like his lips awakened nerve endings she hadn't known existed. The pleasure raked from the point his lips caressed to echo through her body, tightened her nipples and sent heated moisture spilling from her vagina. The sheer eroticism and carnal hunger in each touch, each stroke of his lips and tongue, mesmerized her, pulling her deeper into the chaotic tempest he was building inside her.

As her head tipped back, allowing him greater access to the sensitive flesh, the jarring ring of his cell phone had a moan of denial slipping past her lips.

"Fuck!" Ivan's curse was rough, a broken growl as he pulled back from her, their gazes meeting as she opened her eyes and stared up into the stark hunger in his gaze.

"Goddamn it," he snapped, moving back from her. "I'll be right there."

Flipping the phone closed, he shoved it into the pocket of his slacks and blew out a hard breath as his expression turned rueful. "This will take a while, baby . . ."

She quickly shook her head. "Go . . ." She gave a restless little wave of her hand. "I need to sleep."

She needed to think. She needed to decide what she had to do without sex complicating the issue. Because she couldn't say no to the pleasure, to the pure ecstasy of his touch.

"We'll talk in the morning," he promised, rising from the bed. "We have to discuss this."

"I know." Her hand clenched in the blanket that had pooled along her waist. "In the morning."

His expression turned somber, determined with a hint of the pure arrogant nature of the man himself.

"Get some sleep, love," he said softly. "We'll figure it all out quickly, I promise."

With that, he strode to the door, slipped from her

bedroom. Dropping her gaze to her hands, she realized she was once again running her thumb over the scar on the opposite hand. The cigarette burn had been deep, the embers held to her skin for long moments as her father stared at her with cruel purpose as her grandfather held her hand still with bruising force.

Because as a sixteen-year-old, she'd been unable to hide her complete fascination with the tall, dark Russian who had spoken to her, had invited her to dance and teased her gently. Not sexually, but with a mature man's knowledge of a young girl's complete discomfort. He'd felt sorry for her, she'd told herself over the years. But in those moments he'd stolen a part of a young girl's heart. And over the years, he'd sealed her fascination of him.

Once, she'd dreamed of having a moment in time, a chance to know his touch, his laughter and strength. She'd never dreamed of happily-ever-afters, but she had dreamed of stolen moments, stolen kisses, and passion exploding out of control.

She had her chance now, she told herself. She could take his offer to be in his bed, to be his lover for the amount of time it took her father and grandfather to completely slip into demented rage at the knowledge of it. Even four years ago, the two elder Taites had been desperate to secure that marriage. The importance of it had been drummed into her head that last year.

He would no doubt break her heart.

She touched her lips with trembling fingers. And give her days and nights of pleasure.

He could give her what she'd dreamed of for so

many years, she thought then. If he wanted his vengeance bad enough, then he'd pay any price for it. He'd give her the impossible.

He'd give her the illusion she craved and when it was over, maybe, it would be worth the broken heart.

chapter seven

Stepping from the shower the next morning, as she wrapped one of the large towels around her, Journey came to a sudden stop, her eyes widening at the sight of Ivan as he stood, propped against the bathroom entrance. Tall, imposing, and far too sensual as his gaze moved over her slowly before meeting her own.

"I didn't notice the freckles before," he said quietly, nodding to her shoulders. "They're rather cute."

They were cute?

She hated them.

"They're freckles!" she snapped, off balance with his sudden appearance and a night filled with restless nightmares. "Would you leave? I need to get dressed."

She glanced toward the counter where she'd left her clothes after removing them, only to find the marble counter empty. And she knew she'd placed them there before stepping into the shower.

"I had some new clothes delivered. They're on the bed." He stepped back from the doorway as though in invitation for her to follow him.

"I liked my old clothes," she informed him querulously, following him as she silently cursed his highhandedness.

She'd actually been dreading redressing in the clothes she'd worn the day before. The scent of old grease and hamburgers clung to the material, causing her to wrinkle her nose in distaste when she'd awoken to it.

"No, you didn't." He seemed to read her thoughts. "I'd never allow my mistress to wear those clothes either. If you're going to play this game, my little Syn, you need to look the part."

She frowned at the "little Syn" comment. The play on words didn't amuse her in the least.

Stepping into the bedroom, hesitantly she neared the bed, tucking the towel securely between her breasts, and stared at the clothing laid out. There were several soft, flirty dresses. They were more casual wear though and paired with open-toed heels. A couple of skirts and coordinating blouses, several club dresses more revealing than anything she'd ever worn in her life, and a small mound of sinfully brief thongs and matching lacy bras.

"These will do until I can take you to the shops myself." He moved behind her, his hands cupping her bare shoulders as she froze.

Her stomach clenched in reaction, her heart suddenly racing as the air around her seemed to thin, making her breaths come harder, faster.

"Ivan, I don't know if this is going to work," she whispered, more uncertain now than she believed she'd ever been in her life.

"Of course it will." His head lowered as he lifted a hand to push her hair back and allow his lips to caress her neck.

Heated bursts of pleasure exploded against the sensitive nerve endings, sensitizing her flesh further and causing her nipples to tighten impossibly harder.

Clenching her fingers on the front of the towel, she had to fight to keep her head from tilting for him and allowing him greater access to the area his lips were stroking. The pleasure from that caress alone could become addictive, she thought with dazed appreciation. When he added the scrape of his teeth, the faint flicks of his tongue, it was all she could do not to moan.

A dark chuckle rasped at her neck. "You fight so hard not to feel pleasure from my touch, don't you, my little Syn?"

Syn. He wasn't calling her a sin but using the abbreviation of the identity of Crimsyn.

"It shouldn't . . ." Her breath hitched when he bit down erotically on the side of her neck. "Feel so good."

His hands moved to her hips, tightened, pulled her closer until she felt the thick wedge of his erection against the small of her back.

"Why shouldn't it?" The rasp of his unshaven jaw sent a shiver washing through her as she felt the moisture between her thighs building. "What would life be without such pleasure?"

It was cold and bleak; she already knew that. It was

a constant hunger that made no sense until his touch, his kiss.

She nearly came to her tiptoes when he laid his lips against the bend of her neck and shoulder to deliver a harder, hotter kiss. She couldn't stop that gasp of pleasure or her hands falling to his wrists, gripping them desperately.

"But it's just with you," she protested, her head tilting for him, silently begging for more. "Oh God, Ivan . . ."

The towel fell away from her body, sliding across her nipples as his hands tugged at the material. She was naked before him, hot and dazed, unable, and damned unwilling to even try to learn how to deny his touch.

Just with him.

It was all Ivan could do to keep from bending her over the bed and taking her like a damned animal. Lust thundered through his bloodstream, hardening his dick impossibly further and pushing at his control.

He knew women, their responses, the sound of their voices as arousal filled them. He knew the feel of their bodies, the irregular panting of breaths that signaled the dazed intensity filling them, and he knew she wasn't even aware of the information she gave away. That she'd only felt this way with him.

It wasn't that he hadn't heard such claims before, but before he'd also heard the calculation, the deliberate manipulation, in the words. Something Journey's voice didn't hold. She was so lost in such a simple pleasure, his lips against her neck, that she had no idea what she'd whispered, or the implications of it, the power it gave him.

"Ivan . . ." a soft, pleading moan whispered from her as he lifted her hands from his wrists and raised them until her hands clasped his neck and he could cup the full, swollen mounds of her breasts.

The brush of his fingers across her nipples had her jerking against him in reaction to the pleasure. Her lips were parted, eyes closed, her breathing coming in hard pants as she leaned farther into him.

"So pretty, and so sensitive. Can I suck those pretty nipples again, Syn? Will you get wild for me again?" She had that first time. The harder he'd sucked the little points, the more she'd become lost in the sensations he gave her, that mix of pleasure and pain, of darker lusts and carnal delights.

And he'd wanted to do so much more, teach her things about her body that would allow her to slide past her shyness and tempt him to push her harder.

She arched into his caress, pushing her breasts against his palms, silently begging for more. Her expression was mesmerized, so lost in the pleasure of such a simple touch that it amazed him. She was beautiful, sensual, and she'd been denied, for whatever reason, a lover's touch.

The satisfaction he felt in being the lover to show her this pleasure the first time only intensified his own arousal. What the hell did she do to him and why did he have a feeling he was getting in far too deep here?

A low moan whispered from her lips again as he played with her sensitive nipples. Pretty, pink, swollen with need. As he turned her, his head was lowering to the tight, hard points when a firm knock at her door almost had him snarling.

"What?" he snapped as he felt Journey stiffen in his arms, the haze of sensual pleasure dissipating as reality intruded.

She moved quickly from his arms as he shot her a brooding glare, bent, and jerked the towel from the floor before wrapping it around her once again.

"Ivan, you have a call you need to take," Ilya called through the closed door. "I'll meet you in your office."

Someone's timing sucked.

"I'm going to shoot him," Ivan growled, then turned back to her. "We'll continue this later. I promise you."

"Why?" Her expression was angry now, wary. "You don't have to actually put yourself out to fuck me, Ivan. You can do what you need to do without going that far."

Oh, he doubted that. More to the point, he had no intention of trying.

"We'll discuss it later," he growled, frustration eating at him now.

She had to be the most difficult woman he'd ever met in his life. Even for a redhead she was unusually frustrating.

Turning on his heel, he strode to the door, jerked it open, and left the room. To have disturbed him Ilya would have considered the call important, and the only calls of any importance that he was expecting concerned Journey. And, he hoped, the answers to who or what was behind a team directed to kill her.

* * *

She hadn't worn clothes like this in her life, Journey admitted as she stared at herself in the full-length mirror in the corner of the guest room. The flirty multi-colored skirt ended just above her knees, the white camisole tank meeting the low band of the skirt and dipping just enough at her breasts to be tastefully sexy.

The lace bra and matching thongs were sinfully brief and soft, the sandals she found buried under the skirts perfect for the warm California weather. She felt more feminine than she ever had. Even her pale skin looked prettier, not as bland or unattractive as she imagined. Though the freckles across her shoulders were clearly revealed.

No matter what her face looked like, those freckles would give her away to her family. They were distinctive, though they'd always been covered until now.

If Ivan had his way, her family would soon know exactly where she was and who she was with. Beau, her mother, brother, and sister, and no doubt her cousin Tehya and her husband would descend on Ivan like a brick wall.

She almost grinned at the thought of that. She would have grinned if the reality of the situation were anything but what she knew it to be. She would be in his bed for his vengeance, to put the final nails in the coffins of his enemies.

Her enemies.

Turning from the mirror, she found herself rubbing at the small scar between her thumb and forefinger. The small, circular mark wasn't as easy to see as it had once been, but it was there, a memory of the disobedient child she had always been.

Obedience had just never been her strong suit. It still wasn't. She hated being told what to do, being ordered or forced. It raked against her pride, filled her with a restless anger and an urge to do the exact opposite.

This situation wasn't one she could run away from though. She'd realized that the night before, and digging in her heels in silent rejection of it wasn't going to work either. If she was going to come out of it with some semblance of pride intact, as well as her life, then she had to find a way to meet Ivan on a more even field. Unfortunately, sexual experience wasn't something she possessed. And it was something he possessed in abundance.

What she lacked in experience she could make up for in other areas, maybe. He wasn't exactly immune to her touch. She could give herself to him, learn from him, let him teach her how to ease the sexual needs she found so confusing. And she could follow his lead in learning who threatened her.

Tehya had once told her that she was braver than she knew she was, stronger than she imagined. The other woman had assured her that she could face the life Stephen and Craig left her with her head held high, because they weren't her crimes. And she could refuse any decision made on her behalf that she didn't agree with.

Journey hadn't seen that strength in herself four years ago, but as she faced the fact that someone was determined to kill her she'd felt the complete rejection of allowing them to do so easily. She'd fight, just as she fought to escape the life she was born into. And if that fight involved sleeping with the dark, forbidden Russian, a man who mesmerized her senses, then so be it.

Her fascination with him had haunted her for years. She'd been sixteen when she'd first seen him at one of the social gatherings she was forced to attend as a Taite daughter. And over the years, each time she'd seen him again that fascination had grown.

A silent, secretive crush perhaps, something she'd hidden and only allowed free in the dark privacy of her fantasies. It didn't matter that he was accused of heading a merciless criminal organization. His reputation as a criminal or as a killer had meshed with the fantasies she'd built around him.

Childish.

She was a mess, then and now, where Ivan Resnova was concerned. But why allow her pride and the situation to keep her from those fantasies? And if he failed and she died, at least she wouldn't die without having known what it meant to be bold, to be pleasured.

And if he wanted her to give the world an illusion that would ensure his vengeance, then he could give her a fantasy as well. One that would ensure she had something to carry with her if she survived it.

The only question now was if she was strong enough to stop running and to fight.

Ivan closed the video chat and wiped his hand over his face before looking up at Ilya's somber expression.

"Maxine's in ICU. Carter's stable and the doctors

are certain of a full recovery. Their assailants escaped before Tobias and his team could get there. Carter counted four men, heavily armed, Russian accents. They have no idea which direction they were headed," he told his assistant. His closest friend, Ilya, and he had been working together, watching each other's backs and attempting to navigate the dangerous world they lived in, since they were boys.

The dragon tattooed at the side of Ilya's face flexed dangerously as his jaw clenched, the dimly colored scales appearing almost iridescent for a moment.

"Max and Carter are two of our best agents," Ilya murmured as he sat down wearily in the chair across from Ivan's desk. "Getting the drop on them wouldn't be easy."

That was no more than the truth. Carter wasn't just well trained but intuitive as hell, and Maxine took women's intuition to a level Ivan had never seen before.

"Pull Elizaveta into the house," he ordered. "Tobias and the others will be here in a few hours. Have the plane readied. We're returning to New York."

Ilya's brows lifted in surprise. "Her family is back in the states," he said. Ivan didn't need the reminder. "As well as Beau. They've taken an apartment in Manhattan. Are you sure you want her that close to them?"

Fuck no, he didn't. He'd wanted to keep this in California, give Journey a measure of peace before the game began in earnest. The men chasing her wouldn't have a hard time finding them and Ivan no longer had eyes on them to keep track of their progress or alert him to a possible attack.

"I've no choice." Ivan steeled himself for what he knew was coming.

He'd not yet managed to secure Journey's complete cooperation in this game, and without it there would be no way to convince anyone who knew him that she was his mistress. That she shared his bed nightly when no other woman ever had.

He didn't keep live-in mistresses. He had lovers, he went to their beds, occasionally he had one slipped onto his estate in Colorado when he was there, but only for the night. He'd had a daughter, a child whose innocence he'd wanted to maintain as long as possible. He didn't flaunt his sex life in front of her.

His daughter was with her fiancé now though, planning the wedding she'd dreamed of and overseeing the home she and her fiancé were building in Texas. His daughter was a woman and his own life was decidedly emptier now. A perfect excuse for taking a more permanent lover.

The tabloids and gossip rags would eat it up. The Taites would be puking on their fury.

"Have the house in the Hamptons prepared," he told Ilya as he made the decision. "We'll fly out as soon as the others arrive."

He didn't blame Ilya for his added surprise. The house in the Hamptons had never been used for a lover. It was where he and Amara had hosted the few social events he had thrown in the past, and where his daughter had been raised as a teenager. It was the family's base, their security, not just a residence.

It would only add to the romantic cast that would be thrown on his relationship with Journey.

"Want me to have a selection of engagement rings delivered as well?" Ilya snorted. "Arrange for a meeting with the priest?"

Ivan narrowed his eyes at what he knew was a facetious suggestion. It had merit though.

"I don't like the look on your face, my friend," Ilya said carefully. "Surely you wouldn't go that far?"

Would he? Until Ilya had said it, he hadn't really thought that far, but it wasn't an unpleasant thought.

Ivan shrugged. "I'm getting no younger, Ilya. My daughter is married, moving into her own life now. What man wouldn't consider such a thing?"

He'd make certain his favored gossip columnists received that information.

"And what of her?" Ilya asked somberly. "She's young, Ivan, and far too innocent for this game. Even if that was your wish, what of her desires? She'd want more than such a loosely based relationship for marriage. She'd also no doubt want children."

He shot his friend a brooding look.

There would be no more children for him; he'd made certain of that when he was twenty and realized the danger Amara would always face. Children were to be treasured, protected not just from danger but also from the realities of a parent's past or even future actions. And his life would never be secure enough to allow for a true family, other than his daughter.

The vasectomy he'd had performed had ensured he

was never tricked again as he had been by Amara's mother. Barely more than a child, a virgin to her twenty, whose hands were already stained with blood.

"Call for the plane." He moved to rise from his seat only to sit back at a soft rap at the door.

Ilya rose instead and crossed the office, opening the door, then stepping back and allowing Journey to enter.

His Syn.

That skirt was going to get her fucked, sure as hell. It fluttered just below her thighs, caressed them and teased him with the ease with which it would slide to her hips. The top would be easily lifted, her breasts accessible. And he did so enjoy her breasts.

Her green eyes gleamed with battle; her proud little chin was lifted and her expression determined.

Hell.

Everything he knew about women assured him that she was getting ready to make him insane. And not in a sexual way. *At least,* he amended as he took in the hardened state of her nipples, *not yet.*

"I need to make a video call," she stated, her voice firm as she reached his desk. "Can you secure the call and keep it from being traced?"

His brow lifted. "I was unaware we were going to hide? Though it makes little difference; we'll be leaving soon for New York anyway. Who are you calling?"

"Beauregard Grant." Her smile was tight and cold and for the briefest moment reminded him of the tough-assed hellion cousin of hers, Tehya. "If we're going to do this, Ivan, I get to make the first strike. I want to see his face when I ask him if he sent assassins after me. I want to see his eyes."

He almost grinned.

If he believed in love, he would have fallen in love with her at that moment, he knew.

"Do I get to sit next to you and watch his complete horror when he realizes you belong to me?" he asked her, arching a brow as he watched her closely.

He'd feared for a while that she wasn't as tough as he thought she was a month ago, that she didn't have the pure steel she'd need to go into this game. Perhaps he'd been wrong.

Her head tilted to the side, her eyes narrowing on him. He watched her expression and her gaze carefully, seeing the rapid flicker of something akin to hungry hope.

"Have you ever been in love, Ivan?" She surprised him with the question.

"I have not. What of you?" he countered.

"You're probably the closest I've come to being in love with anyone," she admitted guilelessly, and the sensation he felt in his chest was like a ghostly knife burying in deep. "If you want me to play this game of yours, then you can play mine." She planted her hands flat on the desk and leaned forward just enough to stare him directly in the eye, her gaze flashing with fiery stubborn determination. "The world will believe you're in love. Your staff will believe you're in love. If I don't survive this, and I'm smart enough to know I may not, then I want to know before I die what being loved should feel like. And before you decide, remember this: Tehya and Jordan could hide me, even from you, if I asked, and I know it. I'm choosing to fight, and I'm choosing to allow you to use me for your vengeance. I'll be damned if I'll do that without something just as important from you."

She wasn't angry or confrontational. She was firm, her voice clear, succinct in her demand.

"You want me to fall in love with you?" he asked carefully, just to be certain he understood her. That there was no mistake.

"I want you to give me your illusion of love. I want the romance, the commitment, and everyone's knowledge that I have it, for as long as this lasts. If you can't give me that, then don't expect me to give it to you. And trust me, the only way Beau and my family would ever believe I'd sleep with you is if they believed I loved you."

He was the closest she'd ever come to love, she'd said. No one besides his daughter had ever claimed to love him. And though the statement wasn't exactly a claim, he could question her on it later.

"And if I agree?" he asked, realizing he was actually curious as to her terms.

"No other women. While we do this, I'll have all of you," she added.

All of him? Oh, she had no idea what she was bargaining for there.

"No crying foul, later." He leaned forward, narrowing his eyes on her. "No holding back, no tears when we clash. Understood? You'll get all of me, but by God, you'll give me all of you as well. Everything, Journey."

And she had no idea just how much she had to give. But he did. He knew. And he wanted it all.

"Deal." She didn't hesitate, didn't balk.

Damn, he liked that about her. He'd realized that in Colorado though. The fact that she didn't balk once she'd made up her mind had fascinated him.

She straightened, her chin lifting once again, and for a second he felt as though he were being stared down at by a queen. Evidently, she'd spent far too much time with England's Queen Mother.

But that was okay. His own bloodline carried its own lineage. Perhaps not one as grand, but damned sure one just as royal.

He pushed his chair back slowly and patted his knee. "Then come, love, let's call your former fiancé and inform him that promise has been broken."

Oh, now he was looking forward to this.

"She needs another ring." Ilya spoke, a cool smirk barely hidden as Ivan lifted his gaze to the other man. "He won't accept it unless he sees a mark of ownership, other than the hickey you left on her neck."

He watched as Journey's face flushed, but she never dropped her gaze.

"Very well." He grinned, then lifted the chain he wore from around his neck and pulled it over his head, ignoring the disbelief on Ilya's face. "Grandmother's ring will work, don't you think?" He looked up at Journey, then bid her to him with the crook of his finger. "Should I get on one knee, love?"

She stared at the ring and he saw the dreams. Son of a bitch if he didn't see the dreams in her face.

As she rounded the desk he rose from the chair and drew her to it. When she sat down, he went to one knee, staring into her shocked face, and removed the ring from the chain.

It was his treasured grandmother's. To be held for Amara until his death, or given to the woman who would be his bride.

"Marry me, love?" he asked her softly, staring back at her, watching her hand tremble as he slid the ring onto her finger.

"I'll give it back after the call," she whispered, still staring at it.

"You'll wear it as long as the illusion stands. Take it off and we'll both agree the fantasy is over." Yes, she deserved this. She'd give him what he'd dreamed of, and he'd give her the dream she carried as well.

She stared at the simple diamond, and her lips trembled once, before he leaned forward and covered them with his own.

She wanted the illusion, and perhaps a fantasy wouldn't be a bad thing for her. She was young, innocent, and getting ready to enter a very dangerous game. If the illusion of love would make the coming betrayal easier, then so be it.

He'd give her the illusion of love.

chapter eight

Journey would consider the agreement, the proposal, and the ring later. She knew the fine art of living within a lie and letting the fantasy shape reality when she had to. She'd lived that life for twenty-two years by someone else's rules. This time, the illusion was hers. And it was possibly the one way she'd survive what she was getting ready to do.

"You sure about this?" Ivan asked as she sat perched on his lap, waiting for him to make the video call. Ilya sat across from them, his expression enigmatic as he watched them.

"Of course I'm certain." She frowned, glancing up at Ivan as she folded her hands, engagement ring clearly showing, and placed them on the desk where the computer's internal camera would pick them up. "Are you? Should I reassure you everything's going to be okay?" She slid him a teasing, sideways look to hide her own nerves and the fear she pushed to the back of her mind.

Ivan would protect her. He'd protected Amara all her life. He'd protected himself. He'd see her through this, give her the fantasy she needed to get through it, and everything would be okay.

"The camera won't pick me up until I turn the chair toward it fully. He'll just see you," her newly acquired fiancé reminded her.

"Stop babying me, Ivan," she told him firmly. "I've got this."

"But I do so enjoy spoiling you." He brushed a kiss against her shoulder. "And expect him to get a good look at that mark I left on your neck. There's no way to hide it."

"I had no intentions of hiding it. Now activate the call." She composed her expression, remembered everything she'd learned at a queen's knee during summer breaks, and channeled that inner bitch her older sister swore she possessed.

Just in time for the call to go through and Beauregard Grant's imposing features to flash onto the screen.

"Who the hell . . . ?" The forbidding growl broke off as his irritated features went blank.

He stared at her, taking in her face, her hair. His gaze paused at her neck, went to her hands, took in the diamond, then moved to her face once again.

"Good evening, Beau," she said evenly. "I see you're doing well."

He didn't speak for long moments. Once again, he

took in the reddened mark on her neck and the ring on her finger before his gaze returned to hers.

"Journey?" He frowned, leaning closer to the screen on his end as though in closing the distance he could be certain.

She let a smile tip her lips. "Surprised to see me?"

He blinked back at her, then eased back in his chair, a brooding scowl on his handsome features.

"Why the hell did you cut your hair? And you've colored it?" Displeasure marked his expression.

"I've actually not colored it." She kept her smile cold. "It seems sunlight isn't as detrimental as Mother believed it to be. My hair loves it."

His scowl deepened. "I don't like the color, dammit. That's not you."

Ivan stiffened, the feel of the tension transmitting through his thighs and the hand that lay above her knee.

"I'm certain that should bother me," she assured him blithely, comforted by the fact that it didn't bother her. "But I have other matters more upsetting that we need to discuss."

His gray eyes narrowed on her.

"You've changed, Journey." Something curious, speculative, shadowed his expression.

"I've grown up perhaps?" she suggested. "It happens to the best of us, I hear. Still, not the reason I called."

He lifted his hand, rubbing at his upper lip with a forefinger as he stared at her.

"After four years, at least you finally deigned to

call," he grunted. "Tell me where you are, I'll have a plane sent for you and you can return home . . ."

She let a low, jeering laugh escape her lips. "Really, Beau? Do you believe I'm calling after all this time so you can send a plane for me?" She gave him the look the Queen Mother gave those she considered rather inept and particularly dim witted.

If the look on his face was an indication, he didn't care for it.

"You can return home . . ." he tried again.

"You can call your assassins off," she demanded, surprising herself at her icy tone. "Right now, Beau. You don't want the war you're getting ready to involve yourself in otherwise."

She didn't know if he was behind it, but she knew Beau. She'd known him most of her life; she just hadn't paid much attention to him until her father demanded she accept his proposal. If he was behind the attempt on her life, then he'd give himself away by the time Ivan delivered the final volley to this call.

His gaze moved to her hands once again, her neck, then her gaze. By the time his eyes met hers, his expression was still and hard, revealing nothing.

"Assassins? Journey, I haven't sent anyone to harm you. The men I sent were hired from a security service to bring you home," he stated. "Did they hurt you?" And he actually sounded worried.

"They nearly killed two of my fiancé's bodyguards. To say he isn't happy is an understatement. He's livid. You didn't send a security team; you sent a strike team."

And Ivan had almost lost two people he considered friends as well as employees. More of his people whom he cared for.

Beau stared at her silently once again. His gaze piercing, intent.

"Journey, hear me well," he said softly after several moments. "No strike team, no assassin, was sent for you. Tell me where you are and I'll come to you myself and we'll discuss this."

She smiled back at him mockingly. "That's not possible, Beau," she informed him. "Unfortunately, I don't trust you at all, and my fiancé trusts you even less."

"I'm your goddamned fiancé," he suddenly snarled, arrogant anger filling his face. "That ring and that mark on your neck be damned. Tell me where you are now."

"I prefer to live," she snorted, aware of the carefully controlled tension filling Ivan now. "If you didn't send someone to kill me, then who would? Stephen? Craig?"

"They may as well bare their throats to that goddamned Russian bastard Resnova first," he snarled. "Anything happens to you and the Queen Mother learns of it, then they'll fry. She'll make certain of it. She may not be pleased with you at the moment, but you're still her favorite of her young cousins and she's made it clear she'll blame them if you end up harmed. Now where the hell are you?"

He was livid.

She let her smile soften. She'd learned as a teenager how to compose her expression appropriately when needed.

"I'm with my fiancé," she answered smoothly, glancing at the ring and remembering Ivan as he slid it on her finger.

He'd given her the illusion, the romance.

When she lifted her gaze again, she barely caught the surprised knowledge on Beau's face.

"I'll kill him, Journey," Beau warned her softly. "And if I don't, Stephen and Craig will arrange it. If you love him, leave him now. I won't let you go so easily."

She gave a low, amused laugh. "They haven't managed it thus far and they've been trying for years. And I believe once the two of you meet, you'll change your mind in that regard."

His head tilted just slightly as he kept his gaze on her. Crossing his forearms on the top of the desk, he leaned forward, his expression darkening.

"Journey, be very careful at this moment," he told her warningly. "Very careful."

"Because you're not alone?" She smiled softly. She'd caught the flicker of the shadow of another person moving beyond the computer screen.

"Because you don't want to play this game," he stated with unaccountable gentleness. "You don't want to get an innocent man killed. And no matter how rich he is, he won't be able to protect you. Walk away, sweetheart. Tell me where to pick you up and I'll come for you myself."

The chair turned without warning, giving Beau a clear view of the man holding her.

"Fuck you, Grant." Ivan sounded amused, but the

Russian accent was thicker than normal. "Go ahead and try to take what's mine. I'll gut you."

Beau seemed to flinch.

His gaze went to the mark on her neck again, then the ring, before lifting to meet Ivan's with dawning realization.

"She wears your grandmother's ring." His expression bordered on shock. "Fuck, you're trying to get her killed, Ivan." Anger filled his face, his gaze. "Goddammit."

"Find out who's trying to kill her now, Beau!" Ivan snapped. "If they manage to so much as scratch her, I'll make certain Stephen and Craig die. Then I'll come after you. Orders be damned. You understand me."

Beau shook his head but didn't have time to say anything more before Ivan disengaged the program, a muttered curse slipping past his lips.

"I need a fucking drink," he growled, staring at her as though expecting something from her.

Confusion swept through her. "You want me to give you permission?"

A sound between a snort and amazed laugh left his lips as Ivan muttered something about "idiocy." "No, baby, but I'd never just lift you from my lap voluntarily. I need you to move yourself so I can stomp, drink, and curse for a moment."

Ilya made himself known then with a muttered, "God save us . . ."

Glancing at him, Journey rose from Ivan's lap and

allowed him to get his drink; then he stomped, cursed once, and turned to Ilya.

"Is everything ready to leave here?" he asked the other man.

Ilya nodded. "Tobias and his team will be here in about an hour."

"Have them meet us at the plane." Ivan slammed the glass to the bar. "I want to leave in the next thirty minutes. We're not secure enough here, and an hour gives those bastards a window of opportunity that makes me nervous. Thirty minutes."

"I need to pack." Journey watched him, paying attention to his expression, the angry glitter in his gaze, the calculating expression on his face as he considered his options amid the plan they'd come up with.

"Taken care of while we were conferencing with that whore-mongering royal wannabe," he sneered as he flicked his fingers toward the computer. "They were packed along with my belongings and placed in the SUV about fifteen minutes ago."

Ilya was working quickly on the tablet he'd logged on to, and Ivan was pacing the floor.

Journey sat down in the desk chair, leaned back, and watched both men as they talked, snarled at each other, cursed each other. She remembered the night Ivan had actually hit Ilya in the face and fired him repeatedly. The other man had paid little attention to anything but the blow to his face.

As they snapped and snarled, they might resemble enemies during those moments, but she saw flashes of respect and an easing of Ivan's temper.

He was known to be cool, collected, at all times, and now she understood why. Ilya absorbed that fury that pulsed below the surface and gave Ivan a verbal punching bag while throwing the words back at him. Like a sparring partner, she thought, remembering the kickboxing lessons she'd taken in New York.

Ilya was his sparring partner.

"Ready?" Ivan turned to her, held his hand out, and flashed her a quick smile, his blue eyes once again the dark navy color, his expression not as tense and dangerous as it had been moments before.

She rose and took his hand, allowing him to lead her from the house and into the SUV that awaited them outside.

She hadn't been aware they were leaving so soon, but it made sense. Beau would be able to trace the video call; he'd know where they were. At the very least, his security team would be on their way to the small estate.

"He may not be behind the attempt to kill me, but he's up to something," Journey warned Ivan softly as they neared the airfield he used. "He can't be trusted, Ivan. I know he was working with whatever agency rescued me and Tehya that night, just as you are. But you can't trust him. If he manages to take me, he'll find a way to force that marriage."

His arm slid around her, pulled her to his side, and his lips pressed against the top of her head. "Never fear, Syn," he said softly. "He won't live to consummate it if he does. I swear that to you. He'll die before I'll allow him to take what's mine."

What was his. For now, she belonged to him as no one else did.

She didn't question it; she pushed back the knowledge that she wasn't really his. That was the deal; as long as she wore his ring, she belonged to him.

Her dream, in exchange for his vengeance.

Lifting her head as they passed the gates of the airfield, she gave Ivan a deliberately wide-eyed innocent look.

"Did I mention I get violently airsick? . . ."

"He lied to us," Tehya stated from where she sat beside her husband in Beauregard Grant's office and watched as the MI6 undercover agent spoke on the phone quietly with the head of the Elite Ops unit he worked with.

"Not really," Jordan said, his tone musing. "We didn't ask him if he had Journey; we asked him if he had a woman using the identity she'd assumed."

"Semantics." She glared at her husband.

Sapphire eyes gleamed back at her in amusement. "But technically, still not a lie. Ivan wouldn't bother to lie, but the manipulating bastard isn't above word games. He actually thrives on them, I believe."

She pressed her lips together, not in the mood to be amused.

"Two of his agents are in the hospital and Journey has a team of assassins after her. Who would hire them if not Stephen and Craig?" she asked him worriedly.

"That seems to be the mystery of the moment," he

breathed out heavily. "We have two operations units investigating it, and once I make a call those units will be shifted to provide Ivan and Journey cover. He has the right idea though. The only way to answer that question is to draw them out. And his engagement to her will definitely draw them out."

"He'll get her killed," she protested.

She hadn't had time to really get to know her cousin. She'd tried. She'd hidden who she was, drawn Journey in as a friend, and hadn't trusted her with the truth. And her cousin saw that as a betrayal.

Everyone in Journey's life had managed to betray her, Tehya thought sadly. They'd lied to her, her parents and her grandfather had used her, her sister had ignored her, and her brother had refused to see how desperate she was to escape. Until Journey had simply run from all of them.

At the sound of Beauregard's muttered curse they turned back to him to see him toss the cell phone to the desk before pushing his fingers through the thick, straight strands of black hair framing his face.

"Well, this is a bloody fucking mess!" he snapped, the British accent he possessed heavy with anger. "Stubborn damned Russian bastard. He'll have Stephen and Craig foaming at the mouth in fury." He glared at them as though it were somehow their fault. "And that bloody girl thinks I tried to have her murdered? She's lost her senses."

"She didn't sound as though she'd lost her senses," Jordan pointed out, and Tehya had to agree with him.

"She actually sounded a lot like someone else I know." She caught the smile he shot her and refrained from rolling her eyes.

"That was not Journey." Beauregard punched his finger in the direction of the computer screen. "Hell, she didn't even look like herself. Were it not for that scar on her hand, I would have sworn it was an imposter."

The scar. Tehya's heart ached at the thought of the small burn mark her cousin carried on her hand.

"She's not the girl you knew," Tehya corrected the agent. "She's four years older, Beau, with four years of anger and desperation hardened inside her. She'd not be the same; now we have to figure out how to work with the change in her as well as the situation."

"Ivan's a master gamesman and manipulator," Jordan pointed out then. "But he wouldn't allow Journey to go into one of his games without being honest with her. The fact that she's going along with a fake engagement proves it."

"Fake?" Beau stared at them as if they were crazy. "Jordan, had she been wearing anything other than his grandmother's ring, I'd agree with you. Before the old woman died she made Ivan swear no woman but the one he intended to wed would wear that ring, and anyone who knows Ivan knows that. He's worn it on a chain around his neck instead since her death. He's dead serious about that engagement. And the mark she carried on her neck assures me she's serious enough about it that she's sharing his bed now. The little wench would barely allow me to kiss her."

Well, that was a surprising piece of news.

"Hell, she glowed," Beau bit out, obviously put out that Journey hadn't fallen at his feet as she was supposed to but had not only run from him but also found herself in Ivan's bed rather than Beau's.

Tehya had to admit she was surprised by the fact that Ivan was sleeping with Journey. Besides the fact that she was a Taite, she was more than ten years younger than the Russian. She had been his daughter Amara's friend, and Ivan had never been known to bed any woman who was more than a few years younger than himself. And he damned sure didn't take innocent young women as lovers.

"Where will he take her?" Tehya turned to her husband with the question.

Jordan's expression was thoughtful for long moments before he grimaced. "If he's serious about marrying her, about protecting her, he'll take her to his place in the Hamptons. It's the most secure of his properties, and surrounded by allies rather than enemies. He made certain of that. He'll pull in only his most trusted staff and security, and take a stand there."

"And if it isn't serious?" she asked.

"Then he'll take her to the penthouse. He's never taken one of his lovers to the house. He's funny about things like that. It's the family home, where he has his traditions and where he can be himself. Ivan's rather traditional in a lot of ways," he mused. "Had he been born to anyone other than the monster his father was, he would have married and had a dozen kids. His wife would be too busy being cherished by him and their children to have a wandering eye, and he would have been so devoted to his family that he wouldn't have considered being unfaithful. The man's a throwback."

Strange, she'd never seen Ivan Resnova quite like that, but she had to admit, he did seem to hang on to some odd notions where raising his daughter had been concerned.

"This is a mess, Jordan," Beau stated then, shaking his head. "It won't take Stephen and Craig long to learn about this. Ivan is the one man guaranteed to make those two explode. He always has been. When they learn Journey's not just sleeping with him but wearing that ring, Stephen will have her killed with no thought to the consequences."

"Why?" Tehya shook her head at the information. "That feud has never made sense, especially considering the fact that as far as he and his son know, Ivan's basically just as evil as they are."

Beau was shaking his head as she spoke.

"That ring isn't a fancy stone; it's not worth millions or particularly spectacular. Nothing like the ring I put on her finger. But it's the ring his grandmother was given by Ivan's grandfather. A soldier in the Russian Army. A man who loved her. What issues Stephen and Craig have I've no clue. They refused to say. But you know as well as I, Stephen doesn't release a grudge. And his grudge against Ivan runs deep and black. They won't just try to kill Ivan for daring to touch Journey; they'll have her killed as well."

And their hatred ran just as deep and just as merciless, Tehya knew.

Jordan's fingers curled around hers as she turned to him, her fear for Journey magnifying.

"Beau's right," she whispered. "He'll kill her."

"Let's take care of one set of assassins at a time." Jordan grimaced. "Let's see who's first in line; then we'll take care of Stephen and Craig."

He drew her to her feet as they turned to face Beau.

"I'll contact Ops command," he told the other man. "Then Tehya and I will meet with Ivan. You get on that strike team and find out who the hell they are and who hired them."

Beau nodded sharply and, despite the anger that still filled his expression, his gaze was concerned.

Saying their goodbyes, they left the office, then the apartment. Before leaving, Tehya was aware of Journey's mother standing at the entrance to the sitting room, her lined face somber as she watched them leave.

At least she wasn't drunk today.

chapter nine

The flight from California to New York was uneventful. Once they boarded the plane Ilya mixed her the nonalcoholic drink he always prepared for Amara on longer flights, enabling Journey to nap rather than suffer airsickness.

When she was asleep, the fire and incredible will were dimmed. Her features relaxed, her Cupid's bow lips softened and slightly parted, her left hand tucked at her cheek, the diamond engagement ring resting near her soft flesh.

Ivan knew he really wasn't prone to second-guess himself too often, and once he set a course for himself he didn't often deviate from it. When he'd slid that ring onto Journey's finger and realized it was a perfect fit for her, he'd made a decision in that moment that he was certain would cause Ilya to berate him and Journey to run as quickly as possible from him.

Just as in that moment she stood in front of his desk and declared if she was going to cooperate with his plan, then he was going to give her the illusion of love. In that moment, staring into her eyes, he'd realized his little Syn had no idea what it meant to be loved by a man, by a lover. And something had snapped inside him. He might not believe in the idea of true love, but that didn't mean he couldn't very easily give this woman that illusion. And in giving her the illusion, perhaps he could actually bind her to him. For a while at least. Unless she had that need for children that most young women possessed.

Until she learned that was something he couldn't, wouldn't, give her, then he could allow himself to have her.

There was something about Journey that drew him, made him harder faster than any other woman ever had, and, unfortunately, made him as protective as hell. Because protectiveness and the game they had to play didn't go hand in hand.

She was still a little groggy when the plane landed and on the drive to the oceanside house he owned in the Hamptons. Not as large perhaps as the Colorado estate, but homier and lacking some of the weaknesses he'd found in the other estate.

After escorting her to their room and urging her to nap off the effects of the flight, Ivan gathered his security team together to ensure her protection.

Dinner came and went. He was aware of Journey's movements throughout the house as his aunt Sophia showed her around, though security meetings and various business concerns held him until well after dark.

By the time he was able to break away and make his way to his suite, his frustration was simmering. Beauregard Grant and Jordan and Tehya Malone, as well as Journey's mother, were demanding a meeting. He didn't doubt Jordan and Tehya's concern; Grant's demands and Celeste Taite's only managed to piss him off though.

Stepping into the sitting area of his room, he found Journey curled up in a chair working on the electronic tablet he'd had Ilya set up for her. She'd showered, he saw, and wore one of the silk gowns and matching robe he'd had delivered earlier. The dark violet brought out her green eyes, the soft radiance of her creamy flesh.

Her gaze was somber as she looked up.

"I'm heading to the shower," he told her, pausing as he closed the door.

"Sophia said she left a plate in the kitchen if you're hungry," she told him quietly.

"I devoured it before coming up," he assured her, trying to temper his tone with his knowledge of how quickly he'd eaten the meal. He would always fight to reassure the woman he loved, if he believed in such a thing. "I'll be out in a bit."

He strode to the shower quickly, not certain if he could contain the lust crawling through his system after seeing her in that damned silk nighty and robe.

He was in danger of tearing the damned thing off her.

Son of a bitch, was the illusion he promised to give her affecting his sanity? Because when he entered his personal suite, rather than being irritated by another's presence in it, he thought it felt strangely . . . right. He'd seen her sitting there, and rather than anger, there was just the urge to touch, to taste, to fuck them both into exhaustion.

Crazy.

She made him crazy.

He wanted all of her, just as she wanted all of him.

She did want all of him, right?

She did.

She'd fantasized about him, weaved a hundred fantasies around him, and she'd cried when she'd slipped from his house in Colorado. Just as she'd cried as she'd huddled in that seat on the bus and ridden away from Boulder.

If love existed, then she was in love with Ivan Resnova. She'd begun doubting that such an emotion could even exist in this world. After all, if a girl's parents couldn't love her, who could? If they couldn't love her, then she doubted even a Russian crime czar could love her.

But she could live the dream for a little while. He was willing to give her that. And if this was real, if he loved her, she wouldn't hesitate to go to him. She'd have no hesitation in touching him whenever she wanted to. And she wanted to touch him. Stroke him. Feel him touching her, taking her.

And he wanted her; she knew he did. The evidence

of it was straining his slacks when he'd come into the room and headed to the shower.

She rose from the sofa, dropped the robe from her shoulders, shimmied from the gown, and, naked, padded across the bedroom to the bathroom.

Steam spilled from the tiled enclosure as the sound of water flowing within it wrapped around her. Stepping to the entrance, she paused, simply staring at him.

It was then she saw the tattoo. It wasn't as clearly inked as the one on Ilya's face. It was like a shadow across his heavily muscled shoulder; only the red droplets of blood against the occasional darkened scale showed up clearly.

As his back flexed, the dragon moved. Dark blue eyes watched from within the dragon's face, unblinking, fierce, and filled with fury.

Standing beneath the showerhead, one hand braced on the tile in front of him, his head bent, he was so perfectly, wonderfully male. Bronze flesh, powerful muscles, and completely, fully aroused.

"Be certain . . ." His voice was tight, a sensual rasp whispering around her. "I want you too much to be particularly gentle, Syn."

Syn. No one had ever given her a nickname until Ivan.

"Did I ask you to be gentle?" she mused, her breathing hard, heavy, as she felt her skin sensitizing. "I told you, I wanted all of you."

His head jerked around, his gaze meeting hers, his expression harsh, savagely cast in the hunger filling it. Hunger. For her. He wanted her until his eyes were almost black, his expression stark with lust. And no one had ever wanted her like that.

She stepped into the shower, water spilling over her as he turned to her, watching her with an almost predatory look.

"All of me?" he questioned her, as though to be certain. "No matter what?"

He wouldn't hurt her, she assured herself. If he'd intended to hurt her, he would have done so by now. He wouldn't have offered to protect her.

"All of you," she assured him, and she couldn't help but glance to the heavy flesh straining between his thighs. Thick, imposing. And just for this moment in time, for however long it took him to gain his vengeance and her safety, he belonged to her.

He'd promised. He'd given her a ring he'd held for the woman who might one day be his bride. No other woman had worn it except his grandmother. That was his promise.

Stepping to him, she let her palm touch his chest, the mat of hair that covered it rasping her fingers, the warmth of him sinking into them.

"Ivan . . ." she whispered, uncertain now, aware her inexperience was so vast that she had no idea how to begin taking what she wanted. Especially from a man as experienced as this one.

"Fuck. You're so innocent you make me feel craven," he growled, his hands reaching for her, pulling her to him. "My little Syn. Sweet, innocent Syn."

His lips covered hers before she could retreat, apologize, or do whatever she was supposed to do. But as his fingers threaded in her hair, pulled her head back, and his lips covered hers, the thought slipped away.

Her hands slid to his shoulders, fingers gripped, feeling his flesh, loving it. Needing the stroke of his skin against her. She ached for it. The pleasure of it was addicting.

Reaching up, her hands slid into his hair, desperate to hold him to her as his lips released hers.

"Wait." Breathless, not beyond begging, she brushed her lips against his again and got far more than she anticipated.

If she thought his kisses were hungry before, they now became ravenous. As though the leash he used to control his need suddenly slipped. Her back met the shower tile as he lifted her from her feet. His kiss ravaged her lips, and she loved it. He was wild, his big body hard and tense as he held her against him.

With one hand he lifted her knee to his hips, and she followed with the other one. A moan tore from her lips as the broad crest of his erection became trapped between their bodies, caressing her clit with the throbbing heat it contained.

He jerked his head back, allowing her to drag in much-needed air for just a second. Then one hand gripped the side of her rear and his hips rolled against hers. The hard length of his cock stroked her swollen clit and sent daggers of brilliant heat striking at her womb.

"I wanted to be gentle." His voice was a hard rasp as his lips took stinging tastes of her neck. "I wanted to love you, Syn."

Something clenched and tore at her heart as jagged emotion flooded it.

"Love isn't always gentle . . . Oh God . . . Ivan . . ." she cried out in shock as his teeth raked the sensitive cord in her neck, as his hand gripped her rear more firmly and jerked her tighter against the length of his cock.

She was killing him.

Ivan felt himself losing all sense of control when those damning words slipped from her lips.

Control evaporated, but the determination to ensure her pleasure, to ensure she knew the ultimate in satisfaction, was instinct.

Before she could erode the last semblance of strength he possessed, he reached out and flipped off the water, then stepped from the shower with her in his arms.

Heated towels hung outside the glass cubicle and he made certain to use them quickly. As he knelt before her, rubbing the thick cotton over her thighs, he found himself pausing. His gaze centered on the silky, bare perfection of her inner lips, slick and shimmering with her feminine dew.

"Part your legs." He could barely speak for the lust tearing through him. "Now, Syn."

She trembled, her thighs parting slowly.

"Ivan, I won't be able to stand." Her fingers tightened on his shoulders. "I'll fall."

He licked his lips, the thought of tasting her again raging through him like the need for a fix through an addict.

"I won't let you fall." He jerked the padded vanity stool from beneath the counter. Damn thing had sat there for years unused. He had the perfect use for it. "Sit, baby." Easing her to the chair, he urged her to lean back as he lifted one delicate foot to his shoulder.

Shock and need filled her expression. Her green eyes were the color of emeralds as she stared at his lips.

Deliberately, he let his tongue ease out to touch his lower lip and watched her eyes daze, her face flush, as her lips parted to drag in more air. Staring back at her, lust thundering through his system as he sat at her feet, he eased forward and let his tongue slide through the lush, silky juices coating her flesh.

He groaned at the first taste of her. A hint of sweetness and spice, a delicate, intoxicating blend that went to his senses faster than liquor. And made him hungrier, more desperate, for her than ever.

Parting the swollen folds, he let himself take her with ravenous need. His tongue fucked inside her pussy, pushing past the clenched, saturated entrance before easing free of her and licking along the delicate slit again.

Her clit was swollen, her cries meeting each hard thrust of his tongue or suckling pressure of his mouth. Her hands threaded in his hair again, clenched. Her hips lifted to him and her head fell back along the counter as she became lost in the pleasure.

"That's it, Syn," he groaned as he eased back and tucked two fingers at the entrance to her vagina. "Come for me, baby. Let me feel how much tighter that sweet pussy can get."

His lips covered her clit as he worked his fingers inside her, thrusting into the delicate tissue as his cock throbbed, his cum tightening his balls in impending release.

God, she was straining his control. But he wanted her release, her orgasm. Wanted to feel her coming apart around his fingers and against his tongue.

"Ivan." Her broken gasp was a second behind her ragged cry. "I can't . . ." She jerked, shuddering in his grip, her pussy tightening, tension radiating through her. "Ivan . . ." Her cry was filled with desperation now. "I can't stop . . ."

He could feel her fighting her orgasm, just as she had that first night. The first time the pleasure tore through her and stole her senses. And he wouldn't allow her to stop now, any more than he allowed her to stop it before.

Thrusting his fingers inside her, he curled the tips just enough to reach a highly sensitive spot as he tightened his lips on her clit and held firmly to the hip his free hand gripped.

A low, keening cry filled the bathroom a second before she jerked in his hold. Her pussy clamped around his fingers, milking them as the silky wash of her orgasm flowed around them. Against his tongue, her clit flexed, swelled further, and as he held her to his mouth another cry tore from her. Shudders raced through her; her hands gripped his hair, her thighs clamping with delicate greed on his head.

It was like a drug, making her come. He realized that as he consumed each shudder, each delicate taste and cry that spilled from her. Making his Syn orgasm was addictive.

Journey finally remembered how to breathe, how to process information, as she was carried out of the bathroom and felt Ivan recline back onto the bed, her body covering him, her thighs gripping his.

"Ride me, Syn," he demanded, his voice a dark rasp she couldn't help but obey.

She lifted herself until she knelt above him, her hands braced on his tight abdomen as he cupped her rear and lifted her until the broad crest of his cock notched at the entrance of her sex.

Staring down at him, she was entranced by the wicked sensuality in his expression, the pure hunger gleaming in his near-black eyes.

"Take me, baby," he whispered, black lashes lowered at half-mast, a sexy, teasing grin edging at his lips, belying the bead of sweat easing down the side of his face. "Show me how you want to be fucked."

The explicit sexual demand was more erotic than it should be.

She eased lower, taking the crest, her eyes drifting closed.

"No." The sudden pressure at her hips, stilling her as well as his demand, had her eyes opening in surprise, locking with his. "Let me see your eyes. Let me watch your pleasure, Syn."

Oh God, she didn't know if she could do this. She didn't know if she could keep her eyes opened. But the pressure holding her still eased, allowing her to work the engorged head deeper inside her, and what she saw in his face had a whimper escaping her.

He wanted to watch her pleasure, but did he know

what he was showing her? He stared at her the same way Tehya's husband stared at the wife he loved. His expression absorbed, a glimmer of some inner flame making his eyes brighter.

"Ivan . . ." He promised her whatever she wanted, whatever she needed. Was she bold enough to demand it now?

Rising and lowering, she took him deeper, fighting the need, the hunger.

"I love you, Syn . . ." He whispered the words.

She stilled, his flesh locked halfway inside her, hard and throbbing, his body tense as he held back and waited.

"Take what's yours, love," he invited her, his accent thick, his voice rough. "Take all of me."

"I love you . . ." The words wouldn't still, wouldn't hide. But she knew what he didn't; it was no illusion.

But at the whispered vow his hips jerked beneath her, driving the hard wedge of flesh deeper, harder, before he stilled again.

"Ride me, Syn . . ." A grimace pulled at his expression. "Now, damn you. Fuck me, baby. Give me you."

She was lost.

Staring into his eyes as a cry left her lips, she took him. All of him. Her head tipping back in ecstasy as the fiery pleasure and pain of the hard impalement tore through her.

"Look at me," he snarled, gripping the hair at the side of her head and pulling her head back. "Let me see your love, Syn. Let me see it."

The demand was low, intense. Tortured.

Opening her eyes, she stared down at him as his hands cupped her rear, moving her, taking her as she took him. Just his gaze locked with hers, his erection thrusting inside her. Hard muscles flexed in his arms, his powerful shoulders, and his abs. A sheen of perspiration covering both their bodies as he drove her higher into a pleasure that only built and built. A pleasure that bordered pain, bordered pure rapture.

"Love me, my Syn," he groaned as her whimpers turned to cries, her nails digging into his shoulders. "Sweet Journey. Love . . ."

Her orgasm exploded in a wave of such intense ecstasy, she knew she gave him far more than her heart. It was never an illusion for her, he realized as she watched him, felt his cock drive to the hilt as the blast of his release filled her. Deep, powerful pulses of heat filling her, extending her pleasure, and owning her.

This man owned her, and God only knew if her heart could survive it.

"I love you. Oh God, Ivan, I love you . . ." She collapsed against his chest, shuddering, tremors wracking her body with each wave of sensation tearing through her.

Finally, sated, limp, and exhausted as she lay against his chest, she closed her eyes and let herself just exist within the illusion.

An illusion he allowed.

"I love you, my Syn . . ."

* * *

She was asleep.

Ivan stared at Journey's still features, tracked her deep breaths, and rose wearily from the bed.

Fuck. Where was his mind? What the hell was he allowing in this fucking illusion he was destroying himself with?

Dressing, he slipped from the bedroom, restless, plagued by more questions than answers and a deep, heavy certainty that something was changing within him. Something he didn't recognize.

"There you are." Ilya met him at the bottom of the stairs, alert, armed. "I wondered if you'd show up."

When at the house, he always went through it with Ilya himself every night, just to be certain everything was secure before he turned in to sleep.

And now to ensure his Syn was protected.

Was there any way to protect her from him or the situation? he wondered as he went through the house with Ilya checking windows and doors before he rejoined Journey in the bedroom. If he were a man in love, he told himself, then her protection would be more important than bringing down the two Taite patriarchs.

And he found himself wishing he could protect her from it. He didn't believe in love, had never allowed himself to be weakened by the belief in it, but with Journey he found himself questioning his plans.

If he dropped his need for vengeance, it wouldn't affect his safety either way, or his daughter's. But if he dropped it, Journey would never be safe. Whoever hunted her now wouldn't stop until they killed her, and he had no doubt the threat against her involved her grandfather and her father, in some way.

Pausing at the French doors leading to the patio and pool, he found himself staring into the night, actually contemplating the pros and cons of just having them killed. It would be difficult, the chances of failure were higher than he liked, but he could have it done.

And if he failed he'd lose the backing of the covert agency that so often covered his ass since those bloody years in Russia.

"She's safer here than on other property you own." Ilya spoke behind him, his accented tone quiet.

"True." Sliding his hands into the pockets of his slacks, he let his gaze continue tracking the night rather than meeting that of Ilya.

"You'll break her, Ivan," Ilya warned him. And trust Ilya to never allow a man to forget who and what he was.

"Her conditions," he reminded his assistant. "There are no lies between us."

That was the problem with friends such as Ilya. They didn't sugarcoat a damned thing.

"You slid that ring on her finger easily enough," his friend grunted. "Where's your mind, Ivan? To allow her this illusion is cruel. You'll walk from her as you have from every other woman in your life with the exception of your daughter."

Would he? Could he?

As he stared into the night he realized he'd been giving Journey far more of himself than he'd ever imagined possible. And it had begun further back than the night of her father and grandfather's arrests. It had begun when he glimpsed her discomfort at that party so long ago, and the fact that he'd only wanted to ease it. She'd been a child, but the fear, social unease, and desperation to escape that filled her young face had caused his chest to ache for some reason.

"Ivan, you're too hard for her . . ." Ilya continued, his voice low.

"Leave off." He didn't want to hear what a bastard he was where women were concerned. He knew. "If I rescind the deal she'll run. She'll die. You know that."

And that he couldn't bear, though why she mattered more than other women he'd slept with he had no idea.

"You forget her cousin," Ilya reminded him. "As she said, they can hide her."

He turned to face his friend then, mockery twisting his smile. "She would never be satisfied with that. She's found her independence; being hobbled would only see her boredom pushing her into trouble again. Tell me you don't already suspect it yourself."

Ilya shook his head at the claim. "I don't know, but I saw your face when you gave her that ring. You're risking not just her, but you. And when you risk yourself, I become concerned."

Tilting his head, he stared back at Ilya curiously. "And how am I risking myself?" He was almost amused by the claim.

"You're going to allow yourself to believe this illusion while spinning it for her," he charged. "That's dangerous."

Ivan snorted at the claim. "I'm too old for fairy tales, Ilya."

"No doubt her cousin's husband, Jordan, told himself this as well even as he sank within it." Ilya moved to the bar and poured himself a drink. "Her cousin Tehya has even that hardheaded bastard whispering of love and cooing at their child now. The thing about fairy tales," Ilya warned him, "is how easy it becomes to believe in them."

Ivan simply stared back at him, weighing his words. It wasn't the fairy tale that held a man though, he thought. It was the hunger to fill the night, to find a measure of peace, to know one woman as he'd never known another. To know that one woman who pulled at him as no other ever had.

"Fairy tales or not," he finally said softly, "there's no way to pull her out of this, and no way to truly protect her until it's dealt with. You and I know that well. Where a threat exists, the potential for discovery rises by the day. And of all of us, she's innocent."

Journey, his little Syn. Perhaps the play on the assumed name she'd carried wasn't so far off. She was a woman to tempt a man to sin. To tempt a man to forget the lessons life had taught him.

"Beware the fairy tale, Ivan," Ilya warned him then. "For both your sakes." Nodding at him, the other man finished his drink before turning and heading through the house to his suite and the woman tangling not just his life but also his emotions into knots.

Beware the fairy tale. Because for the first time in his life, he was beginning to wish it wasn't just a fairy tale.

chapter ten

She hated being on display.

Journey had always hated the times her parents demanded she make an appearance at whatever party or function and play the perfect daughter. She'd sworn when she left she'd never allow that again.

Now she wasn't just allowing it, but she'd also helped Ivan plan it. For his vengeance. For her dream.

Was the illusion of being loved really worth it? she wondered as she allowed him to help her from the back of the limo several evenings later outside the exclusive Manhattan restaurant.

She was aware of the flash of lightbulbs, the questions the paparazzi were throwing out to him that he ignored with such arrogance.

Placing his hand possessively at the small of her back, he led her through the door held open by an impassive doorman.

"Mr. Resnova. Miss." The maître d's cool expression was belied by the curiosity in his brown eyes. "Your table's ready. If you'll follow me."

Turning sharply on his heel, he led them through the tables as though every head weren't turning to watch their progress.

Journey gripped the small silk clutch she carried, all too aware of the whispers following them. The whispered, "Taite brat . . . ," probably hurt the most though.

No doubt Ivan had heard it, if the tension in his big body as they stepped to their table was any indication.

Nothing could overshadow the knowledge that they were all but rubbing Stephen and Craig Taite's faces in the fact that she now belonged to Ivan. Not the expensive silk of the short green slip dress, designer shoes, expensive jewelry, or simple diamond on her finger could make her forget why she was there with him.

"I feel like an oddity in a freak show," she muttered after the waiter delivered Ivan's vodka and poured her wine before retreating.

"The most beautiful oddity," he assured her softly with a subtle toast of his glass. "And the most unique."

"But still an oddity," she sighed, refusing to glance around the room.

They were there alone, the only two in the room, as she repeated his warning to herself as she looked up at him.

"In the best of ways, perhaps," he acknowledged. "What makes you an oddity is what makes you the most desirable woman in this room though. A genuine heart, Syn. There are so few of those in the world."

She felt her lips part in surprise at the obvious sincerity, or his perfect portrayal of it; whichever the case might be, she couldn't help but believe him.

Besides, he called her Syn. He always called her Syn when he was being particularly honest or when he touched her. When he possessed her.

How was she going to survive without his touch when this was over? she wondered. She hadn't known how deep her feelings for him could possibly go. But she found herself wishing this was more than an illusion, more and more.

"I remember the first time I saw you." Leaning back in his chair, he sipped at his drink once again. Placing the glass back on the table, he gave her a rather mocking smile. "I felt like the most depraved animal."

"Really?" She couldn't stop the grin that touched her lips as he held her attention.

She knew now what he meant when he said they were the only ones in the room.

"Such a beauty you were for sixteen." He grimaced. "Wearing a dress that covered you from shoulder to foot. Some black shapeless thing." Amusement gleamed in his gaze. "You stood like a frightened doe poised to run."

Because she'd been so very out of place.

"I probably felt like one." She frowned at the memory. "I wanted to dance when you asked me. I knew I didn't dare though."

"I left just after that." Ivan grinned. "I was unaware you and your family were to attend. I felt it best to leave. But I remember the pride and daring I saw in your gaze then. Your head was held high, your expression far from impressed, as you followed the others in your family. I thought then what a beautiful woman you'd make. And, for a moment, wondered what it would be like to be the man that shared that woman's life and her bed."

"You're lying." The words fell from her lips before she could stop them.

The amusement slid from his face and his hand caught hers as it lay next to her plate. His fingers enclosing hers, he leaned forward, his gaze holding hers, warning her.

"I will not lie to you, Syn," he told her softly. "Never, in this regard, will I lie."

She wanted to believe, so desperately. And wasn't she allowed to believe? This was her illusion, the dream she wanted so desperately that she sat here, on display for those who would spread the word until it reached her father and grandfather.

"So." Releasing her hand and glancing at the menu at his side, he sat back as the waiter moved to the table. "Have you decided, or would you like me to order for you?"

She lifted her brow slowly and gave him her order. She didn't need anyone to order for her, even her fiancé.

The meal was exceptionally good, though she drank very little of the wine. Ivan kept her entertained with stories of the security agency he'd opened with his uncle and several other men in Colorado. The meal passed much more pleasantly than she'd expected. They were halfway through dessert and coffee when the peacefulness of the setting came abruptly to an end.

"We are about to have company," Ivan murmured, his gaze never lifting from hers. "Your former fiancé."

Beauregard. Shit. She didn't need this.

They'd planned for it; she'd just hoped she wouldn't have to deal with it.

She placed her fork carefully by the cake she'd barely gotten to taste, as Beau stopped next to the table. She glanced up at him, her brow arching at the brooding anger on his handsome face.

"Journey." He seemed to be forcing the word between clenched teeth as his gaze flicked to the diamond on her finger. "I could barely believe it was you."

"May we help you, Beau?" Ivan leaned back in his chair with lazy interest; his tone, though mildly curious, in no way matched the warning in his dark blue eyes.

"You cannot." His response was clipped and nearly insulting. "I would like to speak to my fiancée alone if you don't mind."

Ivan's lazy appearance quickly evaporated as he slowly straightened in his chair, his forearms bracing against the table tensely.

"You may want to rephrase that," he suggested to Beau, his voice low and rough with threads of fury. "That's my ring she's wearing on her finger, not yours."

That was not part of their plan. And the anger tightening his face damned sure wasn't.

Journey could feel her stomach tightening with panic and fear as the tension between Ivan and Beau began thickening. Where the hell was Ilya? He'd told Ivan he'd be close.

She looked desperately around the room but didn't see Ivan's friend.

"Don't. Please." She stared at Ivan then, nearly flinching as his gaze returned to hers.

The dark blue had lightened and anger swirled in the depths. His expression was savage, fierce, and possessive.

His jaw tightened.

"Journey, you can't keep running." Beau chose that moment to pull the chair beside her from beneath the table and sit down.

Ivan's expression became icy, his gaze hard, as he continued to stare at her.

"Ivan, can we please leave?" she asked, but she wasn't waiting for him.

Gripping her clutch, she moved to push her chair back. Ivan was on his feet and behind her before she could complete the move, his hand catching hers as she rose to her feet.

"Whatever you want, baby," he murmured, though she had no doubt Beau heard him.

Rising as well, her former fiancé glared at both of them.

"Ivan." His voice was like a whip, causing her to flinch.

Ivan cursed beneath his breath, his hand releasing hers and curving behind her back to draw her closer as he moved her past the table and away from the other man.

She could feel her heart racing, a sense of danger gathering behind him, and thought she was going to strangle on it.

She knew Beau and she knew how vindictive he could be. Since she'd learned the truth of her father and grandfather, she'd also managed to figure a few things out where Beau was concerned. He might not be one of the bad guys, but that didn't mean he was one of the good guys.

"He's dangerous," she whispered as Ivan pushed through the doors of the restaurant.

Immediately, two of his bodyguards were in front of them and leading the way to the limo.

"I'm more dangerous," he assured her as the limo door opened and she was pushed inside.

That assurance had her heart in her throat. In that moment, she believed him. There was something so predatory, so savage, in his gaze that she could only stare at him as he sat across from her and pinned her with his gaze.

"Ilya. Home!" he snapped as the other man glanced back at them.

"Of course," he responded. "We have traffic though, and an accident causing a bit of a jam on the way. We'll be quite a bit longer getting back."

Ivan nodded, then slid his hand to the controls on the door. The window separating the front from the back rose slowly, the privacy glass blocking any curious eyes.

"He calls you his fiancé once more and I'll kill him." The statement had Journey staring at him in shock.

He was serious.

This was no act; it wasn't part of an illusion.

He sat there, his expression filled with brooding fury, his eyes burning with it as tension hummed in his body. And he was possessive. So possessive it wrapped around her with comforting warmth, rather than strangling her as Beau's once did.

She wasn't certain how to handle this more temperamental Ivan though.

She licked her lips nervously, aware of him following the movement as anger suddenly morphed to lust.

"I want your mouth on my dick, Syn," he growled, the explicit words causing her breath to catch. "Now, by God. Show me you're mine and I might be able to keep from going back and killing that worthless bastard."

What the hell was wrong with him?

Ivan couldn't define the agonizing lust and fury pounding through his body. The danger of killing Beau was a definite risk though. When he'd stood there and called Journey his fiancée, Ivan had nearly tried to kill him in that moment.

Now all he could see was that bastard standing over Journey, staring down at her as though he owned her. As though Ivan's mark on her neck were of no consequence. As though nothing could mark her deep enough to matter to the bastard.

For one insane moment, the need to mark him to her soul was like a hunger, a greedy, craven need unlike anything he'd ever known. He couldn't kill the bastard determined to take her from his bed, but he could make damned certain she knew who she belonged to now.

As she stared back at him with curious shock, he released the belt and quickly undid his slacks. Leaning forward, his eyes locked on hers, he gripped the back of her head and urged her forward until she knelt between the seats.

"Take me, baby," he whispered. "Just like you did the night before you ran from me."

Gripping the hard stalk, he urged her head lower, lust tightening his balls and thundering through his senses.

God, she was beautiful. Her hair fell around her face like red-gold flames, her green eyes darkened, and a soft pink flush suffused her features.

"Ivan." She whispered his name, her voice soft, her breathing uneven, as the sensitive crest met her lips.

"You're mine, Syn." He couldn't stop the declaration of ownership. His fiancée, his lover, his sweet, soft Syn.

She should fight him, deny him. The hazy thought drifted through her mind as the engorged crest of Ivan's cock pushed past her lips and filled her mouth. She should fight him, but she ached to take him, just like this. The dominance and hunger she could sense spilling from him, wrapping around him. The need for him that filled an emptiness inside her that hadn't made sense until Ivan.

Now she let herself have what she needed, what he needed. The fairy tale would come to an end soon enough. The memories would be all she would have of this time with him if they survived the coming storm.

Tightening her mouth on the thick flesh filling it, she licked over the iron-hard crest, reveling in the tightening of his thighs at her sides, the feel of his fingers tugging at her hair. Heat poured from his body; sexual need scented the air and infused her own driving hunger for this man.

Her breasts swelled, her nipples ached, as her mouth worked over his hard flesh; her sex became sensitive, her clit throbbing.

"Fuck yes," he groaned, his voice tight as his hips shifted, his cock fucking against her lips. "That's it, Syn. Your mouth is so fucking good, baby."

She whimpered, need pouring through her like wildfire. Between her thighs her juices spilled to her minuscule panties, dampening the sensitive folds of flesh.

Curling her fingers around the shaft, she was distinctly amazed at the thickness, the iron hardness, and the heavy veins that ran the length of it.

It was the crest that filled her mouth that held her attention though. How each lick, each stroke of her mouth, caused it to throb, to flex against her tongue.

"So good, Syn. God, your mouth is killing me." His

voice was rougher, darker, the sound of it sinking into her senses like a drug.

His fingers tightened in her hair, tugging at the strands and sending an erotic heat through her scalp.

Who knew having her hair pulled would make her so damned hot? She was burning for him, the need building like a hunger that couldn't be contained. The explicit act in the limo, his hands in her hair, tugging and pulling, his rough groans whispering around her, and her own involuntary moans mixed to an intoxicating level.

"Deeper," the demand came as his hips arched, pushing him against her tongue. "Fuck. You're killing me with your sweet mouth."

Deeper. She took him deeper, working her mouth, her lips and tongue, over the bruising flesh, shuddering as her sex clenched and liquid heat spilled from it.

Ivan could feel the sweat gathering on his forehead as he fought to hold back, to keep his release contained just a little longer. He didn't want to spill in her sweet mouth this time. God, he wanted to come in that tight little pussy, feel her clamped around him from crown to root as the pleasure swamped him.

Her mouth was like a living flame on his dick, moving over it, her tongue licking, stroking . . .

"Fuck. Enough." He had to force the words out, force himself to draw her head back and not push back past those swollen, reddened lips.

"Ivan, please." The hunger in her voice nearly broke his control.

Lifting her to the seat, he pushed her back as he spread her thighs and shoved that damned short dress above her thighs.

The panties were nothing. They barely covered her. Teased him, made him crazy . . .

One sharp tug and they were off her. His head lowered. Smooth moves and a lifetime of sexual experience in the wind. Lust tore through him, gripped his dick, his senses, and shredded his control.

There was no warning, no preliminaries, but Journey realized she didn't need preliminaries. Ivan pushed her back to the seat, spread her legs apart, tore her panties from her, and put his mouth on the swollen, sensitive flesh in the most incredible of ways. Lips and tongue, licking, stroking, kissing, devouring her with greedy, carnal hunger.

As he pushed one leg up, his tongue delved deeper, found the clenched entrance to her vagina, and pushed inside. Each stroke had her writhing with pleasure.

Her hands locked in his hair, hips arched, and her senses exploded with ecstasy. Her cry echoed around her, rife with such incredible pleasure that she couldn't contain it.

As the explosions ripped through her, she was only barely aware of Ivan jerking to his knees. A second later, her eyes jerked open at the first heavy thrust inside the clenching, spasming muscles of her pussy. Her breath caught, her body arched against his, desperate to feel as much of him as possible.

"Ah fuck." The cords in his neck stood out as tension tightened in his body.

Another hard thrust and he buried his length inside her, the sharp pleasure/pain of the impalement dragging another cry from her.

This . . . It was incredible. It was beyond pleasure. Staring up at him, she was mesmerized by the fierce pleasure on his face, the savage need that dominated his expression.

"Ivan . . ." she gasped, held by his gaze, by the penetration of his cock and something she simply couldn't explain.

That something rushed through her, pounded in her blood, her heart, and she knew it had her bound to him.

"Sweet Syn," he whispered, moving slowly, drawing his cock nearly free of her, pausing, then, closing his eyes, worked inside her once again.

Shifting, rising to him, she could feel the tension gathering in her body again, feel the need for that rush of ecstasy rising once again. It was addictive. This, this was worth dying for, she thought hazily as he came over her, his hips driving his cock deeper, his lips capturing hers.

With each pounding stroke inside her she flew higher, racing for a completion she swore each time could never get better yet always managed to do just that.

Tearing his lips from hers, he whispered her name, slid his lips to her neck, his teeth raking the tender flesh. Taking her harder with each stroke, impaling her, pushing to a height of pleasure that left her crying, begging, he drove inside her over and over. Each stroke, each broken male groan, met her cries as the pleasure coiled ever tighter inside her,

"Come for me, Syn." The demand whispered at her ear; his voice graveled, strained, lit the fuse to a release that rocked her to her soul.

Ecstasy tore through her, burned through her senses, and sent her flying, with Ivan. He was there with her. She felt him, holding her, pushing her higher as his release met her own.

How could a fairy tale feel so real?

Craig Taite glared at the video he and his father watched on the electronic pad a guard provided for them. He could clearly hear Resnova's fury when Beau claimed his ownership of the girl. And rightfully so; the boy's father had paid a hefty amount for her when they'd seen her years before Beau had proposed.

Journey had been but thirteen, only months from being sent to France to learn her place, as her sister and her mother had. Beau had been twenty-one, and already a force to be reckoned with. When he'd demanded Journey not be sent to France, then years later that she be allowed her year in America, Craig had stepped aside and allowed the man his way.

After all, he owned Journey, and she was raised to understand that Beau would be her husband when the time came.

His fist clenched in fury. Then the little bitch had run as soon as Craig and his father had been betrayed and arrested. And now, it seemed, Beau no longer wanted her.

He demanded a virgin, even at twenty-one. Stephen and Craig were to ensure she wasn't touched or taken by their business associates and he'd paid enough money to ensure she remained pure.

Until Resnova somehow found her.

"Well?" His father glared at him as the recording from the restaurant ended. "Your men failed."

That had been happening far too often lately. The man he'd been grooming to take his place was obviously not as intelligent as Craig and Stephen had believed him to be.

"*Our* men," he corrected his father calmly. "Never fear, it will be taken care of. Our secondary choice is still an unknown and will be apprised of the situation."

Their secondary choice wasn't as experienced as their first choice, but Craig had faith in the individual. No doubt if this was taken care of and they managed to actually get back on French soil then generations of a very lucrative business were at an end.

Technology, a lack of honor, and too damned many private connections when combined with satellite spying were making such ventures obsolete. The new generation would have to figure this out. He'd be content if he could just get home and regain the reins of his family.

To regain those reins, something had to be done with his younger daughter and that Russian bastard she was now sleeping with. That couldn't, wouldn't, be tolerated.

chapter eleven

Peace reigned for all of two days. Two days that Ivan found oddly comfortable. It was perhaps unfair of him to allow his family to believe the engagement was a love match, but it was one of his fiancée's conditions, and one he'd allowed to stand simply because he had no intention of allowing Journey to escape him.

The fifth day dawned with a burst of warmth and vivid spring sunshine. Spring was well on its way, the cloudy, rain-filled days they'd arrived to drifting off across the horizon. And with the clear skies came the first omen of danger. The fact that it was allies who arrived on his doorstep didn't detract from the knowledge that the danger would be coming.

"Red." He greeted the flame-haired Tehya Malone with a kiss to her cheek while ignoring her scowling husband. "To what do I owe the honor of this visit?"

He grinned down at her, ignoring her frown as

effectively as he ignored the dark look Jordan directed at him.

As though he didn't know why they were there. He was more surprised by the fact that it had taken them this long to make an appearance. Especially considering the fact that two Elite Operations units were positioned in various areas around the estate watching the house with keen eyes. Not to mention precise gunsights.

"Really, Ivan," Jordan drawled laconically. "That was a rather inane question, don't you think?"

He merely arched a brow at the other man and ignored the mockery in his cool sapphire blue eyes while turning to meet Tehya's suspicious green gaze.

"Don't bother with the charm, you lying Russian," she snorted. "Have Journey's belongings packed. She'll be leaving with us."

He was going to regret making an enemy of these two, no doubt.

"Forget it, Red." He turned his back on them as though they weren't capable of killing him without a single regret. "Can I get the two of you a drink? Though I've been informed morning is much too early for alcohol. I believe we do have some sort of fruit juice instead."

His little fiancée had been rather firm about that the day before as she caught him with a vodka in hand before ten that morning.

"Forget it?" Outrage filled her voice as they so obviously followed. "This game you're playing is going to get her killed."

He snorted at that. Making his way to the bar, he poured a glass of the orange juice Sophia had so kindly spiked with vodka for him. He took a healthy drink before turning back to them and lifting the glass in invitation.

Tehya's nostrils flared in anger, though Jordan was amazingly calm, considering his wife's rising fury.

"Ivan . . ."

"Where's that lovely daughter of yours?" He glanced between the two. "I would have thought you'd be home with her rather than rushing here to insert your very pretty nose in my business."

Her eyes widened before she threw her weight to one leg and placed a hand on her hip, her eyes narrowing confrontationally.

"That is my cousin you're endangering, you jacked-up little bastard," she snarled as he lifted his brows at the insult and flicked her husband a hard look.

"My home," he told the other man quietly. "There are rules, Jordan, as well you should know."

Tradition. Here he treated all guests cordially until they dictated otherwise. Male or female.

The statement wasn't lost on Tehya. As she glanced away, consternation filled her expression for a moment.

"You're right," she answered. "I apologize. This time. But those same rules mean you'll have Journey prepared to leave—"

"No, they do not," he growled. "I will of course allow you to see her, if that's what she wants. I sent Sophia to inform her you're here. If she wishes to speak to you, she'll be along shortly." He stared at her warn-

ingly then. "But be warned, Tehya, I won't have her
ordered about or browbeaten. She accepted my proposal with her eyes opened. I won't have her berated
for it."

Tehya's jaw tightened and her green eyes lit with a
furious flame.

"Don't tell me this engagement is anything more
than a ploy to force Stephen and Craig to sign their
own death warrants," she snarled, poking a finger in his
direction. "It's ludicrous. No one will take it seriously."

He finished the drink and with startling control set
the glass on the bar rather than throwing it across the
room.

"Beware what you say, Tehya," he told her softly.
"You are treading perilously close to offending not just
me, but your cousin as well. I would hate to see your
relationship with her deteriorate further."

It was a gentle reminder that despite the danger she
faced and the years she had run from those shadowing her, Journey had never gone to her cousin or Jordan for help. She'd faced life, faced whatever danger
and hardships that arose, alone until she inserted herself into Amara's life with the desire to come to Ivan
for help instead.

"Don't throw that in my face, Ivan!" she snapped.
"She's angry with me. Once I explain . . ."

"Explain what, Tehya?" he questioned, crossing his
arms over his chest, well aware of the concern in Jordan's expression now. "How you spent months allowing her to work for you, with you, and never hinting at
your identity, or your relationship to her? How you

walked away with the man you married while she was fighting to understand the pure evil that filled her family?"

Her gaze darkened, regret filling her face.

"It wasn't like that and you know it," she charged, her tone rough with emotion.

"What I know and what she experienced are two different things," he reminded her. "And it has nothing to do with my engagement to her either way."

A mocking smile curled her lips, and for the first time that hint of a sneer in her smile was more offensive than amusing.

"Really, Ivan? Let's try just an ounce of honesty here. That ring means no more than whatever game you're playing." She glared back at him, as though the look should affect him.

That ring was the final promise he'd given his dying grandmother. Whatever his engagement to Journey had begun as, he was deadly serious about it. He'd been serious about it the moment he placed the ring on her finger. Considering the fact that Tehya and Jordan had worked with him enough over the years to know he would not take a game this far, Ivan found it insulting. He was a bastard, he readily admitted, but never, at any time, had he dealt unfairly with a lover.

"This discussion is over." He glanced between the two. "I'll have Journey contact you sometime today to arrange a meeting outside my home. Good day." He nodded to Jordan dismissively. "Ilya will see the two of you out."

He nodded to Ilya as he stood at the entrance to the foyer watching the confrontation far too quietly.

Turning his back on them once again, he began to head from the sitting room to the wide hall that led to the rest of the house.

"Ivan." Jordan chose that moment to speak. *The bastard.* He owed the other man far too much to walk away.

Pausing, he turned slowly to meet the Irish blue of the former agent's gaze.

"Jordan," he sighed. "I value that respect we've always accorded each other." He glanced to Tehya briefly. "But be warned, I'll tolerate no further insults to either my relationship with Journey or my promises to her. By either of you. Especially here, in our home."

His and Journey's home. Jordan knew Ivan's insistence on certain courtesies in his home and he had always seemed to understand it.

"Understood." The other man nodded slowly. "In Tehya's defense though, no offense was meant. She's understandably upset."

"Which is understood as well." He nodded abruptly, not mentioning there was no understanding for her insulting opinion of his character in regards to his engagement to Journey.

Journey might know no more than to believe it was merely the illusion she so needed, but both Jordan and Tehya should be aware it was much more.

"Do you love her, Ivan?" It was Jordan who asked the question, not a furious Tehya.

"I love her." If love existed, then it was a pale imitation of the commitment he gave her.

For no other reason would he have given her the ring that meant so much to him. And for no reason would he have broken his promise to his grandmother to ensure he loved before allowing any woman to wear it.

Until Journey, until she gave him the innocence she had saved for so long. Until she had walked away and asked nothing in return, despite her need, he had not believed any woman understood honor or tradition.

She believed she loved him, and he would ensure she maintained that belief.

Jordan breathed out heavily as Tehya abruptly lost the smirk and regret filled her expression instead.

"I'm so sorry, Ivan," she whispered, and she meant it. "But you have to admit, your past didn't lend a lot of faith in our ability to trust you."

And still, they'd try to talk Journey from his arms and his life. He accepted it, knew it was coming.

Nodding sharply, he turned on his heel and headed for the opposite door. "I'll send Journey to you."

Before he could reach the door, she stepped into the sitting room, her gaze meeting his, with knowledge, a certainty that no doubt what she heard she believed to be only part of the illusion he promised her.

Dressed in jeans, sneakers, and a light loose-weave spring sweater, she looked like a damned teenager rather than the sensual woman he knew her to be.

Stopping, he waited for her to reach him before drawing her into his arms, against his body.

"I can send them away," he whispered at her ear after brushing a gentle kiss over her lips.

She gave a barely perceptible shake of her head, and in that moment he'd give anything to know exactly what she was thinking. What she was feeling. Hell, while he was at it, it would be nice to know what he was feeling himself.

chapter twelve

Jordan and Tehya left an hour later, the concern in their expressions still heavy when they couldn't convince her to leave with them. Their arguments were valid, the information they revealed on Ivan's past more than she wanted to know. More than she was comfortable with, actually. Some things she already knew, others, some of the more brutal truths of Ivan's life, she hadn't even suspected.

The friends he'd lost the night his father had forced his hand by attempting to take Amara when she was just five, to see her to the English partners he'd worked with. The same ones who had killed Ivan's mother and raped his aunt. At a mere nineteen he'd been forced to kill his own father, cousins he'd cared for, friends he'd believed he could depend upon.

The battle had split the Resnova family in two. Those aligned with Ivan, and those with his father. A father whose cruelties and monstrous actions had finally pushed his son past that final moral boundary.

He'd killed his father, an uncle, a half brother. To save his daughter. Then he'd taken control of the various criminal enterprises his father commanded with a brutal grip and begun molding them, conniving and manipulating men who could have destroyed him until he'd found a way to bring his daughter as well as himself out of Russia. Away from the brutality of his life.

And still, he knew how to love his daughter. He knew how to give an enemy's child the illusion of love.

The sheer will and inner strength he possessed went far deeper than she'd ever imagined before.

God, how was she going to endure this when the time came to leave? When she'd have to return the ring he'd given her and walk out of his life?

She made her way outside the wide patio doors that led to the pool, the thick stand of trees, and then the beach beyond. When she'd asked Ivan about the trees, he'd merely said they kept anyone in a boat from spying on him.

They kept him from being shot at from said boat, she guessed.

Because no matter who he was, what he was, secretly, to the world he was a criminal. To her father and grandfather, he was the ultimate enemy.

Ask him why, Journey. Ask him why they were enemies before you marry him . . .

Tehya believed it was the love match no one expected Ivan Resnova would ever know. Everyone believed that but the two of them, and that was her fault. Because she knew what would destroy the two men Ivan called his enemies, and she'd demanded not just that but also an illusion she could hold on to while he was doing it.

"I can tell from your expression that little visit didn't meet your expectations." Ivan spoke behind her, his dark voice low, questioning.

"My expectations?" She frowned as she stared beyond the pool to the stand of trees, wishing she could see the ocean. "I learned a long time ago not to have expectations."

She'd learned the brutality of seeing them disintegrate just within reach. Sometimes it seemed as though every dream she had ever known and fought to hold on to had been ripped away from her. Because of who she was, the family she'd been born into.

Because she was nothing at all like any of them. Being the girl next door would have been far preferable.

When he didn't speak she turned back to him and wished she hadn't. His expression was savage, his gaze brooding. It wasn't a comfortable look. But it was damned sexy. All that savage anger and brooding male strength ready to erupt. It made her hot. Made her want to rub against him like a cat or something despite the severity of the situation.

There was a tension in him that wasn't present before, but she admitted that tension had been growing over the past days but had deepened since he'd left her with her cousin.

Where it came from she had no idea. It wasn't just the situation; it was something deeper, darker. Something that had her instincts on high alert, her body sensitizing.

"Keep looking at me like that I'll end up fucking you out here for everyone to see." The rough rasp of his voice sent heat curling through her body.

It still amazed her, this hunger he had for her. The way his eyes always slid to her, turned hot and hungry. He should despise her, but instead, he desired her, even now when anger filled him.

"The bad part is that I would probably allow you to fuck me wherever, whenever, you wanted," she told him with a small grimace. "I have no control with you, and we both know it."

All he had to do was hold his hand out to her and she would go with him wherever he led her. This man who had so fascinated her from the moment she'd seen him

He glanced away, his expression tightening for a moment before he shook his head and turned back to her.

"You're damned dangerous," he muttered, sliding his hands into his slacks before breathing out almost wearily.

"Not me." She had to curl her fingers into fists to keep from touching him, from smoothing out the dark frown brewing on his face. "But you've had no other choice but to be dangerous, haven't you?"

To survive, to ensure his daughter's survival, he'd had to be brutally dangerous.

His gaze met hers, knowledge, a deepening fury, and regret filling his expression.

"What did she tell you?" The question sounded casual, but the underlying danger in it wasn't missed by her.

God, how she ached for him. No, she didn't ache for him; the pain tearing through her soul went so much deeper than that as the knowledge of what her family had done to him had slowly come together. When Tehya had told her to ask Ivan what they'd done to him, pieces of conversations, comments, and snide remarks throughout her life had slowly come together to form a horrifying truth.

"Ah. I see they told far more than they should have." Rage flickered in his gaze even as she shook her head desperately.

"They didn't," she whispered, wrapping her arms around herself. "Tehya told me to ask you what Stephen and Craig had done." She swallowed with a tight movement. "But I don't have to ask. The moment she asked the question I began remembering things that had been said." Her lips curled mockingly. "I was always a very quiet child. And I liked to hide and listen to the adults talk."

And she'd always heard far more than she should have, things that had given her nightmares as a child until she'd found a way to block them. With her father's and grandfather's arrests, that block had slowly thinned, then disappeared entirely.

They had raped a young boy's mother to her death as he'd been forced to watch. Stephen, Craig, and Ivan's father. As she screamed for mercy until her voice broke. And then they'd meant to do the same to Ivan.

Had it not been for Ivan's grandfather at the time, he would have died as well that night. Instead, he'd been forced to witness his grandfather's death several years later.

"Amara was always bad to hide and listen as well," he sighed. "She wanted to be near her poppa, she claimed at the time."

There was so much bitterness and pain in his voice. And hatred. The hatred resonated just below the surface, black and heavy with time.

He hated with such power that he'd spent his life attempting to destroy the men who had scarred his childhood. Beginning with his own father. And she'd handed him a weapon guaranteed to enrage both men and break the alliance they'd set up with the powerful Grant family. An alliance they needed to effect a semblance of freedom, and one that Beauregard Grant needed to ensure his acceptance with the associates the two men had so far refused to name.

How could he not hate her as well?

And Ivan was a master gamesman; even her father admitted that, albeit with a voice filled with disdain.

"I didn't want to be near my father," she admitted, her voice almost a whisper. "I was usually hiding from him during those times. He liked to show me off to his friends."

She didn't have to explain the types of friends she was talking about; she saw the knowledge in his eyes, though it did nothing to soften the darkness in his gaze.

"How important is a marriage to Beau where Stephen and Craig are concerned?" she asked him, knowing she couldn't hide any longer, couldn't avoid the truth. "And how important is it to Beau?"

Once, long ago, Beau had been a friend, a confidant. And even then he had been lying to her. Deceiving her. Ivan hadn't lied to her, but she knew there were times he hadn't told her the truth either.

"I'm not entirely certain." He frowned at the question as though not expecting it. "For some reason they believe that marriage is an escape from the American clause of some sort."

It was a possibility, she had to admit. Beau might be considered a bastard son, but he still carried the Grant name, and should he take over the Taite family holdings with his marriage to her, as her father had promised him, then his political influence could be far reaching.

"What would they gain if they have me killed instead?" She could see no possible benefit to that.

"I'm not certain. My sources tell me they're aware of the fact that you're in my bed and that you've agreed to marry me. They are supposedly not acting rationally. With any luck, they'll tip their hand soon."

The satisfaction that filled his voice, his expression, was terrifying to her. He would do anything, sacrifice anyone except his daughter, for vengeance. And though she couldn't blame him, she didn't want to be his sacrifice.

But hadn't she known what to expect? Hadn't she been aware of exactly where this was going? Hadn't she demanded that she be a sacrifice to his vengeance, that she be the tool he used to destroy her father and grandfather?

"But what will they reveal when they tip it?" she asked. "What are you hoping they'll reveal?"

He gave an easy shrug as an icy smile tugged at his lips. "I'm hoping they'll destroy themselves in their attempt to get to me. What are you hoping for, Syn?"

There was nothing warm, nothing caressing, in his tone as there was usually when he used the name he'd given her.

"I just hope it's a peaceful death when the three of you destroy me." Grief seared her chest though and burned her eyes. "I never dared wish for more. And as pretty as this illusion is, I'm not fool enough to believe it will end any other way."

Damn her.

Maintaining even a measure of calm was nearly impossible when he stared into the broken dreams that filled her eyes. No woman should ever look at a man like that. Without hope, with the illusions of the fairy tale he was trying so desperately to make her believe in. And his *Syn* damned sure shouldn't have that look on her pretty, delicate face.

He'd watched his father, then the nameless, faceless partners his father had, attempt to destroy any vestige of kindness inside him. From his first memories he'd known only his father's brutality, then his pure evil. He'd arranged for Amara's mother to seduce him when he was no more than a boy and to conceive a child. A girl child. One he could use to control Ivan. Then Amara would have been a tool to break him.

Had his daughter been a son, then that child would have died at birth. Ivan's legacy demanded it. For the same reasons that his father couldn't kill him, allowing knowledge of a male heir's birth would have been far too dangerous. Ivan would have controlled those families had a boy been born. And he would have controlled the very elite killers that still upheld the traditions of the past.

With no heir, he'd been on his own until he forced those families to honor their traditions. With an iron grip, with blood on his hands and staining his soul, he'd done just that. The Dragons were his now. They followed him. He would lose that control with his death. He was the last male Resnova. He'd ensured it.

"Excuse me," she said when he didn't respond, her voice husky as she stepped farther away from him. "I'm tired. I think I'll go inside now."

"Like hell you will." He reached her before she could turn away, jerked her body against his own, and felt that cauldron of emotions that made no sense to him threatening to explode. "Do you think I'd allow Stephen and Craig Taite to kill you? That I won't do everything in my power to protect you? That I wouldn't place every resource at my disposal to protect you?"

She doubted him, doubted his word to her. She wasn't fighting if she had no hope of survival.

"Can you read their minds?" she asked bitterly, holding herself stiff and unyielding against him. "Can you predict where and when they'll attack and who

they'll use, Ivan? Do you have a magic wand that re-
veals their secrets to you?"

He stared down at her and wanted to assure her that
he had all this covered, that she'd be safe, no matter
what. He wanted to swear to her that he'd never allow
her to be hurt, let alone killed. But that wasn't the world
they lived within, now was it? He'd learned a hell of a
long time ago that such vows only tempted fate. And
fate could be a cruel, malicious bitch when tempted.

"I can promise you that I will do everything in my
power to ensure your safety, even if it means my own
life." He watched her eyes widen, saw her fear deepen.
"I can swear to you, Syn, that the illusion of love you
need so desperately I'll give to you. And I vow to you,
I won't trade your life for my vengeance. If there's
more that you want, then perhaps you should tell me
now."

He wanted to maintain his rage. He wanted to see
the past when he stared into her face, see the horror of
his mother's death, the years spent trying to protect his
daughter, his young aunt. He wanted to be the man he
had been before he took this woman's innocence. Before he stared into her eyes and realized that for whatever reason, she'd saved herself for that moment in
time. For him. And know why that thought had the
power to ease his fury whenever she was around.

He needed to know why that man had changed in
the space of a single night for a woman who carried
his enemies' blood.

Instead, he only saw the woman. Innocent green
eyes, fear, tears, hopes, and dreams, and an emotion

no woman had ever felt when staring back at him. She looked at him as though he was the answer to her hopes, her dreams, and her future, all wrapped up in one man. And it had the power to humble him if he wasn't very careful.

"Your life is important," she said then. "I know that. I suspect I know a few of the men you work with. The night Stephen and Craig revealed who and what they were, I was there, don't forget that. Just as I was there when that team of soldiers, or whatever they were, rushed in. Jordan was with them. And you weren't far behind."

He'd warned Jordan that night that Journey had seen more than she should have and she was more intuitive than anyone had given her credit for.

"And you don't believe your life is just as important, if not more so?" Even he heard the anger in his voice at that point.

The woman would end up making him crazy.

"Oh, I believe it's important." Mocking laughter tinged the bitterness of her tone. "Trust me, Ivan, I don't want to die. But I like to believe I'm a realist. I'll never know a semblance of security . . ." Brushing her hair back with one hand, she looked off for a moment, and he saw the pain-filled hunger and fears that filled her. "No husband, no child, will ever be safe. I'll always be running . . ."

The hell she would be. He wouldn't allow it. She was his, and he'd protect her with everything he possessed.

His Syn still believed in love, and she believed

she loved him. He'd do whatever it took to keep those dreams in her eyes.

As her lips parted, a flash of something at the corner of his eye had his head jerking, had instinct reacting before his brain even processed the fact that a threat was already speeding toward them.

He was a second, a breath, too late. Ivan heard the retort of the rifle, felt the bullet slam into his shoulder even as he threw Journey to the side and fought to shelter her with his own body.

How? Goddammit, how had someone managed to breach his defenses so quickly? In the space of time it took to realize the flash was the sun reflecting off the lens of a rifle's sight and react, it was too late. He couldn't move fast enough to avoid it and he knew it. But Journey, Journey couldn't be harmed. His sanity wouldn't survive it, he realized.

The projectile ripped through the flesh of his shoulder and tore through the other side, exiting his body but causing enough damage that he knew it would weaken him. He could feel the rush of blood as he hit the cement, covering Journey's more delicate, fragile body.

He'd sworn to protect her only moments before, but the vow he made wasn't even a thought as he kept her pinned beneath him and managed to push them both to the only source of protection in the area. The low brick wall that surrounded the patio was his only hope of saving Journey or himself until his men could extricate them.

He could hear Journey screaming his name as he held her close and sheltered behind the low brick wall they'd been standing next to. She wasn't fighting him though; she was holding on to him with a strength he hadn't expected of her. Slender, delicate arms were latched around him like vines, as though he could be torn from her at any moment.

Reaching up with his good arm, he quickly activated the link at his ear.

"Ilya . . ." he shouted into the communications link.

"Stay in place," Ilya ordered, the cool, calm tone ominous. "We have a team coming for you and one heading in the shooter's direction."

He could hear the shouted orders, the retort of return fire from automatic weapons. He knew Jordan's replacement commander at Elite Command had placed men around the property; he wasn't a fool. He was a highly valuable asset and Journey was loved by Jordan's wife. Without him, information as well as valuable hands to move cargo or men beneath the noses of several government authorities would disappear. He controlled the Resnova criminal organization. They needed him.

What he wanted to know was how the hell a shooter had gotten past men as highly trained as those found in the Elite Ops.

Holding Journey to him, her hands gripping his shirt as though he'd be torn from her, he waited for the black-garbed Elite Operations agents who rushed to the patio to join his own men. They created a close, protective circle as Ivan pulled Journey to her feet and allowed the agents to rush them into the house.

She stumbled against him as they reached the safety

of an inner room off the living and kitchen area. A cry left her lips as he gripped her arm to steady her and felt the sticky warmth of blood . . .

Journey's blood.

Shock.

She knew what it was; she'd felt it before. The night her father, grandfather, and Beauregard Grant had kidnapped her, along with her cousin Tehya.

She'd retreated, watched outside herself, disbelieving what was going on around her.

She could see the blood staining Ivan's shoulder and arm, a thick scarlet spreading through the material of his shirt, thread by thread, overtaking it.

Ivan.

It was his blood.

Blood spilling from his body because of her. Because she couldn't accept being sold to the highest bidder when she was no more than a child. Couldn't accept the man determined to possess the legacy her grandfather and her father had built on the depraved greed that filled them.

"They shot you . . ." she whispered, reaching out, watching as her fingers neared the soaked material, seeing the hole in it, the blood pulsing into it.

She could hear him yelling at her, at those around her. Something about her arm, but it was his blood spilling from him.

"I'm so sorry," she whispered, staring up at him, pain and regret lancing her heart and spreading through her body.

They had taken so much from him and forced him to watch it when he was no more than a child. Then, they'd tried to steal his child from him as well, more than once. Now, they wanted to steal his vengeance, steal the only thing she had to hold him to her for a while.

She couldn't let them. He was her illusion. Her one chance to know what being loved by him would mean. He couldn't die. She couldn't let them take him away from her.

As she tried to touch him, tried to force her trembling fingers to hold back the blood, she felt herself wilting. Her legs buckling as pain of a far more physical sort shot through her arm, into her shoulder.

This was getting real now, as she'd once heard Tehya remark disdainfully. Far too real.

"Dammit, sit down before you fall." The rage that filled Ivan's face wasn't comfortable to see.

Hell, were his eyes black now? The blue was so deep, so dark, they appeared black.

"Get that damned doctor in here," he snarled, glancing over her shoulder as she realized that Ivan wasn't the only one who had been shot.

She was bleeding as well.

chapter thirteen

He needed to get drunk.

Hours later Ivan stood, his back to the room and its occupants, hands braced on the bar, and tried to tell himself he really shouldn't upend the bottle of vodka sitting in front of him.

God help him, he really needed to though.

Journey's wound wasn't serious considering the severity of the attack. A flesh wound, the doctor had surmised before Ilya had dragged Ivan from her room. The bullet had torn through his shoulder, clipped her upper arm, then gone only God knew where.

She'd been so pale, so weak, though. Dammit to hell, what had he set in motion here? Where was his mind to involve her in his life in such a way? He should have never done this thing. Only a monster could dare to taunt such evil as her father and grandfather, in such a way.

He could feel the perspiration dampening his back

as his guts roiled sickeningly, the remembered sight of her blood torturing him, reminding him of the danger he'd placed her in.

"Get your drink, Ivan, and stop brooding." Jordan moved to the bar, grabbed the bottle Ivan was intent on, and poured several glasses before sliding one his way. "You'll be happy to know the shooter was caught on the beach and is currently in custody and being interrogated."

Drink forgotten, Ivan swung his head to the side, staring at the other man as murderous fury rose inside him.

"Where is he?" He had to force the words past his lips rather than a snarl of such rage he didn't know if he'd be able to pull back from it.

All he needed was five minutes, no, he'd take five fucking seconds.

"Not a chance in hell." Jordan tipped back his drink, retaining the stare. "We need answers, not another death."

But death would come, Ivan assured himself. A slow, painful death. He'd find the assassin Jordan was hiding, and he'd slit his throat slowly, allow the bastard to feel every second of the knife stealing his life.

Breaking Jordan's gaze, he turned to his drink, drank it in one swallow, and slapped the glass back to the bar.

"How did he get past our men?" How had an assassin made it past three highly trained teams of elite agents?

"According to what the interrogator has learned so

far, he was already here when you arrived. He managed to avoid the agents by creating a very carefully crafted nest in a dune until he could get into place." A grimace pulled at Jordan's lips. "Luck. Then he waited."

Luck. He'd nearly lost Journey because of luck.

Fuck that shit.

"And if another assassin gets so lucky?" he snarled, the rage eating at him like acid. "What then, Jordan?"

"It's not as though you couldn't have expected this." Beau chose that moment to speak.

The bastard. What the hell was in Jordan's mind to have allowed him to actually attend this meeting?

"No one gave you permission to speak, Grant!" he snapped, the savagery brewing inside him now finding an outlet. "And I sure as hell didn't give you permission to express an opinion."

The other man's eyes narrowed.

Oh yeah, Grant didn't care much for his tone or his choice of words. Just as he didn't care for the fact that in their little versions of reality, Ivan was his superior. And there wasn't a fucking thing he could do about it.

"You have an overrated opinion of your position within this group," Beau snorted with mocking disregard of the fury Ivan was doing nothing to hide. "You don't have the power to shut me up, Ivan. Remember that."

That was where he was wrong, Ivan assured himself. In a fight where only experience, sheer strength, and rage mattered, he'd take the younger man down easily.

"Remember your shoulder," Ilya muttered from the other side of the bar. "And Journey won't be pleased if you get your face busted."

But it would be worth it. Journey would get over her anger, and the shoulder would survive.

"Ivan, this isn't why we're here." Jordan, the voice of reason, or so he liked to believe, spoke up as he moved to block Ivan's view of the other man. "We did anticipate a strike against Ivan, which is exactly what this was. The assassin wasn't here for Journey. He was here for her fiancé."

And the bastard had nearly succeeded.

"Sent by the Taites?" Ivan questioned him.

Jordan frowned at the question. "We haven't ascertained that quite yet. Our shooter seems determined to keep that information to himself."

The confident smile that tugged at the other man's lips assured Ivan that Jordan was certain they'd learn that information. But until they did, there was nothing he could do, no recourse he could take. At least not within the parameters of the covert organization he was part of.

Elite Ops.

The privately funded, government-sanctioned organization now had tentacles in some of the darkest corners of the most secure criminal and terrorist operations. They were slowly building a network unlike anything first envisioned. A network both Ivan and Beauregard Grant were part of.

That didn't make them friends. It didn't ensure either of them would work for the greater good rather than his own agenda. It simply ensured they always remembered and worked for what they'd become a part of.

It didn't mean Ivan wouldn't kill him if he crossed the line where Journey was concerned.

"There's nothing we can do until the Taites step over the line," Beau stated the reminder, the mocking edge to it pushing Ivan closer to violence.

"They stepped over the line when they sold Journey to begin with. And as far as I'm concerned, the buyer is no less culpable," Ivan growled.

Beau being the buyer. *Son of a bitch*. His father had paid out an outrageous amount to secure Journey as a future wife to his son.

"She could have been sold to some bastard that gave little regard to taking a child rather than a woman." The negligence in the tone was an affront to those chaotic feelings that rose inside Ivan where Journey was concerned. "You should thank me, Resnova. You took a virgin to your bed because of me. Hell, I should bill you for the price my family paid."

"Enough, Beau!" Jordan snapped, though he didn't turn from Ivan. "The two of you can bait each other when this is finished. Until then, the goal is identifying the final players in the Taites' little circle of friends. Until we learn who is still ensuring their orders are carried out, then Journey will never be safe."

Not Journey, nor many other young women who were born into the elite, privileged world Journey had been a part of.

"Stephen and Craig's lawyers have made several

trips to the federal prison where they're being held."
Tehya stepped to her husband's side, watching Ivan
warningly. "So far, there's nothing to go on to suspect
them of this hit."

"Who else would give a fuck?" He shot her a hard
look as he pushed his fingers through his hair, aware
of Beau's silent watchfulness. "If I die, do they really
believe she'd marry that bastard then?" He gave a sharp
nod in Beau's direction.

A mocking smile curled the other man's lips. "I'd
still marry her; I've made that plain."

Never let it be said Beauregard Grant had any respect for his own life, because as far as Ivan was concerned, the other man was pushing his luck. At the
moment, he'd rather see him dead than living.

But the Taites' knowledge that Grant would still
marry her was probably the only reason she wasn't being targeted along with Ivan. That marriage was
something Stephen and Craig seemed desperate to ensure.

"And your father has made it plain he'll not aid their
return to France without that marriage," Ilya pointed
out.

Beau nodded. "At my urging, yes. It's Elite Command's belief that Stephen and Craig will become desperate enough that they'll slip in their normal care
and reveal who they're sending their orders to. We suspect their lawyers are forwarding those orders, but
until we have proof, interrogating them isn't an option."

It wasn't an option for Elite Command, but Ivan
wasn't bound by the same ideals as Elite Command.

Ilya had already placed someone in the law offices overseeing the Taites' defense to gain the proof needed. If it wasn't revealed soon, then Ivan had no problem interrogating them himself.

"This engagement of yours wasn't exactly the wisest course I would have suggested," Beau stated then. "You should have kept her hidden, Ivan."

"She wasn't exactly safe when I found her!" he snapped. "I was only moments ahead of a strike team that arrived to take her or kill her. I haven't learned which yet."

"And that team is still nowhere to be found. I rather doubt the assassin was part of that crew though. They seemed a bit smarter than this," Beau continued, the mockery in his voice shredding the control Ivan had on his temper.

"I don't believe it was so much intelligence as training," Ilya injected. "They're highly trained and well funded. And Journey Taite does have quite a price on her head where her capture is concerned."

Capture and assurance of marriage to Beau.

Ivan clenched his teeth in fury. The thought of the other man touching her, taking her, was like acid in his brain. Would Beau force the marriage? *Of course he would,* Ivan assured himself. *He'd force the marriage and, no doubt, the marriage bed as well.*

He could stop that from happening, Ivan told himself. He could marry her now. If she was his wife, then simply kidnapping her and forcing her in front of a priest wouldn't be enough to seal a union between her and Beau. They'd have no choice but to confront Ivan.

Killing him wouldn't be enough either, because the Taites knew him and they knew he'd ensure her safety with their marriage. His entire organization would back her. Russian criminals, killers, some of the hardest bastards to ever live, would back her, just as they now backed him when he needed them.

That was the answer. A quick wedding, he would ensure her safety, then give her the wedding women dreamed of later. There was no time for that now, no time to lead her gently into his giving her what she believed was an illusion. Reality instead.

A knock at the office door had his attention shifting, his gaze swinging to the entrance as one of his bodyguards opened the door and stepped back to admit the doctor treating Journey. The wound hadn't been severe, but her pallor had terrified him. She'd been stark white, weak, and nauseous.

Turning to Ilya, he nodded at his friend to pour the doctor a drink. The older man looked harried, his gray hair mussed, deep brown eyes concerned.

"Peter." Ivan nodded. "Is she well?"

A sigh slipped from the portly man though he nodded. "It was just a flesh wound, as I said," the doctor answered, his accent heavy. "She is anemic, but vitamins will fix this fine."

The doctor accepted his glass, took a healthy drink, and met Ivan's gaze once again.

"There's more?" Ivan asked, frowning at the doctor's look and wondering what more a flesh wound could cause.

"She is pregnant," he stated, the look he gave Ivan

censorious. "Perhaps had you allowed the tests I suggested several years ago, you could have prevented this."

Silence filled the room.

The tests. The doctor had suspected that the vasectomy performed so hastily all those years ago may not have been done so effectively. He'd tried to convince Ivan to submit to tests that would prove it either way.

He'd been busy. He hadn't considered it important.

And now Journey was pregnant.

It was all he could do to keep his expression impassive, not to reveal his complete shock, or the satisfaction that made no sense to him.

"No!" Beau snapped, the anger in his tone lashing through the room. "What the fuck have you done, Ivan?"

There was a vein of disbelief, of shock, in Beau's voice. Not that it concerned Ivan. Hell, at that moment nothing about the other man concerned him.

"I suspect she's perhaps four to five weeks along," Peter continued. "She was unaware of her state. Were you?"

The fact that the doctor spoke so easily in front of the others assured Ivan that he'd allowed his closest advisors to become far too familiar with these associates.

He needed time to process this, Ivan thought, amazed, uncertain. Time to make sense of the timing and implications that fate was determined to destroy his carefully built defenses against more children. With the chance of giving birth to a son and a possible male heir to the Resnova holdings.

It would strengthen his hold on the shadowy world he still maintained a grip within. It would strengthen the bonds of loyalty to the families who followed him. And it would be a son. He could feel it, sense the certainty that life, fate, God, whatever the force directing this change in his life was, would ensure it changed irrevocably.

"You son of a bitch. You did this deliberately." Beau pushed the doctor aside, glaring into Ivan's face, pure rage lighting his gaze. "You bastard."

Ivan let a satisfied smile curl his lips. "My woman. I warned you of this, did I not?" he asked the other man softly. "What did you expect?"

Even he hadn't expected this, but he did expect what was coming next.

He barely dodged the fist aimed at his face, sliding aside and giving the other man a hard push into the bar.

Glasses clattered together, one crashed to the floor, and a hard smile curled Ivan's lips as the other man pivoted and came at him again.

Before Ivan could slam his fist into the aristocrat's perfect chiseled jaw, Jordan and Ilya were between them, blocking any blow either of them could make and pulling Beau back.

"You fucking bastard," Beau snarled, glaring at him over Jordan's shoulder as the other man pushed him back farther. "She's not strong enough for this world and you know it. You'll break her, Ivan, if your enemies don't do the job for you."

"And what would you have done?" Ivan could feel the rage crawling through his system, adrenaline pour-

ing through his veins. "Placed her on a shelf to wither
and die? And don't tell me she isn't strong enough.
That woman has a backbone of pure titanium and
you're too damned stupid to see it."

He couldn't believe Beau would dare to call her
weak. Physically, she might not be able to put up much
of a fight, but that woman's mind was like a steel trap
and her stubbornness more than apparent.

"God, Ivan, you've lost your fucking mind!" Beau
charged furiously, his hands fisting at his sides. "They
will kill her. They will not chance that child being born
male. Goddammit . . ."

Ivan's head lifted, nostrils flaring as he fought to
pull in enough oxygen to clear the haze of red from
his gaze. That was his child, just as Amara was his
child. Male or female, it wouldn't matter. But should
it be born male, then the Resnova legacy would be assured for another generation as long as that child lived.
It wouldn't die with Ivan.

And should a male child be born, then the Taites'
lives were forfeit. Ivan wouldn't have to lift a hand to
kill them. The support Ivan had lost when it was
learned he'd had a vasectomy at the young age of eighteen would return, full force.

He was the last of not just a legacy but also a tradition of force. Traditions did not die easily. Not in the
world he still retained control of.

"She will be more protected than even Amara's
mother is," Ivan informed him with brutal assurance.
"The moment the sex of our child is revealed, should
it be a boy, then even her shadow will be protected."

"And until the sex is revealed?" Beau yelled back at him. "God, Ivan. At least with me, she wouldn't have been in constant danger. Stephen and Craig will strike before you can stop them. Before you know they're there. They will not allow that child to be born. So much for that bloody fucking vasectomy of yours, right?"

He was going to kill that little bastard, Ivan thought savagely as the door to the office opened to reveal Journey.

The fiery waves of her hair tumbled about her pale face, her green eyes like emerald fire in her face as her gaze swung to Beau.

The vulnerability that filled her face when Ivan first caught sight of her evaporated, and pure feminine strength tightened her features. In that moment he glimpsed the royal blood that ran through her veins, and the influence of a queen who considered this woman her favorite of her young cousins was fully apparent.

Her gaze moved from Beau as silence descended for the second time, all eyes turning to her, watching her carefully.

She'd changed from the bloody jeans and sweater to a black, flowy skirt that ended just above her knees and a short-sleeved loose-weave heather green sweater. She looked so damned pretty she stole his breath. As arousing as sex itself, and as innocent as life.

What the hell she did to him. He didn't even question that fist that clenched around his heart, that tightened his stomach. It simply was. It was his reaction to her, all those emotions that threatened to burn out of control each time he saw her.

"Well, I see Dr. Jenko didn't waste any time in spreading the news," she stated as she stepped into the room, Ivan's aunt, Sophia, and cousin Elizaveta moving in behind her.

Ivan was aware of the brutal look Beau shot him and ignored it, his gaze on Journey, no one else. He had no idea what she was thinking, how she felt about the child, and he admitted he'd hoped to discuss this with her privately.

"Journey." It was Jordan who spoke first. "This situation is bad now, honey."

A mocking tilt to her lips accompanied her look of amused indulgence. "Really, Jordan? Do you think?"

Jordan grimaced as Tehya took her turn to shoot Ivan a furious look.

Fuck them. Let them be angry. He hadn't meant for this to happen, but he found he didn't regret it either.

His gaze dropped to her stomach, imagining her as she would grow with his child. She would become even more beautiful as the bloom of maternity filled her and shaped her curvy body.

When his gaze returned to hers, he glimpsed a hint of uncertainty for just a moment, as though she wasn't certain of him, wasn't certain of his response.

"Journey, let us hide you, just until the baby's born," Tehya seemed to plead. "I know you heard enough to know how dangerous this pregnancy is to you."

She linked her fingers, facing them all with Sophia and Elizaveta at her back. They would kill for her now,

Ivan knew. They would die to protect her and that baby. Just as he would.

"I've spent years hiding and it did me little good," she stated calmly before inhaling with deliberate control. "I wouldn't mind reserving the option, but for the moment, I believe this is a decision Ivan and I need to make. Alone."

Journey stared back at the implacable, imposing features of the man whose child she now carried.

It made sense now, she thought. The exhaustion, her inability to eat as she once had, that feeling of something not quite as it had once been with her body.

Her body was no longer her own, she thought, softening somewhere deep inside her soul at the knowledge. She carried Ivan's child now, and he didn't exactly seem angry about it.

"Journey, you can't have this child." Beau seemed to be forcing the words between those tight-assed jaws of his.

She wasn't surprised by his unspoken demand, but she was outraged by it.

"Beau, I have thus far refrained from contacting my cousin the Queen in regards to your behavior toward me," she told him politely. "But suggest that I do something so vile to my child again, I'll be on the phone before you can come up with a lie that will save your hide. Are we understood?"

The icy censure that filled his expression assured her that he understood completely.

"There are things you are unaware of," he tried again.

"And I don't need to hear of those things from you!" she snapped back at him.

She hadn't fully trusted Beau since she was a young teenager. There was always that sense that he hid far too many secrets, too many games. Not that Ivan was much better, but with Ivan there had also been that curling heat that filled her whenever she saw him and, somehow, a certainty that he wasn't the villain he was made out to be.

Whichever he was, she guessed she was about to find out though. But that was okay, because he might be getting more than he'd bargained for himself.

chapter fourteen

The illusion she'd bargained for was over, and Journey knew it the moment the doctor asked her if she'd known she was pregnant. Now, hearing the office door close behind her as the others left the room, she met Ivan's implacable gaze and wondered what the hell she should do now.

It was no longer about her. It would never be about her again. This was about the child they had created, and she had to think of that child first.

With all his faults, supposed crimes, and machinations, the one thing she did know about Ivan was the fact that he was a good father. He was an excellent father. Amara had told her many times how her "poppa" had always sheltered her, loved her.

Amara had suffered for the life she and her father had been born into and the choices he'd been forced to make, the other woman had once told Journey. They had both suffered. But she had never doubted his love for her.

He would be a good father. He would love their child; he would do everything in his power to protect their baby. As well as her. Even now, Amara's mother was protected by Ivan even though, according to Amara, they rarely spoke.

Now, as she faced her pseudo-fiancé, trepidation tore at her. How he let others believe he felt, and how he really felt, were often two different things. Just because he'd faced Beau with male outrage and fury didn't mean that was truly how he felt.

Smoothing her hands down her hips, she stared at him as he poured himself a drink, whisky, she suspected, and sipped at it rather lazily. He didn't seem the least angry or put out now that the room had emptied.

"You're watching me as I imagine Red Riding Hood watched the Big Bad Wolf." The corners of his lips twitched in amusement. "Do you believe I blame you somehow?"

"Some men would." She shrugged, watching him carefully. He was far too calm, and yet that tension that radiated just below the surface seemed to be increasing.

"I'm not some men." The reminder did nothing to alleviate her nervousness. "I actually pride myself on that."

Yes, he seemed to.

"This isn't exactly something you expected," she pointed out, off balance and really not certain what to say. "To be tied this way to your enemy's daughter."

He grimaced at that. "Do you know, Journey, it's harder every day to remember you're even related to that family?"

But she was related. She was the daughter and the granddaughter of the two men who had tried every way possible to destroy him. He'd spent his life trying to protect himself against them, against their hatred and attempts to kill him as well as his daughter.

And now there was another child to worry about, as well as the mother.

"I want our child, Ivan," she whispered, watching him carefully as he moved to his desk and leaned against it negligently. "I don't want it taken from me."

Not by her father's or grandfather's schemes or by Ivan for whatever reason. She wanted to hold her baby, protect him or her. She wanted her child to have all the love, all the certainty, of a parent's devotion that she herself had never had.

It wasn't the baby's fault that he or she had been conceived. It was innocent of whatever the past held and deserved a chance to live.

"I have no intention of taking our child from you," he told her, his expression turning somber as he propped his hands on the desk behind him. "I'll simply have to move my own plans forward a bit."

His own plans? What the hell was he talking about? He'd made plans without informing her of them?

She stared back at him, fighting the temper she'd always cursed as he watched her as though she should know what the hell he was talking about.

"And what plans would those be?" Something else

she was unaware of? Another game someone was playing without informing her of it.

"Marrying you of course." His arms crossed over his chest and the sheer arrogance that filled his face had her ready to scream.

Marrying her? Of course? As though he had any such plan to do anything so ridiculous. A pretend engagement and a real marriage were two different things. She took a cautious step back, retreating enough to try to make sense of what the hell he was up to this time.

"I don't need you to marry me." She didn't want marriage, not like this. "Our child will need a father. He'll need your protection . . ."

The low, dark chuckle that came from his chest was just amused enough to almost cover the warning mockery of it.

"And he'll have my protection. Or she, whichever the case may be. Just as you will. You'll also carry my name and sleep in my bed. If that child is born a boy then the legacy he'll be an heir to will demand nothing less."

She shook her head. That made no sense. None of it made sense.

"You didn't marry Amara's mother!" she snapped. "How am I any different?"

"Had Amara been born a boy both the child and his mother would have died before I could have made a move to protect them." The snarl of rage that filled his expression had her heart suddenly racing in her chest. His arms dropped from his chest, his hands tunneling through his hair before he gripped his neck and fought for control. "I am no longer a boy, unable to defend myself, my child, or her mother," he growled, his gaze piercing, intent. "I'm a man, Journey, and as such, I'll claim not just my child but my woman as well."

His woman?

Since when was she his woman?

"There's no one here to convince, Ivan," she cried, trying to make sense of this sudden change in him. "The illusion doesn't apply any longer. The rules have changed and that game doesn't even exist now."

"Doesn't it?" The smirk that curled his lips had her fingers curling in anger. "What you don't understand, my little Syn, is that it was never a game to me. From the moment I slid that ring on your finger, I was entirely serious about marrying you."

He was what?

She stared back at him, eyes wide, certain she had to have heard him wrong. That, or he was lying to her. So far, this farce had at least existed with a semblance of honesty. The thought that he'd choose now to begin lying to her infuriated her.

"You're lying." She was certain of it.

There was no other explanation.

Ivan Resnova didn't believe in fairy tales. He didn't believe in love or happily-ever-afters, in marriage or, even more important, fidelity.

"I hate to disappoint you, love, but it's pure truth," he assured her, watching her carefully now. "I would have never placed that ring on your finger or gone to one knee before you as I did so if I wasn't serious."

She reacted before she thought. Before she knew

what she intended she flew toward him, her hand lifting a second before her palm cracked against his face with enough force to numb her fingers.

"Don't lie to me," she screamed up at his shocked expression. "You of all people. Do not lie to me."

It wasn't the blow that registered as much as the hurt in her expression and burning in her eyes. Ivan watched as the tremors raced through her and her lips shook before she quickly controlled them.

She was hurt. The thought that he would lie to her about what was a lie to begin with completely baffled him.

"You don't want to do that again, love." The words had no more than left his lips when she did exactly that.

Her little palm exploded against his face with enough force to snap the final threads on his control.

For days he'd restrained himself, held himself back with her, unwilling to frighten her or drag her into a sexuality she wasn't ready for. But by God if she was woman enough to smack the shit out of him then she was woman enough to take the man who received that blow.

His hands shot out, gripped her shoulders, and dragged her to him as he pulled her hands behind her back and held them with one of his. With his other hand he gripped her hair, dragged her head back, and his lips were on hers before she could do more than gasp.

Damn. Her kiss was sweet. Her lips parted, took his tongue, stroked it with hers as she arched closer to him.

Sweet, plump breasts pressed against his chest; delicate thighs parted for his leg as he pushed it forward while lifting her closer to him.

Carnal heat flooded his body, thickened his cock further than it had been before, and sent lust surging through his senses. She was like a flame to fuel where his hunger for her was concerned. She was impossible to resist, impossible to release.

As his lips and tongue worked over hers he felt the moan that vibrated against his lips, felt her slowly soften, surrender. Felt the pleasure whipping around them, burning through his senses.

She was lost in a kiss.

The power he had over her would destroy her before he was finished with this game. But he was impossible to resist. His touch was impossible to deny.

She strained against the hold he had on her; the fact that she was restrained, held securely, and unable to resist whatever he wanted only increased her arousal. The suspicion that the careful control he kept over his desires was slipping had anticipation racing through her.

She'd felt the control he exerted over his hunger when he took her, felt it straining, determined to be free. And now it was free and washing over her like subtle flames.

"Sweet, beautiful Syn," he groaned, his lips moving from hers, his teeth nipping at them briefly before his kisses slid to her neck.

Sharp, heated kisses. The rough caresses sent flares

of exquisite sensation racing through her, stealing her breath and her senses. It was like a hurricane, swirling, gaining in power and strength, and robbing her of any chance of control.

"Ivan." His name was a whispered plea as he lifted her, turning her and sitting her on the desk before spreading her thighs with his legs.

"I've got you, baby," he answered, his voice a hard rasp as he gripped the neckline of the fragile sweater in both hands and swiftly jerked the threads apart.

God, he just tore it in half, leaving it hanging on her, framing her lace-covered breasts as she fought for breath.

The front clasp of the bra was quickly undone, the cups pushed from the swollen flesh to reveal the hard points of her nipples.

"Lean back," he demanded. "Offer those pretty nipples to me, my Syn."

She couldn't breathe. She couldn't think. Instead, she leaned back, following his direction as he bent her arms, silently urging her to hold herself up with her forearms. The position thrust her breasts up to him and left her in the perfect position to watch his mouth cover one straining peak.

She jerked as the heat of his mouth seared the sensitive tip. His teeth gripped the tight flesh, his tongue worrying it as she arched closer.

"That's it, little love," he crooned against her nipple before licking it with a hungry swipe of his tongue. "Push that sweet nipple in my mouth."

She felt dizzy, existing on sensation alone as she

arched again, pushing her flesh against his lips and crying out at the feel of the instant suction that surrounded it.

Each draw of his mouth sent spears of sharp pleasure flashing from her nipple to her womb, radiating into her clit and causing her pussy to clench with ever-increasing need.

He repeated the caress to each breast. Drawing the nipple into his mouth, suckling it firmly, his tongue rasping over it with erotic demand.

Her head tipped back, eyes closing, the extremity of the sensations more than she could process.

"My little Syn," he groaned, the heat of his mouth easing from the overly sensitive flesh of her nipple.

Lifting her lashes, she stared up at him as he shed his shirt, the broad, bronze expanse of his hard chest causing her breath to catch. Sending her reaching for him. As she sat up, her lips lifted to his, his name a plea on her lips as he dragged her hands to his belt.

"Release me," he demanded, his lips caressing hers, his eyes staring into hers. "God, Syn, touch me, baby."

His lips devoured hers now, moving over them, his tongue pushing past, kissing her with a hunger she had no defenses against.

Shakily, she pulled the belt loose, leaving it hanging as she unclasped his slacks and slid the zipper down with shaky fingers.

A hard, desperate growl vibrated in his chest as her fingers curled around the width of his erection. Iron hard, straining and throbbing in her grip, the heavy flesh pulsed with a life of its own.

No sooner had she begun to caress the rigid length than she found herself on her back, her skirt pushed to her hips and her panties torn from her. A second later hard hands cupped her rear and lifted her as his head lowered to the bare, aching flesh of her pussy.

Heat suffused her, lashed at the sensitive folds and the swollen bud of her clit. His tongue was an instrument of torture, of pleasure she swore she couldn't survive.

What he did to her shouldn't be possible. She should be furious. She should be fighting . . . but it was so good. So hot and so wicked.

"That's it, Syn," he groaned after delivering a heated kiss to her clit. "Let me have you, baby."

He had all of her; didn't he know that? He terrified her because he owned so much of her.

His lips covered the swollen bud, sucked it into his mouth, and with heated, firm flicks of his tongue sent her exploding, her cries echoing around her as her senses evaporated beneath the ecstasy.

Lost in the waves of heat flooding her body, she was only barely aware of him shifting, moving to her. The first thrust of his erection inside her had a wave of pleasure-pain exploding through her, pushing her higher, deeper inside the chaotic rapture overtaking her.

There were only waves of pleasure. The feel of him stretching her, thrusting inside her with hard, pounding strokes that sent her careening through sensations that only gathered in strength, in pure carnal intensity.

It went past lust; this pleasure seared through carnality. It went deeper, slicing into her soul and carving out another piece of her soul as she lost another part of herself to him.

She simply had no defenses against him, and he knew it. She could fight him until that moment that he touched her, kissed her; then nothing mattered but this. This place of brutal, exquisite ecstasy, a place where she held him, at least in this way, for a single moment in time.

When that final explosion of pure sensation rocked her body, Journey knew there was no coming back from it. He owned her. She belonged to him in ways she hadn't known a woman could belong to a man.

When reality finally intruded, she found herself sprawled on his desk, his lips buried at her neck as they fought to catch their breath.

Languorous, sated, her hands stroked over his shoulders, as she marveled at the play of muscle beneath the tight flesh, the power in his hard body, the strength that surrounded her.

"My sweet Syn," he whispered against her neck, the stroke of his lips against her flesh threatening to rekindle that need for him that she found herself helpless against. "You shred my control."

But she didn't own his heart. He didn't love her, not as she loved him. He wanted her to marry him, to begin a life with him, to raise their child together with him and resign herself to never being loved as she loved.

The complete unfairness of it was enough to bring tears to her eyes. How she had once dreamed of him loving her. She had wanted it so desperately that she had bargained for the illusion of it, believing when this was over she could walk away with her memories.

She'd never imagined she'd conceive his child, or that he'd attempt to deceive her in truth at this late date.

"You're too quiet." He shifted against her, drawing back from her, the still hard length of his cock caressing flesh still achingly sensitive despite her previous orgasm.

As he straightened, he lifted her until she sat on the desk rather than lying across it.

While he straightened his clothes Journey reclipped her bra and dragged the edges of the sweater over her. She was going to have to walk out of this room with her clothes torn . . .

"I'll have Sophia or Elizaveta collect another sweater for you," he stated as she pushed her skirt down her thighs.

Journey shrugged at the offer. What did it matter? she wondered. It wasn't as though she'd had enough sense to her to restrain her cries as he pleasured her. If the others were waiting in the other room they would have heard her.

"The room is soundproof, love." The amusement in his voice had her shooting him an irritated look.

"At least there's that," she muttered, watching as he drew the shirt over his shoulders and began buttoning it.

The grin he shot her was one of pure male satisfaction that only increased the irritation growing inside her. He didn't have to look so damned arrogantly superior. As though he'd won no matter her objections or protests.

"The previous disagreement isn't over, Ivan," she warned him as he pulled his cell phone from the desk.

"Of course it isn't." Confidence all but oozed from him. "I'm certain we'll disagree over it quite often. You're a temperamental little thing, so I really expect nothing less."

She glared back at him. She was going to show him temperamental if he wasn't careful, and he might not survive it.

"Play your games against your enemies, your friends, or whoever else you want, but keep playing them against me, Ivan, and I'll take Tehya up on that offer she made to hide me. And once I disappear, I'll make certain you never find me." Or their child.

She wouldn't tolerate him deceiving her. She'd been lied to all her life, used, threatened. She would not tie herself to a man who saw her as no more than an amusing pawn or the object of his machinations.

Narrowing his eyes on her, he leaned closer until they were nearly nose to nose.

"Run from me and I promise you, once I find you, and I will find you, I'll make damned certain you're too fucking exhausted to ever run again, Journey. I'll fuck you senseless each time I even think you're planning such a thing. Are we understood?"

"Play your games with me, Ivan"—she slid from the desk and stepped away from him carefully—"and I promise you, anything I feel for you will die. I won't be lied to by you. I won't be used without my knowledge and I'll be damned if I'll let you play with me for your own amusement. That I promise you."

She strode quickly to the door, jerked it open, and before she could allow herself to weaken rushed from the room and down the hall to the bedroom she shared with him to change clothes, again.

She had to get away from him, had to hide the tears and the hurt threatening to destroy her now. She pressed her hand to her stomach, the thought of the child who rested there causing her breathing to hitch with a broken sob.

Her child deserved parents who at least respected each other. Parents who cared for each other, even if one didn't love. Her child didn't deserve the life she'd lived, always aware of her mother's tears and drinking, her father's petty cruelties.

And it was a life she refused to live again.

chapter fifteen

Ivan stepped from the office and watched Journey rush up the hall, her head held proudly, shoulders straight with a surfeit of pride. *Damn, she came by that red hair honest, didn't she?*

He couldn't help the grin that tipped his lips. He'd known she'd challenge him in ways no other woman ever had, but damned if she didn't satisfy something he hadn't even known he'd needed until her.

She softened parts of him that had been growing hard and cold, more aloof in the past years than ever before. She made him feel things that weren't always comfortable or easy to explain, and she shredded his control.

His little redheaded Syn, he thought, leaning against the doorframe as the bedroom door closed with a bang.

She didn't believe he loved her, but the realization that he did had been growing over the past week. When she'd disappeared in Colorado, he'd nearly driven himself insane imagining all the dangers that could befall her. And being fully aware of exactly who she was, the nightmares had only increased.

The price on Journey Taite's return was astronomical. Stephen and Craig Taite needed her. They needed her safely married to Beauregard Grant, though even Beau was uncertain of the reasons why. That didn't mean the other man wasn't more than willing to force her into a marriage she so obviously didn't want. He had his own agenda, and ensuring that the Taites' network of terrorists and white slavers ended topped the list.

To secure his position as the head of the Taite family holdings, he needed to secure his marriage to Journey.

Ivan stiffened at the thought.

What would happen to Beau's position among the Taite holdings when Ivan married Journey instead? It was well known Stephen and Craig had personally chosen who would succeed them with their choice of husband for Journey.

No damned wonder the Taites were so desperate to get her back and securely married to the other man. And it explained the attack against Ivan.

"Ilya." He straightened at the thought as his lifelong friend and assistant moved from the living area. "Are Jordan and Tehya still on the property?"

"I've placed them in the guest cottage." Ilya nodded. "Mr. Grant has returned to Manhattan though. He requests that you contact him this evening to further discuss the attack as well as Ms. Taite."

Ivan waved the request away. Beau could wait. As a matter of fact, Ivan preferred that he wait.

"Have Jordan and Tehya return to my office. And I want anything you can dig up on Journey's inheritance as well as any arrangements Stephen and Craig have made for the running of the Taite holdings in the event of their deaths."

A thoughtful expression crossed the other man's face. "A question we should have considered before now," he agreed. "I'll get on that immediately." Suspicion sharpened his expression then. "Do you believe whoever marries Journey will also assume guardianship of their holdings?"

"The son has no interest in running the family holdings, and the elder daughter's husband has his own family business to oversee. If Stephen and Craig were counting their chickens before they hatched and signed something that left that power to Journey's husband, I could have what I need to destroy them."

Because he would marry Journey, inheritance or no. She was his. She brought something to his life that hadn't existed before her. A warmth, a light, he'd fight to hold. If he could destroy her father and grandfather as well with that marriage, all the better.

Could they get that lucky?

He almost grinned at the thought of Beau's reaction. Of course, the other man would detest losing control of the vast, lucrative Taite enterprises. Those businesses spanned not just France but England and America as well.

He should have looked deeper into the reason for the

Taites' determined efforts to see Journey married to Beau, Ivan thought in disgust. Instead, his senses were so distracted by her that he admitted it wasn't always easy to think.

To add to the problems, Journey's mother, brother, and sister were demanding to see her. Their determined efforts at a family reunion were becoming impossible to ignore, he admitted. He'd have to allow them access to her soon, but he could already hear her objections. For some reason, Journey was resistant to the idea of seeing her family just yet.

She rarely mentioned her mother, refused calls from her siblings, and seemed not in the least upset to do so. And that was very un-Journey-like. She'd talked to Amara several times in the past week, as well as cousins who had contacted her, but still refused calls from her mother, brother, and sister.

Making a note to broach that subject once her anger cooled a bit, Ivan turned back to his office and his own business that awaited him. Knowledge of his engagement was sweeping through his own holdings, both legal and shadowed, and his lieutenants needed his assurances that the rumors were true. There were things to take care of, a priest to contact, a wedding to arrange, despite his bride's stated reluctance.

She might have objected to his admission that it had been his plan all along to marry her, but he'd seen the hunger in her eyes, the dreams.

She loved him, but damn if she wasn't a prideful little thing. That stubborn little chin had lifted like a princess staring down at a particularly irritating peon.

It had turned him on, made his dick hard, made him ache to feel her submitting to him.

She would marry him though, he knew. The thought of their child would ensure it, and he admitted, albeit silently, if that was what it took to get her in front of a priest, then he'd take it. He'd convince her of the fact that she owned parts of him that went far beyond love. Parts of his soul that he'd never given to another human being.

She couldn't allow herself to sink any further into that stupid illusion she'd demanded from Ivan. God, how had she allowed this to happen?

Pressing one hand to her stomach, she fought back the tears, the sobs, well aware that neither could help her at this point. She couldn't think if she was crying and allowing the pain to possess her. And right now, she had to think. She had to figure out what was going on and how to help Ivan protect their child.

Their child.

She stared down at the hand covering her stomach, suddenly so amazed, so enchanted by the fact that she was pregnant. She was carrying Ivan's child. A baby.

She'd never really considered having children. Before, she'd simply been unable to contemplate having sex with Beau to begin with, and after she'd run, she'd just assumed she'd always be too frightened of being found to allow any man to tie himself to her.

Until Ivan had taken the matter out of her hands and brought her such pleasure that snowy night in Colorado.

And now, she carried his child.

A child that would love her, completely, unconditionally. No matter what her child did, or where her baby went in life, that love would always follow him or her.

Him, she decided, aware of the silly smile that curled her lips.

Only a son of Ivan Resnova would be so sneaky about the fact he existed. She'd had no morning sickness, and though her breasts had been incredibly sensitive for a week or so right after leaving him, she'd merely marked it down to how often he'd caressed them. His lips had drawn on her nipples, the love bites he'd left on the swollen mounds.

"How do I protect you?" she whispered, her fingers moving against her stomach as though caressing the baby already. "How do I fix this, little one?"

A sound behind her had her whirling around, her eyes widening at the sight of Sophia Resnova standing inside the room, the door closing behind her.

At thirty-three, slender, delicately curved, and with thick, long black hair and dark blue eyes, she could have been Ivan's sister. Dressed in jeans and a dark T-shirt, she wore a weapon strapped to her hip that she hadn't worn before, and her gaze was filled with icy resolve.

"Shall I help you answer that question?" Sophia asked her softly as she leaned back on the wall and crossed her arms over her breasts. "Or was it rhetorical?"

Journey gave an unladylike snort. "Does a Resnova recognize rhetorical questions?"

Not from what she'd seen. They always had an answer for everything. Arrogance didn't even begin to define them.

A small smile tilted the other woman's lips. "You do have a point. So we'll assume it's not rhetorical, and go about helping you answer it."

Sophia could have been Ivan's sister they were so much alike, she thought silently.

Journey shook her head. "I need time . . ."

"My dear, you are about four to five weeks out of time," Sophia assured her. "No doubt your family members will be aware that you carry Ivan's child before the night is out, and will make a move to quickly strike. If you heard what I did downstairs, then you know how very intent they will be on ensuring Ivan's child does not survive to take its first breath."

As if she could have missed that little detail.

Glaring at her, Journey stalked to the end of the bed, her hands latching on to the high footboard and gripping it viciously.

"How have any of you survived your lives?" she whispered, staring back at the other woman painfully. "How were you able to allow any child of Craig Taite's to survive after what he and his father did to all of you?"

Bitterness curled Sophia's lips. "Without the help of my brother, they could not have touched us," she replied, lowering her arms until one hand rested on the butt of the weapon strapped to her thigh. "Our family was a shadow force, they have always been so. We were the powers behind thrones, behind generals. Politics and power did not matter when leaders knew there was a faceless, nameless force watching, always waiting. Russia is a cold, often brutal place, but until my brother stole our father's power from him, Resnovas were always protected, as were those who followed them." The dark head lowered for a moment, and when Sophia looked up at her once again, there was wry knowledge in her expression. "Besides, children are not to blame for the actions of their parents. They can only be held accountable for their own choices."

How anyone could see the world in such a way, Journey had no clue. But this was how she wanted the child to feel. To know that striking against someone weaker, someone not to blame, wasn't the choice to make.

"He wants me to marry him," Journey told Sophia then, her heart, her mind, in turmoil at the thought. "He doesn't love me . . ."

Sophia gave a soft, mocking laugh that silenced Journey's objections.

"Journey, you have no idea of the significance of him placing that ring on your finger. That was his grandmother's ring, the ring that should have gone to his mother at her death. When his mother was murdered, and a year later, his grandfather, on her deathbed his grandmother made him swear by their blood that no woman but one he loved, treasured beyond his own life, would wear that ring and that should she wear it, he would place it on her finger himself." Sophia's expression softened. "From the moment we learned he did just that, every member of his family, every friend, every man, woman, and child that he has protected knew that you were more to him than his own life. That he loved."

Journey shook her head. "It was a bargain we made. I forced it. He wanted his vengeance, and I demanded that he pretend to love me."

"Oh for God's sake, stop fooling yourself." Sophia straightened from the door then. "We'll get back to the subject at hand. You want to protect that child." She nodded toward Journey's stomach. "Then you marry him. You do as he demands when it comes to you and that child and know, if you know nothing else, know that losing either of you would break what is left of his soul. Think about that, Journey. Think of each moment with him, think of the changes in the man you knew before you went to his bed, to the man he became with you. He gave you the man he truly was, rather than the man the world has always seen. Think of that, then tell me Ivan Resnova does not love."

She needed a minute to acclimate, Journey acknowledged that evening after dinner as she joined Ivan, Jordan, and Tehya in the sitting room for drinks. Sophia had given her far too much to think about that she hadn't considered before, and thrown every argument she had straight out the door.

Thankfully, she'd never really enjoyed alcohol, so as the others sipped at their drinks she'd had Ivan pour her water instead and fought to get her bearings, even now, hours after that disastrous argument with her fiancé.

As Ivan and Jordan discussed something quietly on

the other side of the room, Tehya finally did just as Journey had expected her to do. She made her way to where Journey sat, took a seat in the chair opposite the couch where she sat, and stared down at her drink for long moments.

She didn't want what she knew was coming, Journey thought. Of everyone in her life, she'd missed most the loss of the woman she'd counted as her only true friend at one time.

Tehya had been her employer when Journey had first come to America to attend college.

Desperate for a taste of freedom, Journey had risked her father's petty cruelties and applied for a job with the small Maryland landscaping company Tehya had owned at the time. She'd loved landscape design, still did actually.

Tehya had hired her immediately and during those almost idyllic months had befriended Journey. They'd laughed, exchanged confidences to a point, and Journey had learned what true friendship was, she'd thought. And it had all been a lie.

Tehya had known who her new employee was and she'd deliberately developed a friendship with no intention of ever revealing the fact that they were cousins. Journey hadn't learned the truth until the night she and Tehya had been kidnapped by Stephen and Craig Taite.

He was teaching her a lesson, her father had sneered as she stared at him in confused horror. A lesson she would never forget. Oh, he'd ensured she could never forget that lesson or that night. He would have killed Tehya himself if Beau hadn't stopped him.

That night still lived in her horror-filled dreams. Nightmares of Tehya's death, of her cousin's blood spilling over her hands as she tried to push it back.

"I'm sorry, Journey. I should have never lied to you. That was wrong of me, but I needed to know you without my past rising up to harm either of us. And even in that, I failed you," Tehya whispered, the sincerity in her tone heavy with pain. "I'm not asking for forgiveness, but I am asking you to talk to me."

The words had Journey freezing.

Had anyone ever apologized to her before? She didn't think they had. She'd been lied to and deceived all her life, and no one had ever said they were sorry for it or that they regretted it. No one had ever admitted they were wrong until now.

Tehya's past was brutal, she knew. She'd spent nearly her whole life running, first from the father who would have given her to her half brother to rape, then from Journey's father, who wanted nothing more than the inheritance Tehya's parents had left her mother.

"I understand why you didn't tell me." Journey shrugged, because logically, she did understand. But her emotions weren't always logical, and the feeling of betrayal wouldn't let her go.

"I wouldn't, if positions were reversed," Tehya said, once again surprising Journey.

She lifted her gaze to the other woman, watching her somberly as she tried to make sense of the pain and anger that filled her every time she saw or thought of her cousin.

Looking away from her cousin once again, Journey smoothed her hands down the silk pants she wore and tried to tell herself she just needed more time. But she'd had four years, hadn't she? During those years, the memory of her cousin had perhaps hurt the most.

"You could have told me." Journey knew that was the reason why she was having such a hard time forgiving the other woman. "At any time, Tehya, you could have told me and I would have never betrayed you."

She would have loved her, been so thankful she was alive. She would have cried over her aunt's death, her cousin's horrors. And she would have loved her.

"And I was terrified I'd be dragging you into my past and the danger that still existed," her cousin whispered. "I would have killed to keep that from happening, and it happened anyway. The one person I wanted to protect other than Jordan, and you were the one hurt the most."

Journey had to force back her tears, force back the anger. She was still so damned angry over all of it, and perhaps that was the reason she found it so hard to forgive Tehya. She was part of it, no matter how innocent.

Looking away, her gaze moved automatically to Ivan to find him watching her, concern edging at his features. There was something in his gaze, in that look, that invited her into his arms, into his warmth.

"You were my only friend," Journey revealed,

dropping her eyes from Ivan's gaze and returning to Tehya's. "You told me about your dreams for the business; let me share them. You told me about the man you loved and how bad you wanted a puppy. But you couldn't tell me why I was the one you confided in. It was the trust, Tehya. I trusted you with Craig's insistence that I accept Beau's proposal, and my fear of ever returning to France. I trusted you. And I believed in you. I thought you believed in me."

Tehya's eyes filled with tears, and Journey prayed they didn't fall. If they did, there would be no way she could hold back her own. There would be no way to stem the pain and anger or to beg her cousin for explanations she knew likely didn't exist.

Why?

Why had Stephen and Craig betrayed their entire family? They had murdered Tehya's mother, tried to steal her inheritance when they already had so much of what should have belonged to Tehya after her mother's death. Why hadn't her father loved her? Why had her grandfather seen her as no more than a pawn in the depraved double life he led?

There were no answers to those questions any more than they could go back. Tehya couldn't change the decision to protect Journey rather than allow her a bond she had been so hungry for. That with a family member who gave a damn. And admitting to that made her feel petty and childish.

"I did believe in you, Journey, and I still do. But in the past four years haven't you wanted to trust someone with your own secrets, needed to trust, only to fear their reaction or the danger it could bring them?" Tehya asked then. "Is there anyone it would have hurt when the stories of Journey Taite's return began showing up in the papers and on the internet?"

She thought of Amara, Ivan's daughter, and her tears when she'd called several days before. How she'd assured Journey that she could have trusted her. But she understood, Amara had told her, forgiveness filling her voice. She understood her fear and why she'd been so determined to hide.

"All my life, I needed family," Journey whispered then. "My sister, my brother, and I were kept apart, never allowed to develop the bonds siblings have." She looked down at her hands for a moment, remembering the day she'd begged her brother to help her, to keep her father from pushing her into marriage with Beau. And he'd just walked away from her. "I was closer to you than I was to them at any time." She shook her head and lifted her gaze once again. "I understand why; I really do," she assured Tehya painfully. "And I can acknowledge I would have done the same if positions were reversed. It's not that I can't forgive you, Tehya, because you did nothing that should require forgiveness. Maybe it's myself I can't forgive, for not seeing the truth, for not realizing it at a time when you needed me."

Tehya's eyes widened as Journey acknowledged the truth to both of them.

"No, Journey . . ." She shook her head desperately.

"You were fighting for your life and all I was concerned with was trying to find an ally to help me run from Beau." She shook her head, realizing how immature, how thoughtless, she had been.

Her anger at her cousin had been more an expression of her anger at herself, Journey realized. And there was no room for that now. She had much more important concerns than the childishness that had driven her four years before.

"Let me help you now, Journey," Tehya urged her softly, her expression filled with worry. "You and your baby. We don't know what the hell is going on here, or why the Taites want to stop this marriage so desperately. Jordan and I can hide you until we figure it out."

"Hiding me isn't an option," she sighed. "If I disappear, they'll just wait, bide their time, and grow stronger." She knew that for a fact. "Beau was given the CEO position of the businesses with our engagement, so I'm really not certain why he's so determined to carry through with a marriage."

It made no sense. He had what he wanted; why tie himself to a woman he didn't love now? Stephen and Craig were in prison; they couldn't exactly object to him running the companies now.

Still though, Tehya frowned at what she'd told her, watching her intently.

"There must have been a clause in the event the marriage didn't follow through?" It seemed more a question than a statement.

Journey frowned, trying to remember the brief details she'd overheard the week her family had arrived in America for the announcement of the engagement.

"The only thing I remember is overhearing Craig

telling Stephen it wasn't wise to count on Beau's ability to control me before the marriage." Brushing her hair back from her forehead, she gave another shrug. "Too bad, so sad, I guess." Her lips twisted with self-aware bitterness.

"Could Beau's position as CEO of Taite's be dependent on your marriage to him?" her cousin asked then.

Journey laughed with genuine amusement. "I can't imagine either Stephen or Craig being so insane. They were expecting me to run, and if they hadn't been arrested, they would have managed to stop me. They wouldn't take the chance I'd succeed."

She couldn't imagine Stephen, Craig, or Beau being that confident of their ability to control her. Anything was possible where those three were concerned, she guessed, but she simply couldn't imagine that one of them wouldn't consider the fact that her father had been in the process of having her restrained and shipped off to an asylum in France before she'd finally agreed to the engagement.

That had been the reason she'd attempted to talk to Tehya the night they were kidnapped. She'd wanted help to escape, and she'd known Tehya had the connections to help her with that when it was revealed Jordan Malone was her lover.

"According to Beau," Ivan's voice intruded on the conversation then, "Stephen and Craig cut their own throats." Satisfaction filled his voice. "Beau wasn't named as CEO. Your husband, as in whoever you married, was named to take over control of the Taite holdings should Stephen and Craig meet their demises or become otherwise incapacitated. But only your first husband. Successive husbands need not apply."

The pure satisfaction in Ivan's voice was terrifying.

"Did you suspect this when you *decided* you were going to marry me?" she asked him, suspicion flaring at the knowing look in his gaze.

Damn him, she hated that look. Equal parts arrogance and certainty mixed with far too many secrets.

Jordan chuckled at her question and answered for Ivan. "We managed to pry the information out of Beau just before dinner and have spent the time since verifying it. It seems no name was included with the husband part. The moment you marry Ivan, he comes into full control of not just the companies but the family finances as well. Which means he can do what Beau can't and cut off the funds to the Taites' lawyers."

Journey could feel herself pale as her dinner became a leaden weight in her stomach.

"He'll kill you," she whispered. "He won't stop."

"We may have an answer for that." Jordan took the chair beside his wife as Ivan settled in beside her, his arm going over her shoulder.

"Really?" She highly doubted that. "And exactly what is your answer?"

Ivan's low chuckle was far too confident.

"I have the date for the marriage announced in the papers tomorrow, setting it for next summer," Ivan answered her. "That will forestall any hasty moves on their part. Meanwhile, I'll have the priest slipped into the house in the morning, and with Jordan and Tehya as well as my family to witness, we'll have a quiet ceremony. Once everything's official, I'll have notices sent that the marriage has already occurred, but the wedding next year will be for friends and associates, as well as to provide my lovely bride a chance to have the wedding all women dream of."

She stared at him silently, uncertain if she should be shocked, surprised, or simply astounded by his nerve. He was going to enrage Stephen and Craig to the point that their heads would explode.

"You're crazy," she whispered.

The smile he gave her was approving, as though she'd finally figured out something momentous.

"My first act as head of the family will be to cut off the attorneys' fees and payments to the guards and prisoners who make their lives so cushy." Something cold and dangerous flashed in his gaze then. "With those funds cut off, striking against either of us will be impossible, love. And they'll have no chance, period, of striking against our child."

"And you think this will stop them?" she whispered. "Ivan, if they kill you, Beau will retain control of the company, the funds will be reinstated, and our child won't have a chance to draw its first breath."

"Journey, in the event something happens to Ivan, within moments you'll disappear along with his child, I promise you that," Jordan spoke up, defending the plan. "You want to be free of Stephen and Craig? This is the only way. That, or marry Beau."

Ivan snorted at that. "It would be hard for her to marry a dead man, don't you think? I'd kill him first."

And Journey had a feeling he wasn't joking in the least.

She stared at him, remembering what Sophia had said earlier, and comparing this man against the one she'd seen and heard tales of since she was barely more than a child.

Cold. Brutal. Without compassion or mercy, she'd always heard. But that was never the man she had seen. From that ball when she was sixteen to this moment, Ivan's gaze had always held warmth and compassion. He could be teasing, somber, thoughtful, but he'd never been cold to her, or with her. And from that first night in Colorado when he and Ilya jerked her off the streets, he'd been nothing if not protective, sheltering.

She doubted he truly loved her, but she had a feeling he'd never, not in word or manner, act as though he didn't. He cared for her perhaps, and she wondered if that could possibly be enough?

That still didn't mean that this habit of his of playing games with the enemy wasn't going to get him killed.

chapter sixteen

He was determined to push Stephen and Craig Taite into hysterical rage. Once this little plan of his was put into effect, things would explode.

"You're crazy!" Journey turned to face the man determined to make her insane and get himself killed in the process. "Stephen and Craig still have friends, you admitted that yourself. Friends that would help them. You can't play games like this, Ivan."

He merely arched a brow at her and began unbuttoning his shirt, his gaze turning heated and hungry as lust filled his expression.

"Ivan, we need to discuss this." She was on the verge of stomping her foot in sheer frustration.

He'd countered every argument since Jordan and Tehya had left and apparently he was tired of discussing it if his expression was anything to go by.

"No, we can discuss this later. When I'm able to

concentrate on the conversation rather than the sheer pleasure of being buried inside that hot little pussy. Now get naked," he growled.

The shirt fell carelessly to the floor and his hands dropped to his belt as she stared back at him in amazement.

"You just . . ." She waved a hand, flushing at the erotic words.

"Fucked you?" His grin was pure wicked delight. "I know, and it was incredible. I think I'm addicted though. I need my fix."

She couldn't help but blink back at him, aware that he was making quick work of shedding his slacks.

"Come on, baby; you're not undressed enough. I'll end up tearing your clothes off you again." He didn't appear bothered by the thought.

"We have to discuss this first." She was on the verge of whimpering as her body sensitized, her breasts swelling, the flesh between her thighs heating in need. "You'll end up exhausting me. I'll fall asleep, and the next thing I know we'll be married before ever discussing it."

He shrugged, then stole her breath as the slacks were pushed from his long legs, revealing the heavy proof of his erection. The engorged crest and heavily veined shaft drew her attention, scrambling her senses and causing the heated, slick moisture to spill from her vagina. Oh God, she was so weak because she wanted nothing more than to give in and forget about his machinations. At least for a while.

She had to fight for breath, to think, because she

wanted nothing more than to tear her clothes off and spread herself out for him. But he did this every time she tried to convince him that Stephen and Craig could not be anticipated. They had friends and resources they kept carefully hidden, and would pull out if backed in a corner.

"Stop trying to manipulate me," she moaned, knowing she couldn't deny him.

She was the one addicted, she thought. Addicted to his touch, the sound of his voice, his very presence. Otherwise, she'd be able to enforce the fact that they really needed to discuss this. They seriously needed to discuss this.

"Take those clothes off, Syn, or I'll tear them off you," he demanded. "I won't be able to wait long, and I wanted to fuck those pretty lips a minute before things begin to get serious."

Having him fuck her mouth wasn't serious? She disagreed, and so did the sudden hunger for the taste of him.

"I hate you," she muttered as she hurriedly began pulling off her clothes.

"Sweet Jesus," he rasped as she stripped to reveal the lacy black bra, the high-cut panties, and the garter belt that held the silky, smokey stockings on her legs. "Fuck, Journey, if I'd known what you were wearing downstairs then there's no way I could have waited. Leave it," he demanded when her hands lifted to the front closure of her bra. "Just leave the fucking thing on."

He was staring at her like a man starved for sex now. Drugged on the need for it.

"Ivan . . ." She let her hands fall to her sides, staring back at him, still so uncertain when it came to his need for her.

She couldn't think when he did this to her. She couldn't get past her own anticipation and need to find a single, logical thought.

"God, that expression on your face," he whispered. "So innocent, still uncertain of the pleasure I give you or your need for it."

"Uncertain"? "Dazed" was more like it.

She licked her lips slowly, watching as his eyes followed the movement and the lust in his expression increased.

"Innocent?" she asked him softly, wondering just how far she could push him. "Is it innocence that has me aching to have you fuck my mouth? Or your tongue driving inside my pussy?"

Sweet Jesus. Ivan felt his head explode and he swore he nearly came with nothing but air surrounding his dick. Hell, she needed to talk dirty to him some more. The sound of her voice, so filled with feminine hunger, with a sensual wickedness that couldn't be practiced, shredded his control.

Then she moved.

Still wearing heels, the lacy bra, the panties, and the garter belt holding that silky hose on her legs.

He was going to fuck her with those shoes on.

He gripped the base of his dick as she came to him, her movements slow, sensual, her expression both mysterious and innocent.

"Do you want to lay down?" she asked him. "Or stand there while I take you in my mouth?"

He had to tighten his fingers around his cock to keep from coming.

"Why don't I just lay down," he suggested, "and you put that pretty pussy on my mouth while I fuck yours?"

Her green eyes darkened, a flush mounted her cheeks, and he swore her nipples got harder beneath the black lace, teasing and tempting his mouth.

Anticipation burned through him as he lay back on the bed and crooked his finger at her, urging her to him.

"Leave the heels on, baby," he warned her as she paused as though to slide them off.

Her eyes dazed for a moment, her gaze moving along his body to the straining length of his cock.

"Come here, my Syn, let me suck your nipples first," he urged her. "You can take that bra off now."

She was going to cause him to have a stroke. Good Lord above but the woman had an effect on him that he had no defenses against.

She released the clip and drew it slowly from her as she shook her head. "I want you to fuck my mouth first, Ivan." Oh hell, he was going to come if she said that again. "And do like you promised." A slender knee braced her on the bed. "Fuck me with your tongue."

He didn't give her time to come to him and straddle his face. He reached for her, gripped her hips, and pulled her to him, guiding one leg over his head until he pulled the slick, glistening folds of her pussy to his mouth.

He didn't even care if her lips made it to his dick. All he cared about was fucking her pussy however he could. And he did just that. As he jerked her hips down, his tongue found her clit, the swollen little bud sweet and hot against his tongue, in his mouth. He slid his hands to the curve of her ass, gripped the rounded flesh, and pulled her closer as he felt her upper body lowering.

Hell, he'd never survive this. It wasn't possible. There was no way he had the strength to keep from releasing to her mouth too soon. He felt like a fucking teenager ready to blow his first nut.

At the first stroke of her tongue over the engorged head his entire body tightened. His cock strained to be closer and it took everything he had not to thrust past her lips to fuck her mouth immediately. But then there was the sweet, heated moisture spilling from her pussy, meeting his tongue. Ah God, she was so good.

This was going to kill him. She was going to lay him to waste and leave him scrambling to survive the aftermath. Because that tongue of hers was hungry too. It was a lash of sweet, feminine need that all but destroyed his control.

He wouldn't last long. Even as he savored the slick, sweet taste of her, grew drunk on her, he knew once she covered the sensitive crest with her mouth, he could start the countdown. He might make it a few seconds. If he was lucky. God, he'd have to be damned lucky.

She couldn't breathe. She couldn't think.

As she licked over the engorged crest of Ivan's cock,

the clean male scent of him infused her senses and amplified her need for him. His lips and tongue were on her clit, circling it, sucking it, and pushing her to an edge she could barely hold on to. And she saw it as entirely unfair. He needed to be just as crazy, just as damned senseless with pleasure, as she was.

Parting her lips, she surrounded the tip and slowly slid her lips down, taking it into her mouth, sucking him as deep as she could take him as her tongue caressed and licked. The engorged crest that was thick, throbbing as her lips stretched around it. It filled her mouth, silk over iron, pure male heat and lust, and she was so hungry for him.

His hips jerked, burying the throbbing flesh deeper and shredding her control. At the same time, his tongue drove deep inside her pussy, filling her, nearly triggering her orgasm.

Journey fought to just stay sane just for a few moments, a few seconds. But the second she felt the first hungry thrust of Ivan's tongue inside her, she knew she was going to lose her grip on her sanity in no time at all.

Crying out around the wide crest, she tightened her lips on him as her fingers curved around his balls, learned the shape of them, caressed them. Tried to maintain just enough of her senses to give him pleasure as he jerked her into a careening storm of sensation that threatened from second to second to throw her over the edge into orgasm.

Just when she was certain she couldn't hold on much longer, she gasped breathlessly as he lifted her, pulling her from him and tossing her on her back on the bed. Her panties were torn from her, somewhere she lost a shoe, and before she could draw a breath she was penetrated, her inner flesh stretching, pleasure-pain tearing a breathless cry from her as her hips arched to him as he guided her legs until they encased his hips.

As he came over her, his lips covered hers, sharing her taste with her, and shredded that last fragile hold she had on reality. It took three hard thrusts to bury his full length inside her, and on that final thrust she shattered. Her inner muscles clamped down on him as shudders began tearing through her body.

A second later, he groaned against her lips, his hips jerked, his cock throbbing inside her as she felt his release spilling inside her.

It was so good. Oh God, it was so good. What he did to her, where the pleasure he gave her took her, was something she knew she'd grieve the loss of, should he ever grow tired of her.

With Ivan, once he got her in a bed there were always seconds though. Her orgasm hadn't eased when he began thrusting inside her again, each impalement slower now, caressing, stroking nerve endings still sensitive from her release.

His lips moved over her neck, kissing, stroking, then to her breasts, where he sucked first one nipple, then the other even as his cock thrust hard and heavy inside her.

She swore she'd never survive it, but she was always certain she'd never survive it. What he did to her should be illegal. It was probably illegal somewhere.

Her nails dug into his shoulders; she might have raked them down his shoulders at one point. With each draw of his mouth on her nipples, each hard thrust of his hips, he made her beg with ever-increasing desperation.

He held her orgasm back, refused to let her slip from that edge as she reached for the violent, ecstatic explosions she knew would overtake her. Perspiration sheened both their bodies, her breaths were gasping cries, and pleasure became the edge of rapture. Just the edge. Always building, growing hotter, more desperate.

His teeth nipped at a nipple, his lips kissed their way to her neck, and God, finally, his thrusts increased.

Harder, faster.

She strained toward him. Her hips arched to him, the muscles of her pussy clenched around his shuttling cock, and when the explosion came it was catastrophic. It blazed through her like wildfire, overtook her, and shattered her into so many fragments of ecstasy that she was certain she'd never find all the pieces of her soul again.

He held them.

He owned them, just as he owned her.

And God help her, because she had a feeling not only would she never be free, but also she'd never want to be free again. And should he ever release her, she might not survive it.

When he could breathe again, Ivan forced himself from the grip Journey had on him, gritting back a groan of pleasure as her pussy stroked over the highly sensitive head of his cock.

Collapsing next to her, he drew her to him, and listened with a deep core of satisfaction as she too struggled to catch her breath.

He stroked his hand down her back to the rounded curve of her rear, marveling at the softness of her skin, at what she did to him.

He'd bedded some of the most experienced women in his social sphere and at any time during the act he could have risen from the bed and walked away. But with this woman, he wasn't certain anything could tear him from the pleasure she gave him.

"I wish I had come to you sooner," she said, her voice soft as she lay against his chest. "Those first weeks when they forced my engagement to Beau, you were in town. I wanted to. It was all I could do to stay away from you then."

"You attended a party in Baltimore just before Beau announced the engagement. The Masterson estate," he said as he ran his fingers through her hair. "You wore a dress that covered you from the tips of your toes to your neck and to your wrists. I remembered thinking how miserable you must be, and how very lovely you were."

And how very badly he wanted her in his bed.

"I've seen you at a lot of parties over the years, watched you and was very aware that Beau shadowed your every move." He remembered that as well. "I always knew when you were at a party, or social event, and I always saw the loneliness in your eyes. If you had come to me, Syn, I would have made certain you were protected."

He couldn't have helped himself. She'd always done something to him that no one else ever had, made him want things he'd always thought could never be possible.

"I saw it in you as well." Her hand pressed against his chest, directly over his heart. "You were always with some gorgeous, experienced woman and I hated every one of them."

He thought back to those gatherings and found he couldn't remember who he was with, but he remembered looking for her each time.

"I would dream sometimes that you asked me to dance and would steal me away." Amusement and lingering pain touched her voice. "A teenager's dreams at first. That last party in Maryland, the night Stephen and Craig kidnapped me along with Tehya, I ached to dance with you. Just one time, I wanted to feel your arms around me before I was forced to marry Beau."

He tightened his hold on her. He could hear the remembered fear and desperation as she spoke.

"I would have taken you," he admitted. "I knew that, even then. As young as you were, as innocent, I would have taken you myself and made you hate me. What you make me feel isn't familiar, Journey. These emotions are unknown, illogical, and far too possessive."

She lay against him now, silent, waiting.

"You asked for an illusion of love," he sighed. "What I was giving you wasn't an illusion. I don't know love but that of a father for his child. What I gave you was yours to begin with. And it's far more possessive than it should be. Try to leave me and you'll learn this quickly."

She sat up slowly, drawing the edge of the comforter over her breasts and blocking his view of those perfect breasts. He reached out, his fingers gripping the material to pull it away from her when she tapped his hand with her fingers.

"Stop that," she demanded, giving him a fierce look.

He liked that about her. She didn't care about berating him when she thought he deserved it.

"Show me your breasts and I'll be helpless to give you whatever you want." He tugged at the blanket again.

"And of course, within moments you'd make sure that talking wasn't high on my list of priorities." She tried to shoot him a frown, but the grin teasing her lips spoiled the effect.

"No doubt," he agreed, dropping his hand to lay it against her silky thigh as he stared up at her, sobering when he saw the worry in her expression. "I didn't lie to you earlier, Syn," he said, using the name for her that he alone would ever be permitted to use. "The day I slid my grandmother's ring on your finger, I knew I'd marry you. I knew I was never going to let you go, no matter your belief that it was only an illusion."

She stared down at the ring on her finger for a moment before lifting her gaze to his once again.

"You would destroy me if I believed that and it

turned out to be a lie, a trick to somehow punish Stephen and Craig. It wouldn't punish them, Ivan. They wouldn't care if you hurt me," she told him painfully, the distress on her face causing his chest to clench with regret and anger.

She simply didn't know how to accept anyone putting her above their own petty games.

"Since this began, each day I've had to force myself to continue with it, to allow you to be the center of breaking those two. It didn't matter that we agreed it had to be done; still, I wanted to hide you even more than Tehya wanted to help you disappear. You're not a pawn to me, Journey. You're my woman. And no woman has ever been claimed by me, other than my daughter."

His child. And now his Syn would give him a child he'd never believed would be conceived. A child he'd been determined wouldn't be conceived.

"Beau's enraged over us. The engagement, our child." A frown creased her brow. "And it was more than mere anger at realizing I'd never marry him. Why?"

He should have guessed this question was coming. She was far too intelligent for him to ever hide much from, and she didn't even realize it.

"The Resnovas are a very old family, steeped in traditions," he sighed, stroking her thigh as he spoke. "Our line stretches back centuries and we've always held a certain political power, no matter who ruled. Such a lineage garners not just a certain responsibility but also certain loyalties. Loyalties that were lost when it was learned I'd had a vasectomy performed and intended to have no children, other than a daughter. Because it's sons that lead, that ensure the line, the name, always remains."

He frowned, trying to explain those centuries of tradition to her.

"My father was determined that the Resnova name would die with me, because he lost the loyalty of those great families when he turned to criminal enterprises. Once he died and I began legitimizing our holdings once again, drawing away from the depraved practices of my father and bringing a measure of pride to the Resnova name once again, I regained some of that loyalty. But no son." He shrugged. "Tradition. Power and strength came with having a son, because each of the families was sworn to that child's protection. No matter the cost or bloodshed. The Resnova name would carry on. It would lead."

"And there was no longer a chance at a son," she said. "We could have a daughter."

He shook his head and gave her a small grin.

"A man accepts when fate begins weaving his life," he sighed. "You're carrying my son. The Resnova heir." He reached out to her, his fingertips touching her delicate face. "Word has already gone out to the families. They'll now amass, each family determined to protect you and the baby until its sex is known. Once they know it's a boy." He flashed her a smile. "Baby, there's no information pipeline as effective as a Russian's. And no protection as determined. We're a country that's learned to hold on to our traditions and to band together. Resnovas have always kept the political ties, played those games, and protected the families that followed us. And they always lent their protection to our ability to do that."

"But only if there was a male heir?" The sadness in her voice hinted at her disappointment in those families.

"There's rules, whether written or unspoken, to all traditions." He didn't always like it, but he accepted it.

He watched as her head lowered, her gaze on where he caressed her thigh gently.

"I love touching you, Syn," he told her. "I've never enjoyed having a woman in my bed all night, until you. And you I'd never allow to sleep away from me."

Innocent vulnerability filled her face, her eyes.

"Don't lie to me," she whispered. "Don't betray me, Ivan. Let go first. Don't make me live like that."

Had anyone else questioned his word, he'd be furious. But this was his Syn. As illogical and impossible as it seemed, she held a part of him that no one else could, or would, own.

"Never," he swore. "And should any situation, any enemy, force me to do so, I'm quite secure in the fact that you'd know it. I'd make certain, one way or the other, Syn, that you'd know it. Because whether you believe it or not, you know me as I know you. Believe in that, know it, just as I do."

Sliding his hand from her thigh to her arm, he

caressed a path to her neck, where he gripped the slender column gently and drew her lips to his for a kiss as gentle as it was deep.

"Believe in me, Syn, as I believe in you," he asked, drawing back. "Just believe."

chapter seventeen

The announcement hit the morning papers. The marriage between Ivan Resnova and Journey Taite was scheduled for spring of the next year. The bride wanted time to plan her wedding, and it was predicted to be the wedding of the season.

Two hours later, Journey stood next to Ivan in the library of his home and exchanged vows with the man she'd always dreamed of. The wedding bands were his grandparents', plain gold bands he'd pulled from the safe the night before to ensure the fit.

Once the vows were said, a light lunch was served where twenty Resnova family members, Jordan and Tehya Malone, as well as Amara and her fiancé, Riordan Malone, and a dozen Russian family heads who were in the states toasted the couple.

To say she was nervous as hell was an understatement.

It wasn't butterflies beating in her stomach but full-grown birds fighting to be free.

The dress she wore was white, ending just below her knees in a silken fall of fabric, pearls he'd given her surrounded her neck and wrist, and tiny studs graced her ears.

Ivan had taken care of everything, and it went off so smoothly she was almost shocked.

The heads of the families who attended met with Ivan briefly before extending their congratulations to Ivan and Journey and excusing themselves to leave. As each neared the door, a small gift-wrapped box was left on the receiving table.

Presents for later, Ivan had explained, the small smile at the corners of his lips both mysterious and far too sexy.

Throughout the evening and celebratory dinner, she couldn't help but glance at not just the simple gold band she wore but the one Ivan wore as well.

He was her husband.

This man she had dreamed of for so long, fantasized about and ached for, had sworn himself to her. As the evening wore down and the family began drifting away from the huge dining and living rooms, she should have had a chance to ease her nerves, to enjoy her new husband, but the first indication of trouble arrived.

Journey saw the dark look on Ivan's face after a short discussion with Ilya. The other man turned away and headed toward the foyer, the dragon at the side of his face flexing dangerously.

She fought her panic as her gaze turned to Ivan,

watching as he strode toward her, his expression dark as he carefully hid his anger.

"What's wrong?" she asked as he neared her.

"We need to go to the office for a moment," he told her quietly. "Beau and your family are here along with their attorneys with the paperwork we'll both need to sign."

He'd told her to expect it before the evening was over; she'd just hoped it would be delayed, at least until the next morning. The next morning would have worked far better.

Ilya had contacted Beau after the wedding, as he and Ivan had arranged. It should have taken a while for him to get everything together in regard to the legalities of her family's business concerns.

For a moment, she wished she could feel some pleasure or satisfaction in the fact that with her marriage Stephen and Craig would lose any and all access to the funds needed to continue their vendetta against Ivan or their transfer to France. All she could feel was fear and a terrible premonition that there was something Ivan had overlooked.

It simply couldn't be this easy to end Stephen and Craig's reign of terror. They'd never allow it to be this easy.

With Ivan's hand riding the small of her back, his warmth sheltering her back while Ilya moved in front of her, the two men escorted her to the office where Beau, her mother, Celeste, her sister, Celia, and Celia's husband, Albert Edmonsson, and her brother, David, waited.

David looked haggard, she thought. She knew his wife had taken their son and returned to her parents' estate after the elder Taites' arrests. She'd filed for divorce immediately. No less than a year after the divorce had been final she'd remarried and managed to ensure David was deprived of visitation rights based on Stephen's and Craig's crimes and the fact that David had been under investigation as well.

Her brother's handsome face was lined now, his green eyes shadowed. He wasn't wearing the customary silk suit he'd once worn. Amazingly enough he wore jeans and a simple button-down shirt with a pair of scarred leather boots. His hair lay long against his neck, and the once *GQ* clean-shaven jaw was shadowed by an overnight beard. Grief lay heavily on his features as well as anger. But he wasn't the only one angry.

"The prodigal daughter," her sister, Celia, all but sneered as her husband squeezed her arm warningly.

Journey caught the tightening of Albert's beefy hand on her sister's delicate arm, and knew there would be bruises later. But it wasn't rare for her sister to carry bruises.

Celia's auburn hair was cut shorter than it had been four years ago, her hazel eyes seemed more dull, and the maliciousness in her gaze seemed brighter. The stark white blouse she wore with black slacks didn't exactly complement her looks. The clothes seemed to almost hang on her slight frame, as though she'd lost far too much weight.

Her mother stared back at her coolly. There was

little emotion other than anger that Journey could see.
But then, her mother rarely looked at her with anything
but anger in her hazel eyes. The auburn hair she still
wore in a chic, face-framing short cut showed off her
exceptional features. The dark blue dress she wore
was silk, her heels short. And strangely enough, she
looked sober for a change.

Beau stood next to her mother, his expression impassive as he watched her. He wasn't angry, but he was
concerned for some reason.

"Journey, it's good to see you well," Albert alone
greeted her, his smarmy smile reminding her of a ser-
pent's. "And safe."

She inclined her head with imperious haughtiness,
a move her distant cousin, the Queen of England none-
theless, had taught her.

Her mother stood still and silent, hazel eyes cool,
expression closed. If the woman had ever felt even a
spark of love for one of her children, then she'd never
shown it.

"Mother, David." She stopped several feet from her
mother and brother, not really expecting affection.
Damned good thing too, because there was none from
her mother certainly. In her brother's, she saw somber
regret though.

"Your father and I warned Beau to send you to the
Château rather than allowing you to come to America
before your engagement," her mother said then, her
tone as emotional as it would be if she were talking
about the weather. "It was good enough for your sister.
And perhaps it would have taught you your place. And

the inadvisability of consorting with men such as Resnova."

Pity welled inside her for Celia. The Château wasn't exactly a spa or vacation spot. It was a reform center for wayward girls, her mother had stated. And yes, she'd sent her elder daughter there the same day Celia had dared voice an objection to accepting Albert's proposal.

"Enough, Celeste." Beau's voice was dark, warning. "I would have thought your own stay there would have made you hesitate to send either of your daughters. That place is a fucking disgrace."

Celeste's expression tightened at the rebuke. "It's because of my stay there that I'm aware of the benefits of it!" she snapped. "Had she spent a few months in their care she would have been a much more loyal daughter. Not to mention fiancée."

Yes, that was Celeste.

Before Journey could turn on her heel and leave the room she felt Ivan's arms come around her as he pulled her against his chest.

"I thought you were an exceptional fiancée." He chuckled against her ear. "And now, you suit me just fine as my wife."

For a moment, she wanted to cry at the gentleness, the affection, in his low voice. The love. How had she managed to capture this man's love?

"That's all that matters then." She glanced back at him with a smile. "Shall we take care of this meeting so we can get on with our honeymoon?"

"My thoughts exactly." Kissing the top of her head,

he released her just enough to pull her to his side and turn to the lawyers. "I understand we have business to take care of."

The two attorneys were stiff lipped and obviously less than pleased. Opening leather bags, they withdrew several sheaths of papers and placed them on the desk.

"I assume he's acting as your attorney?" The older of the two lawyers nodded to Ilya.

"You assume correctly." Ivan nodded before turning to Ilya with a subtle nod toward the desk.

"Excuse me, gentlemen." Ilya's request was more an order as he neared the desk.

The lawyers stepped aside, their pinched expressions almost painful to see.

"The papers are pretty straightforward," Beau stated. "I prepared most of it myself and made suggestions for the rest of it."

Now, how interesting, Journey thought. She hadn't known that.

"You created a contract you believed would allow you your freedom while running the companies only to lose it to some dirty Russian," Celia murmured with an edge of amusement as her husband shot her a dark look. "Won't your father be pleased, Beau?"

The look Beau shot her was filled with knowing mockery. "No more pleased than he would have been otherwise," he snorted. "Never fear, Celia; this will in no way affect his regard for me, one way or the other."

"Cease your little insults, Celia." David spoke then, the chipped-ice sound of his voice a shock.

She'd never heard him sound so hard, so cold. And

she'd never known Celia to pay attention to anything he said, until now. Normally, she only listened to her husband, father, and grandfather. On rare occasions she listened to her mother.

"He's right." Ilya looked up from the papers. "Simple, to the point. I need a few more minutes to go through the addendums, but so far there's nothing that needs to be addressed."

She wanted him to hurry, to finish this. She wanted her family to leave, to allow her to enjoy the night and the pleasure to be found in her husband's arms. He had made this day perfect, and having it spoiled by the snide cruelties her sister and mother could deliver wasn't her preferred ending to the day.

"You disappoint me, Journey," her mother said as she gripped her purse before her and gave Journey a hard look before directing her gaze to Ivan. "To rebel is one thing; to marry the man determined to destroy your family is another thing altogether."

And what of this woman's husband and father-in-law? How many lives had they destroyed? How many young women had died or lived in sexual captivity because of them?

"Is that what you're trying to do, Ivan?" Journey asked him as though genuinely curious. "Strange, I thought you married me because you loved me."

"Indeed, I do." He tucked her closer to him then. "So much, that nothing matters more than ensuring you're protected. No matter who threatens you."

Her mother's grimace was one of distaste. It emphasized the lines and bitterness in her expression, and as she reached up to brush back the front of her perfectly styled hair Journey realized how much her mother had aged in the past four years.

Then, those hate-filled hazel eyes turned on Ivan. "Of course, it has nothing to do with that brat of yours she's carrying—"

"Enough!" Journey snapped, her chin lifting, anger surging through her. "You have no right to consider my and Ivan's child in any way, Mrs. Taite. Now you'll speak respectfully in our home or I can have one of our security personnel escort you from it. Choose now."

The shock on her mother's face would have been amusing under different circumstances. But this was her child, her and Ivan's baby; after the hell Ivan had suffered at the hands of this woman's husband and father-in-law, Journey would be damned if she'd allow such disrespect in their home.

"That goes for all of you." She turned to the others, each in turn, meeting their gazes furiously. "I have no problem in ordering you thrown from our home."

Silence filled the room. All but Beau and David turned their gazes from her.

Their expressions were closed, implacable, but there was no anger lurking in their gazes.

"Bravo, love," Ivan murmured at her ear, and in his voice she could hear the dark undercurrent of fury though she knew it wasn't directed toward her.

But what none of them realized was that the look Ilya directed toward them was one she hoped to never see turned her way. It was predatory, murderous, before he directed his attention back to the documents he was going over.

"Ivan." Beau stepped from the family and paced a few steps from them. "I'm available whenever you need me to give you a rundown of the business. There are quite a few holdings . . ."

"Let's deal with the paperwork first," Ivan stated as his fingers stroked over Journey's hip almost comfortingly, "One thing at a time."

She knew why Ivan was unwilling to discuss the subject. He had no desire to run the companies, and despite Beau's silence on the details of the contracts, he intended to leave the business in the other man's hands. It had actually been Jordan's suggestion.

Ivan's main concern was cutting off the funds, the attorneys, and the ability to hire assassins. They'd already signed papers that morning that ensured the Taite holdings and profits would be placed in secure accounts, accessible only by Journey. He had his own fortune, Ivan had informed her; he had no desire to add hers to it.

It was nearly an hour later that Ivan, Beau, Ilya, Celeste, and David added their signatures to the documents. Collecting Ivan's copy, Ilya stepped from the desk and left the room.

"Beau." Journey turned to him, keeping her voice firm. "Ivan and I have agreed that we'd prefer you maintain the CEO position. You and Ivan can discuss the package deal we've come up with if you're interested."

Beau looked between them speculatively, nodding slowly. "At your convenience."

"As for the two of you," Ivan growled as he faced the attorneys. "Your firm, as well as the two others previously used by the Taites, and your services will no longer be required. Neither for the Taite business concerns, nor in regards to the criminal charges brought against Stephen and Craig. Ilya has directed our attorneys to contact you at the start of the business day tomorrow to secure all files and concerns regarding Taite holdings or defendants."

They didn't speak, either to object or to agree. They stared back at Journey with imposing disgust instead.

"Thank you for your time, gentlemen," Ivan expressed, his voice anything but polite as the office door opened and admitted two of the Resnova bodyguards. "Our men will see you out now."

"This is a mistake, Resnova," the older of the two men bit out as he jerked his briefcase from the desk.

"I'm certain it is," Ivan agreed. "But the mistake was your clients'. They can rot where they are as far as I'm concerned. And without the funds you've ensured they had access to, rotting is probably exactly what they'll do."

Nodding to the two bodyguards, he watched with narrowed eyes as the attorneys were led from the office and the door closed behind them.

Journey turned back to her family, realizing that her mother's and sister's animosity no longer had the power to hurt her as it once had. She'd accepted it in the years she'd been running from them. Celeste and Celia had been broken and remolded at the Château beneath the so-called treatments they'd been given to ensure they obeyed the wishes of their parents as well as the husbands they'd never wanted.

Celeste handled it with alcohol; Celia handled it with biting sarcasm and a hatred for anyone else's happiness. She was never certain how David felt. He'd begun distancing himself from the family years ago.

"Poor Journey." It was Celia who finally spoke, and for once Journey detected something like regret in her tone. "You think you're safe, don't you?"

"Shut up." The hold Albert had on her arm had to be painful. "Come on. It's time we leave."

"Of course it is." Celia gave a hard, brittle laugh as her bull-like husband drew her to the door and from the room.

Celeste simply stared back at Journey, her lips compressed and fear shadowing her eyes.

"I'm ready to leave, David," she stated regally when she broke from Journey's gaze. "I'll wait for you in the car if you don't mind. I find the company here rather tedious."

Her mother found her rather tedious.

The thought was almost amusing. All her life she'd fought for this woman's approval, for her love, only to realize Celeste Taite simply had no love inside her for anyone.

"I'm tired," she told Ivan softly. "And it's my wedding night. Are we finished here?"

"We are," he assured her, then turned to Ilya. "Finish this for me if you don't mind. My wife is tired."

Before she could guess what he was up to Ivan swung her into his arms and carried her from the office to their bedroom. It was her wedding night, and all she wanted to do was cry.

It was nearly midnight when Ivan stepped from the bedroom, fighting the rage coiling in his gut at the memory of the wounds Journey's mother and sister had inflicted on her heart. Not that she had cried or raged. The strength she carried inside her didn't often give way to tears.

Temper, yes, but rarely tears.

He'd held her, nothing more, allowing her to absorb his warmth as she talked. She'd told him of years of disinterest by her mother, her sister's seeming hatred, her father's determination to keep her brother separated from all of them. There had been friendships ruined by her sister's spitefulness, her mother's drunkenness, until she'd simply grown weary with the fight to have a friend.

Until Tehya.

She'd finally grown silent before slipping into sleep and leaving him to stare into the darkness with raging fury. No child, no little girl especially, should have to live so isolated from any love or tender care. How she'd survived, he couldn't imagine.

Nodding to the security guard positioned outside the bedroom, he strode down the hall and made his way once again to his office. The text Ilya had sent to his phone moments ago was surprising. Information concerning the Taites' outside connections had been found and he thought Ivan would want to see it.

Oh, he definitely wanted to see it, Ivan thought. Whoever was managing to carry out Stephen's and Craig's orders had to be stopped, quickly. He'd be damned if he'd tolerate another risk to Journey.

Reaching the office, he stepped inside, his gaze narrowing at the sight that met his eyes as he slowly eased the door closed.

"I'm rarely surprised," he said, allowing a mocking smile to tilt his lips. "But you've managed it."

Ilya was unconscious on the floor in front of the desk but breathing. Barely. Sitting behind the desk was none other than Journey's brother-in-law, Albert Edmonsson. Stocky, with a receding hairline, his brown eyes narrowed with anger, his pale face flushed, he stared at Ivan with a gleam of almost rabid triumph.

Standing with him were four men Ivan remembered from Russia. Former soldiers he'd released from the Resnova payroll when he'd learned they were working for his enemies as well.

He should have just killed them. But the thought of spilling more blood at that time had been distasteful. He wouldn't find it nearly so distasteful this time.

If he survived.

"Excellent security by the way." Albert smiled, and Ivan realized how much he looked like a rabid little gnome when doing so.

"Really?" He arched a brow at the statement. "I

could disagree with that, considering you managed to bypass them."

Three teams of Elite Ops agents outside, his best personal security inside, and still five of these bastards had gotten past them all.

"Yes, well, perhaps you should have more men on the grounds." Albert shrugged. "The four Anton and his men took out weren't much of a challenge, you know."

Four. There were eight men outside and he knew it.

"It seems Ilya was right," he sighed. "He wanted to assign more, but I thought they would be better placed in the house." He shrugged as though it didn't matter. "Live and learn, I guess."

Anton Vladeski, the commander of the other three soldiers, a tall dark-haired bastard with a streak of cruelty a mile wide, smiled at the comment.

"Or learn and die," he stated, his accent heavy. "Tonight, Resnova, you die. Just as your very good friend Ilya did."

Ivan stared down at Ilya's body again, aware it was hidden from the others where it lay. He sighed, watching as the other man's finger moved just enough to assure Ivan that he was indeed alive and, he hoped, had managed to get out an alarm of some sort.

He couldn't depend on it though. The blood that had eased from beneath Ilya's body in a heavy stream seemed to come from his chest. Ilya could be far closer to death than he at first seemed.

"Killing Ilya was a stupid move," he stated, crossing his arms over his chest and directing his attention to the men behind the desk once again. "His family won't rest until they hunt you down. Did you warn Edmonsson of that? Did you tell him who Ilya's brother was?"

Anton's expression never changed, but Ivan saw the concern in his gaze.

"The old families, no matter the country, aren't what they used to be, no matter what you like to think," Albert assured him, his lips twisting with disdain. "No matter how they like to believe they are. Besides, no one will ever know we were here. Once you're dead and that brat Journey's carrying is disposed of, then she'll marry Beau, and Stephen and Craig can regain the reins to the business once they're transferred out of the states."

And Ivan had to laugh at that one. A deep, amused chuckle filled with knowing condescension.

"He really believes that, doesn't he?" he asked Anton. "Tell me, Vladeski, do you really believe it will be so easy? Do you really think Ilya's brother, your esteemed Russian President, will allow his baby brother's death to go unavenged? Surely you know him better than that."

And he didn't. Ivan saw it in his eyes, in the flicker of fear in his expression. The former soldier knew damned good and well it wasn't going to be that easy. Now that he was aware of why it wouldn't be so easy, he would understand the hell he faced if Ivan escaped.

If.

No matter what Albert Edmonsson had convinced Vladeski of before, in the moment, Anton knew he'd die. And if the expressions on the three men with him were an indication, they knew they'd be following him.

"Ignore him. No one will ever know we were here," Albert ordered, his voice sharp. "Now go find his little whore. The doctor's waiting to relieve her of her brat as soon as we take care of things here." He turned back to Ivan. "The documents you signed earlier, if you please. We'll need to destroy those as well."

As well. The son of a bitch meant to have his child aborted?

Ivan narrowed his gaze on him, rage beginning to burn through him.

"I'll kill you," he promised as two of his men eased from the room, exiting by way of the once secure door leading to the gardens outside.

Albert only grinned. "I'll have you killed before you can move. Go ahead, Ivan, try me."

He was going to do far more than try him . . .

chapter eighteen

Journey came awake the second a hard hand covered her lips, muffling any sound she'd make as she felt weight straddle her hips, holding her in place. Her eyes jerked open, panic racing through her as she fought to extricate her arms, to free herself from the binding pressure holding them down.

It took precious moments to recognize Elizaveta's face above her and the fact that it was Sophia Resnova restraining her hands. She froze as she realized who they were and the implications of their presence there and the fact that she couldn't see Ivan.

He would have never sent these two women after her. He would have come himself if there was danger, if he could have.

"Silence," Elizaveta hissed, her head lowering to allow her to speak close to Journey's ear.

Journey nodded quickly.

"Riordan, Jordan, and several others are in the room as well. We must get you out of here." The dangerous softness in the other woman's voice terrified her. "Sophia has clothes for you. Dress quickly."

Elizaveta lifted her hand and slid from her quickly before she and Sophia shielded her from the shadowed male forms that stood alertly, armed and ready.

"Ivan?" She whispered his name as she quickly pulled on jeans and a T-shirt before sliding her feet into the sneakers Sophia held out to her.

"Safe for now," Elizaveta assured her, but there was an edge to her tone that assured Journey that something was wrong.

"Where?" She jerked her arm back when the other woman would have gripped it.

Her gaze went to the half-dozen men behind the women, waiting, tense and alert, at the patio doors they'd obviously come through. Ivan wasn't with them. She would have recognized him, even dressed in black with his face shielded as four of the men were.

"Come with us," the bodyguard hissed. "Ivan cannot do what he must if you aren't safe."

And just what was Ivan doing?

Journey stared into Elizaveta's, then Sophia's eyes, fear curdling in her stomach as she fought against the panic beginning to tighten her chest.

"Where is he?" Her voice trembled and she jerked her arm back again as Sophia reached out to her this time.

"Do you want him to die?" Elizaveta suddenly

hissed. "Because if you are taken, he will die to protect you and his child. Now let's go."

This time, she let them take her arm and lead her to the door. One of the men stepped outside, checked the area quickly, then motioned them forward. She was surrounded by bodies as they rushed her from the bedroom. As the patio doors closed, the sound of her bedroom door crashing in had Jordan cursing and the women urging Journey into a run.

Whatever the hell was going on, it seemed time had run out.

Ivan felt the subtle vibration of the simple, supposedly old-fashioned watch he wore against the inside of his wrist indicating Journey had been whisked from any danger. She was safe; that was all that mattered.

Evidently, Ilya had received the same signal. From his periphery Ivan watched as Ilya moved two fingers slowly. Journey and his child were safe; nothing else mattered. She'd be taken with Amara and secured in a safe location.

Now it was up to him, Ivan thought. He'd have to find a way to distract Albert, Anton, and Anton's cousin Igor. Ilya was conscious but no doubt out of any fight. The bleeding seemed severe enough that Ivan feared the other man might well be unconscious soon.

"What's taking so long?" Albert asked, his weapon still leveled on Ivan as he questioned the soldier.

"They haven't reported in yet," Anton answered. "We're on radio silence until they have her."

Ivan smiled. A slow, controlled smile filled with satisfaction.

"I'm going to guess it was your team she's been running from since Colorado," he drawled. "What makes you think you'll have any more success tonight than you did at any other time?"

The other man couldn't hide the shadow of concern in his gaze.

"Because she doesn't have you to help her now," Albert pointed out, his tone filled with hatred. "Had you left things alone, then she would have already been married to Beau, and Stephen and Craig's plans would be in play. But you had to play the hero for her, didn't you?"

"The rewards were well worth the effort," he assured Journey's brother-in-law.

"I bet they were." Thick, heavy lips pursed in disgust as Albert glanced at Anton again.

"Your men aren't going to notify you of their success, Anton," Ivan informed him. "Because they're not going to succeed. By now, my wife is safe, as well as my daughter, and your men are dead."

Igor turned to Anton, his expression concerned.

Igor wasn't a man who liked it when things didn't go according to plan. Anton was rather adaptable himself, a trait Igor didn't share.

"They are fine," Anton assured his cousin. "We're still within an acceptable time frame for the job."

Anton liked to lie to himself when a job was going to hell; it made him undependable, made his team ineffective.

"You know better than that, Anton." Ivan chuckled though he could see the tension rising in the three men. "You know me. I would never leave the safety of my wife, my children, to chance. Your men are dead or they would already be here."

Igor shifted uncomfortably as Anton glared at Ivan.

"Igor!" Albert snapped. "Go check on them."

At Anton's nod, Igor lifted the automatic rifle he carried closer and moved to the door. Opening it cautiously and glancing outside, he slid through the narrow opening before closing the door behind him.

"Who are you going to send to check on Igor when he doesn't return?" Ivan questioned the other two men. "You should have known better than to face me like this, Anton. Not with the resources I have. Do you think I'd only position four men outside? Have I ever acted the fool where my security was concerned?"

He hadn't. If there was one thing Anton knew, it was that Ivan took his security extremely seriously.

Anton shifted the weapon in his arms, the rifle gleaming dully in the low light cast by the desk lamp.

"He's bluffing," Albert assured the soldier, evidently far more confident than Anton at the moment.

Albert's weapon hadn't shifted, the barrel still aimed directly at Ivan's heart. But only two remained, Ivan consoled himself. He was weaponless, Ilya was bleeding like a stuck pig on the floor, and he could see the nervousness building in Anton.

This wasn't going to end well if he wasn't very damned careful.

"Just walk out of here, Albert," he suggested as

though weary of the game. "I'll give you and Anton safe exit just for the hell of it. But you kill me and you won't have a chance. Beau won't have the Taite holdings; my wife will be so well hidden until Stephen and Craig are killed that you won't have a hope of finding her. And to add to that, when my people get their hands on you, and Anton, and they will, they'll make you scream before they ever allow you to die."

Even Stephen and Craig had known that. It was the reason why they struck everywhere but at Ivan directly. They always worked behind the scenes, always kept their own hands clean, because they knew exactly what Ivan could do.

Anton stepped back from Albert slowly, his gaze centered on Ivan.

"Walk away," Ivan encouraged him. "Your men are dead. Your cousin's dead. Unless you want to join them, get the hell out of here."

Albert rose slowly to his feet. "Stay where the hell you are, Anton," he growled. "As long as we have this bastard we're safe. And as far as we know your men already have that little bitch."

His wife was no little bitch, Ivan thought, icy fury beginning to build inside him.

He hadn't made the offer to Albert to walk away. That bastard was dead. Then he'd deliver the body to Stephen and Craig Taite personally. This fucking game was over. Journey was no longer a pawn, nor would Ivan allow her to be threatened again.

He met Anton's gaze once again and watched the soldier swallow tightly.

"Ivan doesn't bluff," Anton said then. "And he's right. If my men had not failed, they would be here by now with his woman in tow."

Ivan calculated the distance between himself and the desk and his chances of reaching the weapon he could glimpse just beneath Ilya's arm.

Anton stepped farther away as he swung the rifle around and leveled it on Albert. Evidently, he didn't trust the other man nearly as well as he'd pretended.

Now if he could just get lucky enough to have the two men kill each other. It would save him the trouble of killing either of them.

"Can't you see what he's doing?" Albert hissed. "He's playing with your mind, you dumb bastard."

"Let him go, Albert. We'll sit here and wait this out together," Ivan suggested. "We'll see who arrives first. Your men, or mine."

Ivan knew who would arrive first, but waiting really wasn't on his agenda. For one thing, he wasn't comfortable allowing Ilya to lie on that floor bleeding to death. Secondly, he had no doubt his men as well as the Ops agents were outside that secured steel door just waiting to push their way inside.

"Get out of here, Anton," Ivan ordered him. He was damned tired of playing with these two. "The offer has an expiration date."

Anton was beginning to look decidedly nervous.

"Shut the fuck up." Albert swung back around, the weapon leveling on Ivan once again.

As he turned, Anton slid behind him, moving for the door while keeping his eyes on Albert cautiously.

"You troublemaking bastard," Albert sneered, still not smart enough to realize the position he was in. "When his men get back here with that little bitch I'll rape her in front of you before we deliver her to the doctor to flush that brat out of her."

Ivan wished the other man were just a little bit closer. He'd rip his damned guts out with his bare hands. He dropped his arms from his chest, forcing the tension threatening to overtake him to keep him prepared instead.

"Get back here, Anton." Albert swung back to the soldier, his weapon leveled on the other man, his finger on the trigger.

Instantly, Anton aimed his rifle back at Albert, his expression turning cold and hard.

"I kill you and Resnova will thank me for it!" Anton snapped. "Be thankful I'm willing to just walk away."

Albert's weapon shook, rage contorting his face as he stared at the man he had believed would actually follow his orders in the face of Ivan's vengeance.

"Walk away, Anton," Ivan stated softly. "Albert and I will just wait and see who comes first. The soldiers he sent after my wife, or my men."

All Anton had to do was open the damned door. By this time, Ivan knew the Elite Ops agents were in place, backed by the Resnova security.

Anton reached behind him, his fingers gripping the doorknob as he balanced the weapon using the strap attached to his shoulder and the finger lying against the trigger.

Ivan was ready to move. From the corner of his eye he watched as the soldier turned the doorknob, easing it around, the locking mechanism releasing.

Anton's eyes widened as a sudden force threw him forward. Ivan threw himself to the floor, quickly covering Ilya's body as gunfire erupted through the room. Ilya grunted, cursed weakly, and Ivan almost grinned at the response.

"Ivan!" Jordan and Riordan were there within seconds, the gunfire silenced, the room filling with black-clad agents, their faces covered, identities hidden.

"Ilya's wounded." Ivan levered himself back before gripping the hand Jordan extended to him and allowing him to help him to his feet. "Gregor." He turned to the uncle stepping into the room through the hall entrance. "Get Peter in here. Let's see how bad Ilya let them wound him. I think he likes bullets."

He grinned, staring down at Ilya as he shook his head, his face still resting against the floor.

"Fuck you, Ivan." His voice was weak, but he was talking. Breathing.

Albert and Anton, however, weren't nearly so lucky. Both men were sprawled out on the floor, staring sightlessly up at the ceiling.

"The others?" he asked Jordan.

"They opted to fight." Jordan shrugged. "We opted to kill them."

Yeah, that was Jordan; he didn't waste a lot of time when it came to taking care of the enemy. A risk wasn't accepted as far as the other man was concerned. A man couldn't come for vengeance if he was dead.

"Journey and Amara?" He turned back to Jordan, needing to know, to hear, that they were well.

"With Tehya, Sophia, and Elizaveta," he was told. "They're both fine. Journey's not so happy that we dragged her from the house without you, but she's safe."

The other man slapped him on the shoulder as Ivan inhaled deeply. She was safe; that was all that mattered. His daughter, his wife, his child. They were safe. Nothing else mattered.

"We have Beau coming in," Riordan said then. "Five minutes out. We notified him just after we got Amara and Journey off the property."

As they spoke, Peter arrived with several security personnel and a gurney used to transport his patients to the basement when walking wasn't happening.

Ilya cursed, swore he was killing every one of them, but finally settled back on the makeshift bed while Peter worked quickly to stop the blood flow from his chest. The younger man was pale, the front of his white shirt saturated with blood, but the tough son of a bitch was still cursing as the doctor applied a compress to his chest and ordered the two men to get him downstairs.

Watching him leave, Ivan rubbed at the back of his neck wearily, glanced at the window, and saw the darkness outside had begun easing. Dawn was coming and with it, he hoped, an end to the bullshit he and Journey had been fighting. Stephen and Craig wouldn't last long without the funds that had sustained them, and enough pressure on the attorneys and they'd reveal whatever they knew where the two men were concerned.

As he watched Ilya disappear down the hall, a prickling along the back of his neck had him turning slowly to face the door once again.

She stood just inside the room. She wasn't staring at the bloodstains on the floor from the two men the agents had hastily carted from the house. Nor was she concerned with the black-masked men milling around.

Those green eyes, so damned pretty and bright, were locked on him. Her red-gold hair framed her face, the bright waves mussed, concern marking her expression.

She was staring at him like no other woman ever had. With stars in her eyes, with love filling her face.

His Syn.

He opened his arms for her, watching as she sprinted across the room, all but jumping into his arms so he could lift her against him, hold her to his heart. And he held her tight. He couldn't stop himself. He buried his face in her hair, whispered her name, and felt like going to his knees to thank God that she was safe. She was his.

His Syn.

Beau stared at the couple from the doorway, his hands in the pockets of his slacks, watching Ivan Resnova's face as he held the delicate, sobbing woman in his arms. And in his face Beau saw love.

Hell.

He breathed out heavily at the sight and had to finally accept the fact that the plans he'd had in place for a decade weren't exactly going to work out.

He could have married Journey, cared for her, kept her safe. He wouldn't have risked his heart, wouldn't have risked having a woman he couldn't afford to lose should the worst happen. When a man loved, he weakened himself.

Beau had no desire to weaken himself; he still had work to do, had his own ghosts to vanquish.

Journey would be safe though, Beau thought, which was all his stepfather was concerned with. Of course, he would have preferred Beau to have married her, but he'd accept Ivan. All that mattered was ensuring she was safe. Having her happy would be an added plus, Beau thought.

There were still details to get through, information they all needed to go over, and certain roles that would have to be played for a while longer.

Disposing of the Taites was only part of the plan. Unfortunately, he couldn't allow the disposal to appear as anything other than the repercussions of their own ignorance. They'd allowed themselves to be caught and placed themselves perfectly for Resnova's vengeance. Journey's arrival in Ivan's life hadn't been what Beau would have wished, but it would work out for the best perhaps.

He'd make certain it worked out for the best.

"Beau." Jordan eased over to him, his gaze questioning as Beau shifted his attention from the couple to the other man.

"Jordan." He nodded. "Hell, did we even suspect Albert was part of this?"

Jordan's lips quirked in amusement. "I suspected everyone, Beau, but I can't say I wasn't surprised. I was."

Beau nodded slowly. "It's not over," he warned Jordan. "For Resnova perhaps, but not for myself. You know that."

Jordan simply nodded.

Yeah, he would know that, Beau thought, his gaze going to Ivan and Journey once again as they shared a slow, almost chaste kiss. It was all the more intimate for the restrained passion inherent in it.

"Never thought I'd see it," he murmured. "Ivan Resnova in love. It's enough to make a man believe in miracles."

"Or love," Jordan said softly. "It's enough to make a man believe in love, Beau."

Some men perhaps. Never him.

He knew better. He knew the dangers.

Love wasn't for him . . .

epilogue

Three days later . . .

It was three stupid days later before Ivan was free to return to their bed.

Ilya needed surgery, and of course they had to be there with him.

On the heels of Ilya's recovery was the report that Stephen and Craig Taite were willing to discuss their criminal connections as well as any associates in their activities. That took more than twenty-four hours and by time he returned home, he was exhausted. He'd fallen into bed beside her and no sooner than his arms surrounded her, sleep had taken him.

She'd lain for several hours just staring at him, amazed at the man she'd found him to be versus the man the world believed him to be. This was a man who she'd learned had worked since he was twelve years old, twelve years old, to bring down the monster his father was. And nearly six years later, when his father had tried to take Amara and sell her to the men who had raped and murdered Ivan's mother, he'd taken matters into his own hands.

But he hadn't broken the vow he gave at twelve to aid the men trying to help him and the organization that vowed they'd be there when he needed them. And they had been there. They were still there.

His strength, his ability to find kindness and compassion within himself, and his love for her, still amazed her.

And his effect on her amazed her.

He woke her with kisses. Deep, hungry kisses as he framed her face with his hands. Slanting his lips across her, his tongue stroking against her own, he had the need that had only grown over the days, burning brighter than ever.

With each caress, each deep kiss, she let herself fall into the chaotic sensations once again.

There were a few preliminaries. Three days, the threat of losing Ilya, the knowledge that Stephen and Craig could never hurt them again, that they were safe, their child was safe, had taken a toll. The ravenous need to come together, to touch and be touched, couldn't be denied.

With his lips still on hers, their kisses growing more frantic by the second, Journey gripped Ivan's shoulders, her legs parting, lifting as he came between them, and she felt the engorged crest of his erection pressing into her.

Her cries were muffled by his kisses, but nothing could contain the pleasure. Arching to him, her knees gripping his hips, she moaned, cried out against his lips, and reveled in each rush of pleasure. Each thrust inside her, each powerful lunging stroke of his cock through the clenching tissue of her pussy had her flying. It was like touching paradise each time he took her, each time he touched her.

Rising to him, her nails clenching his shoulders, knees tightening on his hips, she felt the pleasure overwhelm her and her orgasm rush over her like a tidal wave.

Tearing his lips from her, Ivan buried his lips at her shoulder, his release exploding inside her, adding to and pushing her own pleasure higher.

But it was the words he groaned at her shoulder that had tears spilling from her eyes, her heart clenching at the eruption of emotion that joined the pleasure tearing through her.

"My heart . . . My Syn . . . God help me, I love you . . ."

It wasn't an illusion. This was her reality.

She loved. And she was loved in turn.

Whatever the future would bring, whatever they had faced because of their parents' pasts didn't matter. They loved, they were loved. And the fairy tale was real.

Dear Readers,

I hope you enjoyed *Dagger's Edge*. I know Ivan and Journey enjoyed showing off for you. With *Dagger's Edge* completed, I'm looking forward to returning to the cowboys and teaming up with Veronica Chadwick once again to bring you *One Tough Cowboy*, coming Winter 2019.

I really think you'll enjoy this first cowboy romance from me and Veronica. Happy reading to you, and thank you so much for continuing on this adventure with me.

Lora Leigh